R.H.
GRÜND
WORKS

I0769093

OTHER BOOKS BY R. H. GRÜND

Room of Cloth

Simulacrum

Abattoir

R. H. GRÜND
A NOVEL
INFLUENCE

R.H.
GRÜND
WORKS

Why this is hell, nor am I out of it:
Think'st thou that I, who saw the face of God
And tasted the eternal joys of Heaven,
Am not tormented with ten thousand hells
In being deprived of everlasting bliss?

Mephistopheles (Marlowe's *Doctor Faustus*)

ONE

Virginia curled her fingers and toes, settled more snugly under her blanket, and waited for the video to load. Her cat, Felix, stretched himself out by her side. Finally, the black of Virginia's laptop gave way to a dark bedroom much like her own, gave way to another girl. The girl on the screen was older, her skin darker, features sharper, but her eyes were sad. Virginia's gaze lit up as she watched.

"My name is Minerva King," said the girl on the screen. She had been crying, dabbing at her eyes with a tissue, wiping at her nose with her sleeve. "My therapist said it might be good to talk about what I'm feeling, so I thought, why not include everybody? So, here we are. I'm twenty-one years old. I live in Oakland, California. I just got out of college. I've been modeling—" She paused and broke into nervous laughter. "God, what am I doing? No one's even watching this."

Virginia waited, locking onto the sad eyes through the grainy resolution of the webcam. The girl, Minerva, drew a breath. She looked off at something out of view of the camera, maybe off into the distance of a window. Virginia liked to think she was looking out towards the dark ocean, the nighttime sky. They were free out there in California, after all. They lived in a world of boundless possibility.

"My dad died," Minerva went on. "Not recently. When I was a lot younger. It's been almost ten years, and it still bothers me sometimes. I dream about him, and it's scary because sometimes, he looks different. His face isn't what I see in the pictures. He's shorter, or he's taller. Maybe his hair's a different color. People say, he's still with you, he's in your heart, but obviously, he's not. It's not my dad—it's just a video reel, and the film's giving out. Getting old.

"Anyway"—she cleared her throat—"this isn't supposed to be about my dad. It's more like, what happens if these things don't go away? What happens if they stay with you? That's what keeps me up. Like, twenty years from now, am I gonna be over it? Or am I just gonna *think* I'm over it? That's really it. I guess, leave a comment and let me know what you think. And if you want me to make another video, let me know that, too."

She smiled briefly, even the tiniest flicker of her lips seeming to brighten up the dark room, and then the video ended. Virginia sat there afterwards and scrolled the comments. Two years had passed since the video was published, and messages still poured in:

It's gonna be ok

Too real babe! Love from PA

Very resonating

youre gorgeous! don't be sad

Thank you. I lost my mom recently and really needed this. You put everything I couldn't say into words.

Somewhere in that list was Virginia's own comment, already a year old now:

im so sorry, i cant imagine. my dad didnt die. he just ran away. and my moms still crying about it. but you didnt turn into a monster like she did. you became an angel. just look at all the people watching you.

That impromptu video had started it all. Thousands and then millions of viewers flocked to the "minerva queen" channel over the two years that followed, and over time, Minerva's videos transformed from nighttime confessionals and therapeutic talks to cooking tutorials, fit checks, and modeling Q&As. She started streaming modeling gigs, auditions for commercials, and nights out with her housemates, Michelle and Sue, and her other friends. They were all beautiful, of course, but none of them at the level of Minerva, whose olive skin and picturesque face set her apart. Virginia hadn't been able to resist the emotional vulnerability of the early videos and the array of neon-bright bars and pure-white beaches that followed. She perused religiously the forums dedicated to Minerva and maintained her own private collection of memes and images. She became one of the "goddess's worshippers," as the most devoted fans called themselves. She didn't follow any other streams, and why would she? Minerva had it all. More than that, she was happy. She had a place in the world. She had people. Despite the things that had happened in her past, despite the challenges she faced, she stayed calm, stayed strong. She shone like a fire, serving as a beacon to light the way for everyone else stuck in the dark.

Virginia closed her laptop. Darkness overtook her room, but she wasn't afraid. She lay back, pulled Felix against her, and closed her eyes, knowing that somewhere out there, Minerva had wrestled with the same fears and won. Virginia fell asleep, her dreams a refuge of brightly colored streets and a majestic, cerulean sea.

TWO

Two days later, after a week of scouring the woods with flashlights and shouting her name, they found Suzanne. She had gone far, like an animal limping into the underbrush. The rope had snapped, and her body lay in the moss and dirt, riddled with insects, already rotting.

When the news reached her family, Virginia's mother scoffed, and her sister wailed. For her part, Virginia wasn't sure what to feel. It didn't seem real, but at the same time, Suzanne was always taking off, always disappearing for a day or two at a time. She had always been looking for an out—always talking about leaving, about starting down the highway and never looking back. Anywhere but here, she always said.

One would think a small, Central Texas town like theirs to be quaint, but Oasis was the opposite of its namesake: overcast and somber, dense with dark forestry. The highlights on the main street were the partly condemned theater and an ancient ice cream shop. Time had stopped for the town, which was the last thing Suzanne would have ever wanted: being frozen in place, stuck in a routine she couldn't get out of. It was easy to say the town had killed her, but Suzanne made the call, hadn't she? Instead of running away, she'd opted for the rope. Honestly, if Virginia felt anything, it was anger. It was classic Suzanne to talk big about running away and then choose the option that would definitely be more dramatic, that would get everyone to see her as a victim.

Maybe Virginia would go to Hell for thinking that, but screw it. Suzanne had been a bitch by the end, always insulting her and making fun of her own goal of leaving, as if Virginia wasn't good enough for it but Suzanne somehow was. And when Virginia tried to introduce Suzanne to Minerva, to get her to watch even one of the videos, Suzanne had laughed in her face and said it was stupid to follow some dumb wannabe model. It hadn't been long afterwards that Suzanne became even more depressed than usual, even more withdrawn and quiet. Then she disappeared. Then they found her.

Well, Virginia wouldn't end up like Suzanne. She'd make it out of Oasis, and she knew where she would go: California, where Minerva was. Maybe she hadn't actually met Minerva, but she *knew* her. Minerva wasn't some random girl, not some wannabe model—she brought people together and inspired them. What had Suzanne done but complain and bring others down?

"Minerva makes me feel good," Virginia whispered to Felix, the glow of the laptop on her face. "She makes me feel safe. That's more than Suzanne ever did."

With Suzanne gone, Virginia wouldn't have to tolerate the long silences anymore. She wouldn't have to hear about how gray everything was, how colorless and soundless. She wouldn't have to deal with the constant frowning and the complaining and the negativity. She wouldn't have to deal with being associated with a "freak" or a "loser." Her life no longer revolved around Suzanne Grayson. She was free!

She did, on occasion, think back to one of the last things she said to Suzanne: "If it's so bad, then just die." But any regret or worry or grief was quickly solved by turning on the laptop and watching Minerva. If Virginia had watched the stream obsessively before Suzanne's death, she doubled down afterwards. Every moment of her free time outside of school was devoted to the blue skies and glimmering studios of Minerva's life. And as Virginia watched, she planned and imagined what her own future in California would look like.

In the meantime, regular, boring life continued.

At dinner, her sister, Janine, broke down again. "I just can't believe it. She sat at this table! She ate with us!"

Virginia had to stifle her laugh. Her sister seemed to get more hysterical as she got more pregnant.

"She was a smart kid," remarked Davy, Janine's husband, as he piled his plate with potatoes. As usual, he seemed about ready to fall asleep over his food.

Janine turned to Virginia. "Did she ever say anything to you? Did you have any idea?"

Yeah, Virginia almost said. When *wasn't* Suzanne talking about leaving?

"Oh, quiet down, Janine," said their mother. She sat at the head of the table, her flabby, varicose-veined arms swinging as she topped her plate. "The girl's dead. No use crying about it."

"Mama, how can you say that? She was like Ginny's sister—"

"She wasn't her sister. And no spineless fool like that's ever gonna be associated with this family." Mother Blue snapped off a drumstick from the cooked chicken at the center of the table. "That girl always looked like death. Just a matter of time before something happened."

No one said anything else. Janine sniffled, dabbing at her nose with a napkin. Davy busied himself with his food. Virginia watched the pale folds of her mother's jowls, the sags of her cheeks. Mother

Blue was foul, vulgar, cruel, but in this case, Virginia agreed with her. Suzanne was always headed this way. Why was everyone freaking out over it?

It won't happen to me, she thought. I'll get out of here. I'll make it to California.

After dinner, she hurried to her bedroom. Suzanne was dead, just like her mother said. This wasn't Victorian England, as she learned in school, when one wore black for months and swore off smiling. She lay in the dark, snuggling comfortably against her pillows, and balanced her laptop on her knees. With Minerva, there was no reason to be unhappy, no reason to cry or complain as Suzanne often did. As Virginia logged onto the stream, the screen bright with the clear sky and crystalline ocean of the Oakland coast, all thoughts of Suzanne disappeared.

Virginia was rarely able to catch Minerva live, but she made a point to always catch the recorded streams in the evening before bedtime. Today, Minerva had taken to the beach in a turquoise two-piece, chatting with beachgoers, dipping her toes in the water. Virginia watched her cocoa-colored skin speckled with sand, her hazel eyes glowing bright with the afternoon sun. Minerva's ombré curls grew richer and more golden as the sunlight waned. At night, as Minerva enjoyed frozen margaritas with her girlfriends, Virginia closed her eyes and imagined herself among their number: older, wiser, prettier, sexier, confident, no longer a virgin, no longer afraid.

When the stream was over, Virginia shut her laptop and sat still in the dark. She clung to the warm sunlight, the salty air, the chilled glass. I'm there, she thought. I'm there. But inevitably, the sensations, already only half-real, eroded. She taxed her imagination, exhausted her creativity, but the beach melted into the black formlessness of her bedroom. Try as she might, she was *not* one of Minerva's girlfriends. She was just lame, unremarkable, run-of-the-mill Virginia Blue, not even old enough to drink. She was chunky-cheeked and small-framed, neither attractive nor unattractive. Her gray eyes did not catch the light but rather clouded and turned opaque. She was pale and ghastly, so much that if she disappeared into wisps of smoke, no one would be surprised. The sun did not shine on the likes of Virginia—or Suzanne for that matter.

She rolled over. Suzanne again. Suzanne always. Why? Why couldn't Suzanne just leave her alone? Why did she have to kill herself and make everything about her forever, as if it wasn't enough that she complained and cried every minute while she was alive? It didn't make sense to hate life so much but want all the attention all the time. What right did she have? Or maybe this was her revenge—what better way to spite all of them than make herself impossible to forget?

"I was there for you," Virginia said into the dark. "I was there for everything. Your dad drinking. Your mom's drugs. And it still wasn't enough. You still wanted to run away. You still needed every single other person to care. Well, now you have everything you want. Now you can finally be happy."

She waited, half-expecting Suzanne to rise up out of the darkness and answer back. But of course, she didn't. It didn't matter how many people talked about her or for how long. She was dead, and dead people couldn't be happy or sad. They were gone. Just turned into dust no matter what the Bible said.

She cradled Felix and scratched behind his ears, his purrs reverberating through her arms. "It won't take long," Virginia told him.

"Everyone will forget about her. And then we won't have to worry about her anymore."

THREE

In the morning, she found the family in the kitchen. Janine sat at the table mending socks. Davy waited for the coffee to finish. They were meek in their respective pale gown and shabby suit, especially in the proximity of Mother Blue. She dominated the room, both in size and presence, situated at the head of the table like an enormous sentry. Despite the newspaper she scanned with her dark, pinched eyes, Virginia knew she overlooked nothing.

"I'm going to school," Virginia said.

Her mother wrinkled her nose and flipped to another page of the newspaper. "We're going to evening Mass, so you better be back early."

"Yes, Mama. I will."

"You try getting out of it again, and I'll take that computer of yours. I swear it."

"She knows, Mama," said Janine. "Ginny—"

"I'm talking to Virginia, not you," interrupted their mother. Those pinched eyes rose from the newspaper. "Spending all your time on that damned thing. Skipping Mass. Next you'll say it's because of Suzanne."

Virginia shook her head. "No, Mama. I'll be home for Mass."

There was nothing else from her mother, just the crinkle of the paper as she flipped pages again. Janine smiled at Virginia and winked. She was shrill and weepy, thin as a stick apart from her bulging belly, with baggy eyes and a nasally tone. Most of the time, Virginia found her sister annoying, but in light of Mother Blue's fury, Janine was almost saintly, a port in a whirling storm.

Virginia walked down the cracked, overgrown walkway from their front porch, past sun-bleached, wind-torn Texan and American flags. Their neighborhood was only a couple of blocks from the main street of Oasis. The town was practically prehistoric, stuck in time, and Mother Blue seemed to Virginia much the same. Janine had once shown her pictures of a young woman, thin and beautiful with waist-length hair the color of chocolate, but Virginia still couldn't believe that was their mother in her youth. No, Mother Blue had always been Mother Blue, huge and eternal and unchanging. She was there at the beginning, all fists and screams, and she would be there at the end, long after they were all dead, laughing at them and calling them weak for dying—even if she was the one who killed them. Janine had told Virginia how she'd had to set her shoulder when she was a teen, how she'd have to hide her bruises with long sleeves and turtlenecks. It was a wonder to Virginia that thin, fragile Janine hadn't broken a long time ago (in every sense), but magically, once the clock struck midnight on Virginia's eleventh birthday, the fists came for her instead. It was kind of like a sick rite of passage. Janine was going to be a mother—she'd made it to adulthood. But now it was Virginia's turn to take her share.

Over time, she'd learned the triggers, the words and actions that would attract her mother's rage. The rare punch still landed, usually on the late nights when Mother Blue groped for the whiskey, but for the most part, Virginia lived in an icy truce with her mother. If she behaved, spoke only when spoken to, went to church, and did her chores, she was largely safe. Maybe when Virginia left, Mother Blue would turn her anger once again on Janine and potentially even her baby, but that was the price Virginia would have to pay.

The baby didn't deserve what Mother Blue would do to it, but Virginia couldn't save her family. She could only save herself.

Once at school, she shuffled to her locker, sneakers dragging on bruised tile, face hidden by her unruly thicket of hair. Clumps of students dispersed to grant her passage, as though she repelled them by an innate magnetism. "There's Ginny," she heard one girl say, and the chatter quieted to whispers as she passed.

Even with Suzanne gone, they still avoided her. Virginia raised her cuff and took a whiff—there was just the faint vanilla of her body cream, but she thought briefly that Suzanne's dead smell clung to her. That stink had been like a cloud around Suzanne, reeking of rotten fish and sour milk. She glanced down the hall at Suzanne's locker, and its entire radius was empty, as if that smell remained and drove everyone away. Had it always clung to Suzanne? Had there been a time when she had been clean and clear, or had she been marked from the beginning, doomed to her fate?

Virginia's classes that day dragged on, but besides doodling, she would rest her head on her hand and stare out the dusty windows and daydream. The life of John Adams went in one ear, and the formula for sodium chloride floated out the other. Minerva's sunny adventures took up most of Virginia's headspace, and she sketched herself in the margins of her notebook, embellishing her bosom, polka-dotting a tiny bikini of black ink, using her blackened eraser to color in a graphite tan. But these mental escapes were foiled again and again. The hint of that sour smell wrinkled her nose, and she'd look up invariably towards Suzanne's empty desk with annoyance. Give it up, she thought. Haven't you had enough?

But Suzanne stuck around. At Mass that evening, wedged between the girth of her mother and the frailty of her sister, Virginia had to listen to the priest drone on and on about the senseless trag-edy of Suzanne's death, about the mystery of so much despair at such a young age when there was so much love surrounding her. Right, Virginia thought. The alcoholic father, depressed mother, and bullies were full of so much love. She could say nothing, of course, unless she wanted to suffer the wrath of Mother Blue, who fanned herself with a crumpled program and licked the perspiration from her fuzzy lips. Instead, Virginia sat quietly and mumbled along with her prayers. Hail Mary, full of grace, the Lord is with thee. Blessed art thou among women, and blessed is the fruit of thy womb, Jesus. Holy Mary, mother of God, pray for us sinners now and at the hour of our death. Amen. Amen. Amen.

She did the same at the rosary and then the funeral. Both were closed-casket—the most she saw of Suzanne was a photo outdated by two or three years, one of the rare instances when Suzanne was caught on camera smiling. Virginia watched as the townspeople paid their respects to Suzanne's red-eyed, mournful parents at the front pew. They were crying, getting pity just like Suzanne was, but they were part of the reason she was dead. It's sick, Virginia thought. Nobody gets what they deserve. And when you try to care for someone instead, when you try to be there for them, it just gets thrown away. It makes more sense to be cruel. Makes more sense to ignore.

The one person who shed no tears was Mother Blue, who sat be-side her at the rear of the church, fanning herself again and complaining about the heat. She refused to even pretend to grieve for such a spineless child—her words—and had only gone to the rosary to put an end to Janine's begging. As usual, Virginia said lit-tle, keeping her thoughts to herself and simply playing the role of bereaved best friend—*only* friend. When it was all over, the casket in the ground, the services concluded, everyone returned home, she lay in bed with Felix across her knees and the glow of her laptop, the glow of Minerva, awash upon her face. As long as Minerva's light was over her, the shadow of Suzanne had nowhere to hang.

FOUR

One weekend morning, as Virginia caught up on an old stream, there was a rap at her door. "Ginny," came her sister's nasally voice, "Ginny, can I come in?" Of course, Virginia didn't hear her, didn't even see her until Janine was at her bedside, fingers poised gingerly (threateningly) on the rim of the laptop monitor.

Virginia's eyes snapped up to her. "What?"

"I've been calling you." Janine smiled. "You want to come for a walk?"

"I'm busy right now."

"Come on. It won't be long. Besides, you shouldn't spend so much time on the computer." When Virginia still didn't budge, Janine placed her fingers atop the computer again. "You want to show Mama you're good, don't you? Don't want to make her worry?"

They walked laps around the block, stepping carefully over cracks in the decades-old cement, ducking adeptly under low-hanging branches. Janine looked funny to Virginia, so slender apart from the enormous mound leading her around. She was constantly bent forward, cradling her belly, wincing every so often from some invisible pain, drawing careful, protracted breaths the way a runner in a marathon would.

"She's kicking a lot now," Janine said. "Won't be long."

Virginia gave her a sideways glance, hanging a little behind in her torn jeans, playing with her overlong sleeves. "Why even put yourself through that?"

Janine laughed. "Don't tell Mama, but we didn't plan it. Me and Davy talked about a kid, but maybe not for a while, you know? This just happened."

"I won't ever get pregnant. Looks awful."

"You say that, but just wait, there'll be a boy—" Janine paused. "Do you even like boys?"

Virginia scoffed. "I'm not gay, Janine!"

"Okay. Just occurred to me we never talked about it. Never talked about anything, really."

She stopped and leaned against a tree to catch her breath. "I know I haven't been a good sister. Haven't been around the way I probably should've been. But I'm around now. You ever need to talk—about boys—about Suzanne—I'm around. I'm here."

"Everybody keeps going on about Suzanne," Virginia said. "She got what she wanted. What's so bad about that?"

"Don't say that, Ginny! You know it's a sin to take your own life."

Virginia shrugged. "Maybe she just thought Hell's better than this."

Back in her room, she lay across her bed, swinging her socked feet behind her, watching Felix arch his back and curl into a new position to sleep. She reached out and stroked his fur. "No one gets it. Not Janine. Not Mama. Suzanne's the past now."

And the future? That was easy—Minerva was the future. Minerva could do anything, be anyone. She wouldn't mope around because of some dead girl. There wasn't time at all for that. Not with so much possibility.

The following weeks saw the residual effects of Suzanne's death slowly, but finally, fade away. Suddenly, Janine was no longer crying but fretting once again about the baby and the oncoming due date. Mother Blue resumed her critiques of the government, the liberals, and whomever else she thought responsible for destroying the country. Virginia lost herself in Minerva's streams, her fan sites, gradually going to sleep later and later, sometimes forgetting to refresh Felix's food or empty his litter. "Virginia Blue," her mother roared, "you let this cat stink up the house one more time, and I will make sure he never comes in again!" Slowly, her grades slumped, too. She dozed off in class, had trouble keeping track of lectures. This led to another instance of Mother Blue's fury one night. "Getting called in the middle of the day while I'm working, slaving away," she growled. "You know how embarrassing that is? Knowing your daughter is making a fool of herself and this family?"

"She knows, Mama," Janine said breathlessly. "She knows—"

"Hush, Janine. Don't make excuses for her. Virginia! You look at me when I'm speaking to you."

Virginia raised her eyes to her mother. Mother Blue's face contorted. Her nostrils flared. Her beady eyes narrowed further.

"You watch how you look at me. You think I'm wrong to be embarrassed? You think it's funny? Or you mean to do it? You mean to make us all look like fools?"

"No, Mama. I'm sorry. It won't happen again."

"What's that?"

"It won't happen again."

"It better not." Mother Blue turned away, snatched her cigarettes from the table, and lumbered onto the porch. "That computer of yours is the problem. I don't care if you earned it with God's own money—I'll wreck it."

The screen door banged behind her. Davy continued reading his magazine as though nothing had happened. Janine refused to even chance a glance over her crocheting. Virginia stood simmering, staring after her mother's form in the deep blue pall of the evening. She rushed to her room and slammed the door. "She's a mean, fat bitch," she whispered to Felix, pulling him into a hug. "It's not my fault. I didn't send Daddy away."

She flipped open her laptop. As usual, Minerva would light the way to something better.

One late afternoon, Mother Blue summoned Virginia from her bedroom. "They need me at the store," she announced. "Your sister's hung up, and Davy's working late, too."

"Okay, Mama."

Mother Blue had hardly taken two steps out of the house before Virginia returned to her bedroom and unpaused the latest stream. Minerva and her friends were sampling hot sauces, alternating between bites of chicken wings and spoonfuls of ice cream. It almost didn't matter what they were doing—in fact, it didn't matter at all. All that mattered was that Minerva was on screen, smiling, laughing, living. Virginia watched and watched. She could have stopped breathing and wouldn't have noticed.

Meanwhile, Janine cried out. She collapsed against the kitchen table, her legs drenched, her face flushed and strained. Her screams left her as if delayed, erupting from her throat long after her mouth had warbled. She latched onto the leg of a chair, but no amount of struggle could get her to her feet.

Virginia heard nothing through her headphones. She didn't notice Felix's head snap up or his ears flatten. She might as well have not been in her bedroom at all, instead trying on dresses with Minerva, instead cracking open crawfish and sampling wines. Maybe minutes passed, maybe hours, possibly even days, and then her door flew open. Mother Blue charged inside. Pure red, with an incongruous, incredible speed, she wrenched Virginia from the bed by her hair.

"Mama!" the girl shrieked, dropped on the floor in a heap, her headphones torn away, her laptop hoisted over her head.

"You been in here this whole time," her mother snarled, staring at the laptop screen with disgust and confusion, "watching this trash while your sister was out there losing her baby! Your niece! My granddaughter!"

"I didn't know, Mama! I'm sorry!"

"You'd have known if you were good for something! No better than that damn Grayson girl!"

She raised the laptop higher.

"Mama! Please! I'm sorry!"

The laptop crashed down in an explosion of glass shards, plastic keys, and silicon circuits. Both mother and daughter looked upon the mangled machinery, the mauled motherboard. Mother Blue's jowls quivered, heralding another rage, but she only turned and marched out of the room, snatching Virginia's phone along the way. Virginia remained frozen in shock, eyeing the shattered screen and exposed circuitry in disbelief. Felix, head low, tail between his legs, emerged tentatively from beneath the bed. When he sniffed her hand, Virginia took him into her arms and sobbed into his midnight-black fur.

It was dark and starless outside when Davy nudged open her door. "Ginny," he whispered into the darkness, "you want to meet your niece?"

She rode silently in his truck past the fleeting glow of gas sta-tions and corner stores, walked wordlessly into the fluorescent light of the hospital. From behind a window, they looked over the new-borns in the nursery. Davy pointed out a baby in the front row. "There she is," he said, his voice welling with a mixture of pride and nervousness. "Her name's Coral."

Virginia stared at the infant swaddled in pink, the baby so still she would have thought it dead if not for the chest lightly rising and falling. She turned to Davy, speaking in little more than a hoarse whisper. "Janine?"

Janine slept softly in a nearby room, paler than Virginia had ever seen her and somehow even frailer. Davy stroked her arm. "I brought Ginny, baby," he said, kissing her brow.

Janine roused, her eyes fluttering open. She saw her sister and smiled. "Ginny. You made it. Did you see her? Isn't she beautiful?"

Virginia approached the bedside. She eyed Janine from sweaty hair to sallow lips, from ashen skin to bleary eyes, and then the shock holding together her quivering lips and watering eyes broke.

Janine held her as she cried. "It's okay, sweetie. Everybody's safe. Everything's okay."

Back in the darkness of her room, Virginia clutched Felix to her chest and conjured with all the force she could muster the Califor-nia sunshine and Pacific spray. She willed what she could of Minerva's hazel eyes and infectious smile. But all the images quickly faded, and there was Janine again, near death in that hospital bed. There was Suzanne, shuffling down the corridors of their school and lounging lifelessly on her bed. There was Suzanne curled up in the forest, reeking of that awful dead smell.

Days passed. Janine and the baby remained in the hospital. Virginia evaded her mother as best she could, sleepwalking through her classes, so silent and negligible that no one even glanced at her. She hadn't realized how much the gray sky of Oasis seemed to press down without the sugary blue of Oakland to counter it, nor had she realized how suffocating the air was, how rife with Suzanne's dead smell. Maybe it really wasn't Suzanne, after all, but indeed the town, indeed the stagnant ground rotten with generations of bodies. The only thing separating Virginia from Suzanne had been Minerva—without the streams, without the comfort of Minerva's teary-eyed authenticity, without her contagious, carefree joy, how would Virginia last? Every day, she felt more sluggish, more tired. She couldn't sleep, hearing the rustle of bugs somewhere in the walls, dreaming about wading in black tar and stumbling through dense fog. "I'm not sorry," she whispered. "I won't be sorry. You left *me*. You don't deserve me crying for you. So just leave me alone. You hear me, Suzanne? Just leave me alone!"

But no matter how much she pleaded or begged, how much anger she threw out into the dark, the smell only got worse, her nightmares only more vivid. It was like Suzanne's death had been the first domino to fall, and now things were just getting worse and worse. She found herself scratching at her neck and under her sleeves, imagining things crawling over her. If only she could sleep. If only she could find a way to see Minerva again, to rest and recover and forget about all this other stuff.

Then, coming home on an especially overcast day, stinking and teetering from exhaustion, Virginia stopped in her tracks before reaching the driveway.

Lying in the street, motionless, was the vague, dark shape of an animal. She knew immediately it was Felix. The face was contorted agonizingly in mid-wail. The black fur was streaked with muddy blood. Her heart like a stone in her gut, Virginia scooped up the rigid carcass and sat on the porch, plucking and smoothing out the intractable fur. Now, the awful dead smell shrouded Felix, too.

"Oh, Jesus, Ginny," a dark-eyed, long-faced Davy moaned to her. "I just wanted him to go out for a bit. You know, it's Janine who brings him in. Ah, Christ. Fuck—"

She said nothing to him, didn't even look at him. Even when her mother's enormous shadow enveloped her, when the great mouth spat its invectives, she didn't budge at all. But when Mother Blue seized Virginia's arm to pry free the dead animal, Virginia resisted. She hardened against her mother's strength, pulling her arms closer together, entombing the broken mass of fur, flesh, and bone against her chest, behind her knees. Her face tightened. Her mouth solidified into an unbreakable line. Another pull, harder than the first, and still she held, her hair falling over her face, the first tears prickling her eyes. A third tug elicited an indignant whimper. At last, a fourth and final jerk freed the animal and threw Virginia onto her stomach.

"Get a bag and throw this out," Mother Blue commanded Davy, and as he scampered away, Virginia rose, snarling as though feral, baring her teenaged mouth in a display of primal rage. She hissed and shrieked and pounced, but the wide arc of Mother Blue's palm sent her sprawling against the wooden floor of the porch.

"If you weren't my daughter—and I wish you weren't—I'd do worse," said Mother Blue. She balled her hand into a trembling, thick-veined fist. "You care more about some damn cat than you do your own sister, your own niece." She seemed about to say more but simply shook her head and walked into the house.

Quietly, Davy reappeared and bagged the dead animal before retreating inside. Virginia didn't stir from the floor, her eyes and nostrils burning from that awful, reeking smell, from the sensation of bugs crawling over her tongue.

She sat in the utter blackness of her room, feeling legs over her skin, hearing chittering in the walls and in her head. Her tears dried in sticky clumps on her cheeks, and she had to try hard to control her erratic breathing. Then, as if a switch went off, she moved. It was late, past midnight, when she emerged from her bedroom in her ratty black parka, her backpack slung over her shoulder. As Mother Blue and Davy snored in their respective rooms, she went about quietly selecting cans of rice and beans, jars of fruit preserves, an assortment of granola bars. She folded away the money Janine kept wadded up in an old coffee pot. She fingered Davy's key ring and unhooked his pocket knife and truck keys. Her pictures of Felix—him as a kitten, him asleep in flower pots and on her windowsill, his head poking out from under her covers—she kept safely tucked underneath a quilt Janine had made her when she turned twelve.

As she backed out Davy's truck and turned onto the road, the headlight beams disappearing into the misty distance, she had only one thought: Suzanne had been right. Any place was better than here.

FIVE

She drove over an hour before the low-gas indicator chimed on in dull amber. Fuck—she had forgotten all about gas. The truck trundled on a few more miles before grinding to a halt on the long, desolate stretch of highway. Virginia sat with clammy hands on the steering wheel, peering past the headlight beams at the empty road, the endless fields, the dark expanse of sky and its handful of scattered stars. After a long, steadying breath, she cut off the engine and started into the night with her bag, a weak flashlight guiding the way.

She tried not to think of Felix, but he came to her in fits. Him as a kitten, scrounging through her dolls and pawing at a cast-aside sock. His blood-caked fur between her fingers. Her dressing him in T-shirts, posing him with sunglasses. His body sluggish and loose upon her knees, as though he were mud or putty. The excited swish of his tail and the flare of his green eyes as she filled his food bowl. The rigid mask of anguish that dressed his dead face.

No conjuring of Minerva helped. Felix kept coming back, and with him, her mother, Janine, Davy, and yes, even Suzanne. She didn't want to think of them—she'd never see any of them again, anyway. And so what? She was better off without them. Janine was pathetic. Mother Blue was a monstrous bitch. Davy was a careless piece of shit, and it was his fault that Felix was dead. Suzanne was a coward who had run away from her. They'd all worked together to make her life in Oasis an absolute pile of shit from day one. But what about Coral? She felt a pang at the thought of the little baby in pink, but the baby wasn't blameless, either. She was a trap, an anchor designed to pull Virginia back into the mess she was leaving behind. She wasn't about to feel guilty, and she wasn't going to sacrifice herself to protect some little human she didn't even know. Flesh-and-blood family hadn't amounted to much, and some baby wouldn't change that.

They're the past now, she told herself. The future's out there, with Minerva, with the sun and the water and the dresses and the drinks. You can be yourself out there. You can be whoever you want to be.

She kept telling herself that, repeating it in her mind like a chant, as much to convince herself as to keep her mind off the cold, off the ache of her already throbbing feet, off the nagging anxiety bristling at the back of her head. The sound of an oncoming car made her heart leap, and she turned to see lights rising behind her. She ducked into the nearby brush, clutching Janine's quilt tight around her shoulders, struggling to keep her jaw from shaking. She waited for the sound of the wheels crunching on the asphalt to churn into the distance until only the chirps of the crickets and the rustle of branches remained. She continued on, avoiding the road, keeping to the thicket, the cold and pain and anxiety all the stronger for the break in momentum. You can't get caught, she thought. Then it'll be for nothing. Mama hurting you will be for nothing. Felix dying will be for nothing.

But the exhaustion weighed, and not long after she broke from the road, her legs gave out on her. She sat against a tree, hugging her knees, rubbing her arms. Beyond the cold and the fatigue, there was fear: fear of the dark and the things that roamed out here. Virginia had been scared of the dark as a kid, desperate for a nightlight and denied one every time she asked. "Ain't nothing there," Mother

Blue told her. "It's what's in your head that's coming out. And a good little girl wouldn't have anything bad in her head, would she? She'd only have Jesus."

Except Jesus never made her feel any better. She'd had to learn how to deal with the dark and everything it hid away on her own. How to tolerate it and wait patiently for the light to return.

It dawned on her for the first time what she was doing, the material things she was leaving behind. Food. Shelter. Electricity. No nightlight would help out here even if she had one. But it was worth it to get away from Mama's constant anger and Janine's nasally voice and Davy's cringe commentary. She just had to square up and find courage. Minerva did it—she'd come out the other side of her father dying. Virginia had sat with her in the middle of the night, listening to her talk about the car accident that claimed her father, how she had dealt with therapists, how she had suffered night terrors and sleep paralysis as a result. My dad's also gone, Virginia had thought, tears icing her cheeks. Only he wasn't dead, of course— just a deadbeat who ran off. Her problems were nothing compared to Minerva's, but Virginia liked to think they were connected in a way, both survivors, heroes of their own stories. And look at what Minerva had accomplished, navigating the modeling world, making videos for millions of people and inspiring them to come together and be better. Her father's death hadn't stopped her. The night terrors hadn't held her back. She'd been brave, no matter how painful the loss, no matter how scary the dark.

Virginia searched for that same strength, digging as deep as she could. Mama was right about some things even if she was a monster: there was nothing there in the dark, only fears and doubts and insecurities. Virginia kept telling herself that, asking herself what Minerva would do, and soon, without realizing it, she dozed off.

Moments later, her eyes opened.

The dark had settled deeply around her, so thick she thought she could actually touch it, actually feel it with her fingers—but when she tried to raise her arms, they didn't budge. They were glued to her sides, just as her knees were frozen against her chest. She scanned desperately with her eyes, but there was only that thick, dense darkness hanging all around her like a blanket. The dark buzzed with the flutter of wings and crackled with the swarm of legs. She fought to move, but her limbs remained stuck in place. Then a twig snapped.

Her eyes darted to the sound. Something approached, gliding through the tangible dark like a ship passing through deep fog. A black paw landed first, followed by a bloody, furry leg. The small face that emerged next was scarred, the green eyes dull and lacking their familiar brightness. A twisted, too-long body slunk out, followed by crippled legs and broken tail. Only when the full animal appeared did the sour, musty dead smell reach Virginia in force. She felt the tears gather and stream down her paralyzed cheeks. Felix, she tried to say. I'm sorry. I'm sorry. I should've been there. I shouldn't have let them do that to you. But although her mouth moved, no sound left her throat. The cat's battered form weaved closer and closer, until the blood-caked paws topped her knees, until the ice-cold whiskers brushed her cheeks, until the stomach-churning dead smell filled her nostrils—

A voice called her name and startled her awake: "Virginia."

Her eyes shot open. A man crouched before her, his off-white suit tinged blue in the moonlight, a satin tie reflecting dimly under his neck. A masquerade mask, painted a deep navy blue and trimmed with elaborate gold, covered his face. She thought it a tiger at first, but no—it was the visage of a cat, with pointed ears at the top. A thin, nearly invisible wire around his head, digging so deep as to almost draw blood, kept the mask grafted to his face. His eyes were shrouded in shadow, submerged so completely Virginia would have doubted he had a face at all if his voice didn't sound again.

"Good. You're awake. You'll freeze out here, to say nothing of animals."

His voice had a tinny quality, bouncing off the interior of the mask. There was a crunchy undertone: the mask stretching and compressing with the movements of his jaw and the flexes of his muscular neck.

"Who are you?" Virginia managed at last. "Were you following me?"

The man was silent, but she felt his hidden eyes studying her.

"Of course I followed you," he said, standing. "We planned this together, after all. Making your way to Dallas, buying your bus ticket—finally meeting Minerva. That was many nights, you and I."

She stared. "Felix?"

He raised black-gloved hands. "Indeed."

"But—but that doesn't make sense—"

"I suppose you would be confused." He adjusted his lapels, his cuffs. "I'm liberated. To think, Mama's cruelty wrought a blessing."

"Mama?"

"Yes. How selfless of Davy, trying to deflect your anger. After all, he is no blood of yours. Or perhaps he feared Mama's wrath. Didn't we all? Every moment in that house spent trying to placate her."

He looked upon her disbelieving face, her chattering teeth and trembling shoulders.

"You still don't understand? She took me by the nape of the neck and flung me out. Her retribution against you, Virginia. Impossible to fathom such hatred towards one's own child—but we know the story very well, don't we? Insecurity and self-loathing projected onto a prodigal daughter. Sixteen years of resentment culminating in a violent explosion." He paused. "Why the tears? You, of all people, have the least reason to cry over her."

"Mama wouldn't," Virginia said. She couldn't help the tears, much as they surprised her. "She hit me, but she would never do that to Felix—"

"Mama *did*," the man said. "She enjoyed it, too." He knelt before her again, took her cheek in his hand, wiped away a tear. "Your mother has done you a kindness. Her hatred spares your own. You can let go of her—let go of all that past life."

She didn't say anything, couldn't say anything. Could any of this be real? Mama killed Felix? And this was his ghost or—

"That word fits well enough," he said. "But there is little point in quibbling over my reality. You'll freeze without a fire."

She watched him break branches and stomp sticks with decisive, violent precision. Soon, flames were lit. The warmth and glow tugged at her, drawing her forward. As she warmed herself, the man withdrew a can of beans from her bag. With the same adeptness with which he assembled the kindling, he unsealed the can and, using a forked stick as makeshift tongs, warmed the can over the fire. "Eat," he urged her, and she did, stirring the beans slowly, blowing on each spoonful and testing the heat with miniscule sips. As the beans cooled, her appetite swelled—she ate more rapidly, and the man regarded her, the sparks of the fire illuminating a pair of dark eyes at last. Were they green, just like Felix's?

"If you're really Felix," she said at length, sniffling, her spoon scraping the bottom of the can, "tell me something he would know. That not Mama or Davy or Janine would know."

"Not even Suzanne?"

She shook her head. "Not even Suzanne."

The fire crackled. The man stoked the flames with the same forked stick, turning over blackened stones, casting embers into the air.

"Not long after we met," he said, "you entertained a radical idea. You would leave, just as you are now, to seek out your father."

She stared at him.

"You wrote a letter to him. I remember its words vividly—you dictated them every night. In your crude crayon, you must have produced at least ten drafts, none satisfactory. Finally, one rainy night, long after your mother commanded you to sleep, you finished the letter by the glow of a toy flashlight. You folded it, used a sticker to ensure it was sealed."

Virginia shivered. She swallowed down new tears.

"Of course, you never sent that letter, never left to deliver it personally. To this day, the letter sits at the bottom of your drawer. Maybe tomorrow, or the day after, as they hunt for clues as to your whereabouts, your mother will read it. Perhaps she'll share it with your sister. They'll commiserate together."

He paused, watching her. "Do I need to recite the words?"

"No," she said quickly. "No. I—I believe you." She smiled through a fresh wave of sobs. "It's really you, Felix? You'll help me?"

He nodded. "Yes, Virginia. It's really me. And I am here for you always."

She rushed into his arms, fully crying now. He held her, stroked her hair. "No crying, Virginia," he soothed. "You have nothing to be sorry for."

"But Mama—and I—"

He held her apart and wiped away her tears again. "As always, I am here to serve you. You never have to apologize to me."

She smiled, laughed, and soon enough, exhausted with relief, fell asleep again, this time into a deep, restful slumber.

When she woke up, the sky was dim and gray. She rose from the quilt to find Felix hunkered before the crackling, dying fire, warming pieces of cornbread she had brought with the canned food. He held out the plate. "Come, while it's warm."

She ate quickly, surprised by her hunger. Between chewing and chasing down the bread with water, she spoke to her new (old?) companion.

"What about you? Aren't you hungry?"

"Not at all," he said. "I don't need to eat. I don't need to sleep."

"So"—she hesitated—"you're really a ghost?"

He chuckled. "Yes. I did die, after all."

"And did it hurt? Was it scary?"

"You don't need to worry about me, Virginia. Besides, without that happening, I wouldn't be here now. I wouldn't be able to watch over you."

"I'd never leave you behind," she said, and he laughed.

"Nor would I leave you. But a cat seems to me limited in its ability to keep watch or prepare food. Now. Finish eating, so we can depart. We need to take advantage of the light."

When they had broken their impromptu camp, scattering the fire pit and obscuring their tracks, she followed Felix out of the brush and into the open field. "Can we make it to Dallas today?" she asked. "Or do you think it'll take longer?"

"Longer," he said. "We need to keep our footprint as small as possible."

"Okay." Virginia took his gloved hand. "Let's go."

SIX

They kept to the wooded areas, out of sight of the highway. Daytime was difficult, the sun hard to bear, but nighttime worse, with limited moonlight to guide the way. After another day of walking, exhausted and stinking, Virginia looked over what little remained of her canned food and granola bars and cursed. "We would've been to Dallas by now if we still had the car," she said. She looked up at Felix with alarm. "We can make it, right?"

The man raised his hand to his chin and surveyed her. His close gaze felt strange and uncomfortable, no matter how many times she reminded herself that this was Felix. The problem was he didn't *feel* like Felix. When he was a cat, Felix's presence alone had been enough to soothe her, to help ease the anxieties and fears. He would wedge himself between her legs or curl up on her lap. When Mother Blue was at her worst, Janine at her most annoying, Suzanne at her most avoidant, Felix never strayed from her side. She could always count on him to be there—he didn't have to wear a nice suit or say weird things. How could it even be possible that he was here? Sure, she could figure ghosts were real—when she was younger, the kids at school would trade stories of doors opening and closing on their own, of windows rattling and plates falling without explanation—but shouldn't ghosts be the way they were when they were alive? Felix should still be a cat, not a person. Yet he knew so much: details about Virginia and Suzanne, Janine and Mother Blue, that no one outside the house could know. The only one who would know, who could know, was Felix—precisely because he had always been by Virginia's side.

"We will need to find more food," he said finally. "You're exhausted and eating more than you should be."

"I'm sorry, I—"

He raised a reassuring hand. "It's all right. I believe there is someplace close." He turned in the direction of the highway, head poised as if scanning, and then pointed. "There—a diner."

How did he know? No matter how she craned her neck, there was nothing but gray countryside and empty sky all around. Still, the mere mention of a diner immediately made her stomach growl, roused by the images of waffles dripping with syrup, of plates running yellow with loosed egg yolk. She grimaced—the memory of Mother Blue's pancakes came next, followed by her fried chicken, her grits. Virginia had enjoyed many such breakfasts, especially when she was younger.

"Ah, yes," Felix said. "Mama's cooking is delicious. Only ever outdone by her yelling. And who could forget her wonderful hitting?"

Virginia shivered. It was like he could read her thoughts, see the directions in which they wound. It went beyond just knowing things about her, things only Felix would know. But as weird as the situation was, as strange as this new Felix seemed, he was helping her. Without the car, she didn't think she could make it to Dallas by herself, especially with her supply of food running so low so quickly.

They kept moving, and true to Felix's word, the sign of a diner rose over the horizon. Virginia was about to cross the parking lot when Felix took her arm.

"Don't forget—no one else can see me. You must act like you're alone."

It was true: only she could see and hear him. She didn't know why, and he couldn't explain it—maybe it was some kind of "ghost rule," she thought, something to do with their connection in life that kept him here after death. But it had real consequences, especially because she had to keep a low profile. Word had probably already spread from Oasis that she was missing, and she wasn't far enough away yet to be reckless with how she acted. Doing the wrong thing, saying the wrong thing, would just dump her back into the hell that was her home—and how much worse would it be after what she'd done?

She tried to be casual walking into the diner, acting as if she didn't stink, as if she hadn't just appeared out of the wilderness. She sat quietly in one of the booths, playing with her fingers, having trouble figuring out where to put her eyes. "A menu," Felix said, sitting across from her. She took one from the stand at the end of the table and tried to look as seriously as she could at the pictures of poached eggs and BLT sandwiches.

A tired-eyed waitress came by, thin and blonde, wrinkled at the mouth and around the eyes. "What'll it be?" she asked, sliding out her notepad. "Need more time?"

Virginia hesitated, stealing glances at the waitress, trying not to stare and finding it hard not to do so. It became clearer and clearer with every glance that, despite the wrinkles, the waitress wasn't much older than Virginia was—maybe nineteen or twenty-one at the most. What was her story, working in this rinky-dink place that seemed as antique as Oasis? Overstressed college student who commuted out of Dallas? Burnt-out single mom just trying to make ends meet? Getting older didn't solve any problems by the looks of it—Virginia knew that from Janine, anyway. Time and age only seemed to introduce new issues.

The waitress turned. "I'll swing back—"

"No," said Virginia, "sorry. Can I just get a couple of fried eggs? And a side of bacon?"

"Sure. Coming right up."

Felix lifted a finger.

"Oh—and can it be to go?"

The waitress left to another table, and Virginia sucked in a big breath. The menu was clattering, and she realized with quiet surprise that her arms were shaking.

"It's okay," Felix said. "You did well. Now, count the money. Good—the eggs will be over five dollars, the bacon an additional three—"

She folded out the wrinkled bills, smoothing them as much as she could. When the waitress returned with the plastic-bagged take-out, Virginia had to resist the urge to bolt and run. She manufactured her best smile, stilled her trembling arms as much as possible, said her "thank you" maybe a little too loudly, and then she left, bag swinging at her side, cheeks burning red.

"Once we get to Dallas, there will be less need to conceal you," Felix said after they left the diner behind them. "The city is large enough to hide you and make the departure to California simple."

Virginia hoped he was right. It was true that she had planned running away for a long time, always caving to the little chorus of doubtful voices that warned her it was too dangerous, too far, too risky. She had criticized Suzanne for never making good on her promise to leave, but Virginia had been just as cagey about her own plans. She was seeing now that there had been decent reason to be nervous. Things weren't going all that smoothly, and after paying for the food, the money she had taken from Janine's stash didn't seem nearly as much as it did before. No matter what, she needed enough for the bus fare: the golden ticket that would pave the way to her new life. Nothing could threaten that.

The sound of thunder drew her eyes up. The horizon darkened with storm clouds, and a sudden gust of cool air cut through the thin cotton of her hoodie and raised the hairs on her arms.

"Rain," Felix said. He pointed now in the direction of what he said was a barn.

"How do you know?" Virginia asked, rubbing her arms. "First the diner, and now a barn?"

"I'm not sure myself," he said after a moment. "Maybe death has yielded even more gifts for me."

Virginia didn't say anything else, following him into the countryside. Not long afterwards, the sky above nearly black, the heavy wind rattling trees and blowing up dust, they found the barn. The uneven paint job, peeled and stripped over many years, exposed the beige mahogany underneath. Felix pulled open the doors, and the interior drew Virginia in with stale, humid air and the stench of old wood and ancient manure. She lingered inside, stepping over scattered strands of hay and fallen planks of wood. As Felix shut the door, and darkness overtook the barn, the rain started to fall.

After eating, bundled in her quilt, sitting in a dry corner and licking her fingers of residual grease, she watched as Felix paced the length of the barn. A small fire burned nearby, keeping at bay the chill of the storm. Rain leaked through the holes in the roof, collecting in puddles on the ground. Being stationary again had intensified her anxiety and left her with nothing to do but dwell on her fears and doubts. They centered on Felix now. It was true that he didn't eat, didn't sleep. He didn't seem to get tired or even angry. Problems came up, and he had answers for each one. He seemed to know so much—seemed to know everything.

"Felix," she said slowly, tentatively. "What was it like?"

He paused his pacing, peering through one of the holes in the roof. He caught rainwater in his palm and whisked it away.

"Dying?" he asked.

She nodded. "Everything after, too."

"I told you before, Virginia," he said. "You don't need to worry about me."

"I know. I'm just curious, I guess. Like, this whole thing is crazy. If you're here, that means ghosts are *real*."

He chuckled. "True enough." He paused and thought on his answer.

A sudden boom of thunder shook the barn and made her jump.

"Dying was painful," he said at length, undisturbed by the storm, "but what came after is hard to explain."

She waited, trying to calm her panicked heart.

"Imagine being free of your body," he went on. "Being free of the chemicals and hormones, the bones and muscles. All the restraints that held you back in life. Total freedom, and with it, what feels like total knowledge. Suddenly, I was aware of ideas I never could have expressed in earthly life—ideas that were nonetheless so intimate, so tied to my sense of self. Ideas I never could have known with such a pitiful excuse for a brain and such a weak, temporary body. Ideas I had known before, in previous lives. In many other forms."

Still shaking, Virginia wasn't sure she understood. But her curiosity pushed her on.

"What happened? Where did you go?"

"Go?" he asked. "But aren't I here? Aren't I still with you?"

"Yeah, but—"

"That's not what you really mean to ask, is it?" He drew closer, kneeling before her, the dark eyes behind his mask searching her own. "What do you really want to know? Could it be Suzanne? Whether she is safe? Whether she is happy, wherever she is?"

Virginia was quiet. She avoided his gaze.

"I thought you hated her," he said. "Why the change of heart?"

"She left me alone," Virginia said, "but that doesn't mean she deserved to die."

"And I did?"

"No! Of course not. I just hope things are better for her. That it was worth it."

Felix stood and linked his hands behind his back. Virginia watched him, afraid she had said the wrong thing, offended him in some way. Of course she was happy he was here—how could she not be? But that also meant so many other things. People and animals didn't just die. They stayed on somehow. They changed. Was Suzanne still herself? Or had she become something different, something that wasn't even human anymore? Was she a cat now? Was she even here anymore, like Felix, or had she gone to another place, like Heaven? Had she, as much as it terrified Virginia, gone to Hell? Because of everything she did while she was alive, the sex and the drugs?

"Truthfully," said Felix, "I have no idea what's become of Suzanne. But I can only imagine she experienced a change like mine. A realization of what she really is."

"Do you think she might still be here? Like you?"

"If she is," Felix replied, "she clearly hasn't made an effort to see you."

His words chilled her more than the rain or the wind. It was true: Felix was here, but where was Suzanne? For months, Virginia had suffered in the aftermath of Suzanne's death. She had lost access to Minerva, lost Felix, and never, not once, did her supposed best friend visit her.

"She's abandoned you, Virginia," Felix said. "Not just once, but twice. Your entire friendship was never about what she could do for you, but rather, what you could do for her."

Virginia sat silently, burying her face in her hands so she could hide her tears. But somehow, she knew Felix could see through her hands, see through her whole being. The final threads of faith in Suzanne were the hardest to snap, but they were also the most embarrassing.

Felix resumed his pacing. "Look to the future, Virginia. Minerva is waiting. She wouldn't abandon you. She *won't* abandon you."

She knew he was right. Minerva had so many friends, so many followers, and she made time for all of them. Suzanne? There had been nobody except Virginia, not even Suzanne's parents, and look how she had treated Virginia. Everyone at school was right: Suzanne was a freak, a weirdo. She'd kept everyone at arm's length, and all the crocodile tears at the funeral couldn't change that.

"You're right," Virginia murmured, and she settled back as comfortably as she could. Just keep going, she told herself. Don't be afraid or anxious. Minerva's waiting. And when you get there, all this will be like a bad dream, a nightmare that you had to pass through to wake up.

SEVEN

The storm continued, and Virginia ended up spending the rest of the day in the barn, slipping in and out of sleep as lightning flashed and thunder raged. Felix was quiet, hovering like he had been doing, but she sensed his impatience in the quickness of his pacing and the rigidity of his posture. She wanted to get to Dallas, too, but there was nothing to do with the storm.

When the rain finally stopped, Felix roused her with a biscuit she had saved as well as the few remaining slices of bacon. No amount of sleep seemed to make her feel rested, but eating energized her enough to get her on her feet. Outside, the sky had cleared to a heavy blue, the grass a gleaming green. With her bag once more over her shoulder, Virginia started walking after Felix. The walking was definitely the worst part since leaving Oasis. No matter the hours they trudged, they never seemed closer to getting anywhere. But Felix assured her they were on the right track. They would get there soon, provided they kept a solid pace and were no longer delayed by the weather or having to hide.

Eventually, cresting a hill, they found themselves overlooking a farmhouse. In the late morning light, under the blue sky and against the lush, green backdrop, the white, clapboard house and its adjacent windmill seemed taken straight from a painting. In the distance, cattle grazed—the animals watched blandly, chewing their cud, as Virginia and Felix approached the house.

Virginia was about to ask why they were going to the house when they should have been avoiding people, but the sight of a nearby well wiped away all her concerns. She practically ran to the well and strained her muscles pulling up a pail of cold, glistening water. The sight of the water revived her thirst and hunger, to the point she wondered if anything she had even eaten or drunk over the past few days had mattered at all. She guzzled down water, not caring that it splashed over her mouth and drenched her chest.

As she drank, Felix surveyed the house.

"No vehicle," he said. "We should see what we can find inside. There may be more food, better clothing for the rest of the journey."

Virginia barely heard him, so focused as she was on draining the water. When she looked up, Felix was gone.

"Felix?" she called. "Wait!"

She followed hesitantly, instinctively staying low, keeping her eyes on the far-off road. Without Felix by her side, her anxiety spiked again, and she dreaded what might happen if even a single person saw her. Would they take her back? Would they arrest her? Would she have to sit there while Janine and her baby cried over her, while Davy squirmed in the corner, while Mama screamed at her and hit her?

She found the front door open, swinging lightly, noisily, on aged hinges. A wind chime on the porch clanged ominously to her right.

She spoke nervously into the house. "Felix? Are you there?"

He didn't answer her. She stood for a long time on the porch, sensing somehow that if she stepped inside, she was going to cross some kind of line, some fuzzy boundary. She wasn't like Suzanne—breaking the law terrified her, even though she had technically stolen Davy's car. But that was different. That was personal. If she went inside this house, she'd be breaking into a stranger's home, somebody totally unrelated to Oasis and her family and all the shit she was leaving behind. And she couldn't justify that no matter what she told herself.

But you have to find Felix, she insisted. And you can't let anyone see you.

One anxiety overcame the other, and she crept inside, the wooden floorboards creaking beneath her sneakers. Lining the foyer were sideboards topped with decorative china depicting flowers, roosters, mountaintops. A grandfather clock ticked down the hall, and she dreaded the mechanical cuckoo springing out at any moment.

"Felix?" she whispered, speaking so softly she almost didn't hear herself. Carefully, she went up the carpeted stairs, reaching into her back pocket for Davy's knife. She had no idea what to do with it were someone actually to spring out, but it felt good to hold it. It was something Suzanne would do, she thought absently, Suzanne who, for all her faults, was never afraid of getting in some guy's pickup or going into a store with a fake ID to buy beer.

She paused and tightened her grip on the knife. Oh, just forget about Suzanne already, Jesus Christ. Always Suzanne. *Always* Suzanne. Remember what Felix said. She abandoned you. She left you behind and went off wherever people go when they die.

A breeze ruffled the white drapes of a window on the second-floor landing. There was still no sign of Felix, no sign of anyone at all. Virginia reached an open door, holding out the knife shakily, imagining that something might jump out from around the corner—

"What do you plan to do with that? You'll more likely hurt yourself before anyone else."

She swung around to Felix filling up the doorway.

"Shit!" she cried. "You scared me! Where did you go?"

He ignored her and moved into the room. "The bedroom," he announced. "Anything valuable will be here."

Virginia eyed the woodwork armoire and floral-printed bed, smelled the rose-scented perfume hanging heavily in the air. She hadn't known her grandmother, but this felt like what that lady's room would look like and smell like. The sensation made her feel even worse about what they were doing—they weren't just violating someone's space, but an old lady's.

"We shouldn't be here," she said. "This is somebody's house. We can't just steal stuff."

Felix glanced through the armoire's drawers, flicking through a stack of letters, sifting through tubes of lipstick. "Losing the car has delayed us badly," he said, "and you saw as well as I did that your sister's money will only get you so far. What if it's not enough to reach California? You'll be trapped in a city you don't know. And Minerva will be out of reach."

"But it's not right."

He chuckled. "You sound like Janine. Why are you afraid?"

She straightened up. The challenge was reminiscent of Suzanne, the way she would mock and laugh whenever Virginia tried to be brave.

"I'm not afraid," she said.

Felix moved aside. "In that case, show me."

She hadn't expected to be challenged like that, and having those dark eyes so intently on her made her skin crawl. She breathed in deep and went for the armoire, forcing herself to throw open the drawers and rifle through the amassed jewelry, the various perfume bottles and makeup. After a moment of searching, she lifted a necklace—the silver chain glinted in the light from the window, and the embedded piece of garnet shone a deep, passionate red.

"Beautiful," Felix remarked. "Likely valuable."

Virginia turned it over. "It says something: 'To my beloved Caroline. Yours, Harold.'"

Not just a grandma, after all, she thought, but a wife, maybe even a widow. She hesitated and put the necklace back.

"It's not ours," she said. "And we shouldn't be here, anyway."

Felix watched her. "As you wish," he said at length.

They returned downstairs. Virginia walked onto the porch, and then her heart dropped—coming up towards the house was an old woman in denim, a wicker hat atop her head and a basket of lemons on her arm. This was the old lady the house belonged to, and now everything was about to come to an end. All the nightmarish scenarios flashed again before her eyes. Sitting in a jail cell. Enduring Mother Blue's inevitable rage. Being stuck in Oasis forever.

The woman spotted her and stopped. With a quick, penetrating glance, she seemed to see through Virginia just like Felix often did. Virginia felt her cheeks burn with shame, embarrassment, fear. She thought vaguely that it would be nice to disappear, to sink into the wood of the porch and keep sinking until she was gone, sucked up into the planet's core. But that didn't happen, of course. It would have been too easy.

"Can I help you?" the old woman asked, removing her hat and letting her gray hair loose in the wind.

"I was just seeing if anyone was here," Virginia blurted. "I ain't been inside—"

"What's your name?"

"Huh?"

"Your name, sweetheart."

"Oh. It's Virginia—"

Felix's hand wrapped around her arm. "Not your real name," he reminded her.

The woman approached. "What was that?"

"Suzanne," Virginia said quickly. "My name's Suzanne."

"Well, Suzanne. My name's Caroline." The woman smiled. "Why don't we go inside? How about some lemonade?" She raised the basket hanging on her arm. "I just picked these, and they'll need squeezing."

In the kitchen, Virginia fidgeted at the small table, watching as the woman squeezed the lemons and broke ice cubes from a freezer tray. Felix stood by the table, but just like the waitress at the diner, the woman couldn't see him—she moved around the kitchen as if no one was there.

"May not be sweet enough," Caroline said, bringing two glasses to the table, "but we can always add some sugar if you'd like." When Virginia didn't drink, the woman gestured to the glass. "Go ahead. It won't bite."

Virginia drank and nearly recoiled. Caroline laughed. "I guess it is sweet enough."

"Sorry," Virginia said. "I don't drink stuff like this. Mama's strict about what we eat."

"Nothing wrong with a little lemonade." Caroline sipped from her own glass. "You have a lot of arguments with your mama?"

Above Caroline's shoulder, Felix shook his head.

"I didn't think anyone was here," Virginia said, changing the subject. "There's no car."

"My son took it into town to get some work done. He'll be gone till tomorrow."

Virginia nodded, sipping that bitter lemonade, looking around at the green-hued kitchen. The antique, crystalline knobs on the drawers and the aged, rusted stovetop reminded her of the kitchen back home. She could clearly picture Mother Blue before that stove, pulling out drawers by their decades-old knobs and rummaging for the egg beater or rolling pin. Maybe it was Janine cooking today, in front of the stove with the baby on her hip, and Mother Blue at the table smoking her cigarettes and coughing, flapping her newspaper, saying what a relief it was to finally be rid of Ginny. Davy would be there, too, in his flimsy shirt and tie, like a kid playing pretend at an office job. They would go on, with or without her—they were the past, but they would still go on.

The old woman eyed her, in particular the bag at her feet. Maybe she saw the momentary longing in Virginia's eyes, the ambivalent desire. The weakness.

"I'm all alone tonight," she said, "and you look like you could use a break. Why don't you stay the night?"

"I don't know," said Virginia. "I should probably get going."

"I insist. I don't care for being all alone here."

Virginia glanced at Felix. The dark mask, without expression, nonetheless seemed to communicate to her its disapproval. Were the eyes narrowing, the ears flattening? But the thought of a bed, any bed, however old or dirty, pulled at her. Her feet hurt—her back hurt. She could only imagine how badly she smelled. Sleeping on the ground and in the barn for the last few days had only made her more and more tired.

I've got to be strong, she thought, letting the idea of an actual bed wash over her. Only way to make it to Dallas and then California.

"Okay," she said.

Caroline led her to a small, nondescript guest room on the ground floor. There was a bare bunk, an empty bookshelf, and a pile of dust-covered boxes. Virginia put down her bag and tested the bunk's mattress. The springs strained under her weight.

"We'll find you some sheets," Caroline said. "For now, why don't you come out with me? I've got more fruit to pick."

Not far from the house, in a shaded grove more picturesque than the farmhouse itself, Virginia followed Caroline with a second basket and collected more lemons. Caroline pointed out the apple trees, which she said wouldn't be ready again for a long while. Virginia looked around nervously for Felix, thinking she would glimpse him through the branches, but he was gone, disappeared.

"Harold," Caroline said, "that was my husband—he had a big green thumb. The trees here are like a memory of him. Proof he was here."

She stopped and plucked a particularly rich, shiny apple from a drooping branch. Virginia marveled at it, reminded of the beautiful red garnet of Caroline's necklace. Her cheeks burned again, her fear tiny now compared to her shame.

What memory would she leave behind? What would be her proof? She thought of those questions throughout the rest of the day, as she helped the old woman cook dinner, as she drew a bath and soaked in the lukewarm water. Everything up until now had been about escaping, making distance from Oasis and her rotten family. She and Suzanne had been bonded by that shared dream, maybe even more than the fact that they had been left out by every-one else. Or maybe their dream had been forged specifically *because* they had been cast out. Either way, they'd always thought about what was coming, not what they'd leave behind, and they'd espe-cially never wondered if leaving anything behind was even important.

In the small guest bedroom, clean after what felt like forever wandering the countryside, Virginia drifted fingers through her shampooed hair and rubbed her heavy eyes. It felt good to be clean, to be fresh. Even the dead smell that had been hanging around her since Suzanne died was gone. She could lick her teeth and rest easy, not worried she might run her tongue over what felt like the roving shell of a beetle, not concerned that, when she scratched her arms, her hands would come back riddled with roaches.

The door nudged open, and Caroline peeked in at her. "Sorry to interrupt. How's everything?"

"Perfect," Virginia said. "The food was really good, too."

"I'm happy to hear."

Caroline waited, and then she came inside and sat down next to Virginia. She measured her words carefully before she spoke.

"Are you in trouble, Suzanne?"

Virginia's heart skipped. She knew where this line of question-ing was headed, and her mind flooded once again with all the possibilities. The police had gotten to Caroline, or she'd seen some-thing on the news about a girl missing from Oasis. Maybe Janine came on to do an interview, crying and slinging snot out her nose. Maybe Mother Blue had spat at the reporter or called the police useless for not being able to find one little girl. Of course, that assumed Virginia's mother even cared about finding her. She had been ready to disown Virginia the last time they saw each other.

"It's okay if you don't want to tell me," Caroline continued. "I just want you to know you're safe here. I'm not gonna kick you out. You want to stay here tomorrow, and the day after that, or another week, or even a month—you go right on ahead. You take your time until you're sure you know what you want to do."

Virginia said nothing, could say nothing, her throat suddenly clogged, her eyes abruptly wet. There was a blurry vision of the Oakland beaches, the sun high in the sky, the water crisp and clear. Minerva was there, and Michelle and Sue and all the other girls. But as vivid as the vision was, it was getting blurrier by the day. Every bone and muscle in Virginia's body hungered for the bed and the fresh sheets and regular baths and good food. There wasn't cigarette smoke here. There wasn't screaming or fighting. No one was going to barge in and bring fists down on her head. No one was going to throw out her cat and not care one bit if it lived or died. No one was going to kill herself and leave her alone, all alone.

"Well, I'll see you in the morning," Caroline said. "We'll get the rest of those apples. How's that sound?"

After she left, Virginia lay in the dark, looking up at the crescent moon through the window, the shadow of the windowpane fixture long across the bed. She was calm, she realized. So, so calm. Unbelievably calm. So calm she started to shake, started to cry. She didn't know what to do. God, if only she knew what to do!

The shadows at the foot of the bed shifted. She scurried back, trying not to scream even as she recognized the black gloves and white lapels.

"What are you doing, Virginia?" Felix asked, his gentle tone betraying something deeper and darker underneath.

"I don't know," she said. "I'm scared, Felix."

He stood over her, silhouetted by the moonlight. "Scared of what?"

"I don't know. I just am."

"I thought your resolve was stronger." Although she couldn't see his face because of the mask, she could hear how his lips curled into a smile. "Clearly, you're not committed if a little bit of food and a nice bed is enough to deter you. Frankly, I'm disappointed."

She swallowed down her tears. "I didn't say I was going to stop."

"Oh, no? Then why cry? Why agonize?" When she didn't answer, he continued. "Stop if you'd like. By all means, stay here. But eventually, you will need to go back. Need I remind you how she hit you? How she insulted you? Imagine how ferocious she will be when you return."

She turned away from him. "Stop it, Felix."

"I have experience with fear. When I was alive, I could only process it in a crude way, as though I were two-dimensional in three-dimensional space. I knew it only as a brute."

She said nothing, but she shook.

"In that state, fear is all-consuming. Like anger. Grief. Hunger. The pure instinct of an animal is admirable. The fear as I lay there, crying out, paralyzed, in absolute agony—there are no words to describe it."

Images invaded her mind again: images of that broken body and blood-caked fur upon her knees, too long, too rigid, too loose. Still he talked. His voice grew deeper and slower.

"Screaming for that pain to end, wishing for an end of any kind. Failing to understand the power that ruined my body. Just a tire as you know—just several thousand pounds of metal and rubber, moving at all of thirty, perhaps forty miles per hour. But enough to be godlike to such a small, stupid animal. Enough to induce pain and fear that a hundred suicides could not abate. An unimaginable terror."

"Why are you telling me this?" Virginia asked through her tears. "You don't think I wanted to die, too? I didn't want that to happen to you, Felix! I never wanted that!"

"But it did happen, Virginia. The same mother to whom you will return subjected me to that. Without reluctance. Without remorse."

She was silent. He was right, of course. Mother Blue was wretched—Mother Blue had killed him. She ruled that house and judged everyone and everything in it. She did with them what she wanted when she wanted. And she would be the final destination if Virginia stopped. Caroline was just a bump in the road, a little pit stop before circling back to the hell of the Blue household.

"I understand your fear," Felix said, his voice once again gentle and unassuming. "Who wouldn't be afraid, running from all she's ever known, braving uncertainty? But the fear doesn't have to control you. You can overcome it. You can harness it as fuel to steer towards what is really, truly good for you."

He leaned over her, so close that his hot breath tickled her ear.

"Who never judges? Who treats her friends and family with love and kindness? Who is magnanimous, beautiful inside and out? Who accepts all and rejects no one?"

"Minerva," Virginia said quietly.

"Yes. Would Minerva have murdered an innocent animal in cold blood? Would Minerva have rejected her own daughter?"

Slowly, Virginia removed herself from the bed. She dressed. Quietly, stepping lightly upon the creaking wood, she left the house and started again on the path towards Dallas. Felix was right: going in any direction but forward meant returning to Oasis and her mother. There wasn't any other option even if her insides screamed and begged for her to turn back after that brief, blissful stay at Caroline's home.

Deep in the thicket again, the night sky sprawling and star-studded above, she held up the photos of Felix to firelight. Maybe she couldn't go back, but at least she had reminders of the good things—

Gloved hands came from behind and snatched away the photos.

"What are you doing?" Virginia demanded.

"You don't need these pictures," Felix said, and then he dashed one into the fire. Virginia nearly dove for the flames, but there was nothing to do—the photograph blackened and shriveled into an ashen contortion.

"Stop it!" she yelled. "Give them back!"

She lunged for the photos, but he circled around her and let the remaining pictures fall into the flames. They watched as the fire did its work. The fight almost literally drained from Virginia—she fell to her knees, tears streaming down her face and gleaming in the firelight.

"Why did you do that?" she sobbed. "That's all I had left of him!"

"I'm right here, Virginia," he said. "You need no pictures to remember me."

"But you're not the same! You're different!"

"Yes, I am—because that's what I must be to keep you safe. To make sure you arrive where you need to. Look at how close you were to disaster just now. You would have stayed there if not for my intervention. You would have been drawn back into Mama's orbit, and then you would never have escaped."

He pointed to the fire. "If you want to reach Minerva, you have to burn it all. All of your past. All of whom you were. You can't leave a single piece of it behind, lest it tempt you back."

What more was there to burn besides the pictures? She looked down at the quilt in her lap. Not the most impressive or most expensive gift she had received from her sister, but the one she had chosen to bring all the same. The one she had pulled around herself during the long nights. The one into which she had cried when it dawned on her she would never meet her father, when she realized finally that Suzanne was dead.

She tightened up as she had against Mother Blue. She shook her head. "No. You can't make me."

Felix did not waver. "Virginia. Virginia, look at me."

"No."

"Virginia."

Reluctantly, she looked up at the mask, the feline features morphing in the erratic light.

"You will never be free of your mother if you refuse," he said. "You will never reach Minerva. And even if you did, what would she want to do with you? Why would she, of all people, accept a coward? A spineless, broken girl unable to free herself from her tormentors, her abusers?"

Virginia stood before the fire, fists clenched, arms trembling. She didn't want to accept his words, but he was right. Minerva would accept her into the circle because she herself was perfect, pure-hearted, but did Virginia deserve that if she couldn't let go of the past? Did she want to be someone who was pitied, or did she want to stand shoulder to shoulder with Minerva and the other girls, responsible for herself, able to protect herself? If she wanted to stand among them, she couldn't be a coward. She couldn't be like Suzanne. She couldn't be like her mother.

"Well?" Felix asked. "What is your decision?"

Virginia held up Janine's quilt. She almost felt her there, standing alongside them, thin and nasally, but not angry with her, never judgmental. Maybe she had never stopped Mama, had never put herself in the way of the punches, but would Virginia have done any different in her shoes? At least Janine hadn't added to the cruelty. At least she hadn't made it worse. She'd been something *not bad* about Oasis. She'd been something almost, kind of good.

Virginia threw the quilt into the flames, watched the threads come undone and disintegrate, watched the colors turn a uniform black. Bye, Janine, she thought, her tears finally seeming to run out. Maybe she was too tired to cry. Maybe she'd just run dry.

"Good," said Felix. "I'm proud of you, Virginia."

She wrapped the other blankets around herself and lay down to sleep. She looked away into the distant, dark horizon. She didn't say anything else.

EIGHT

Days later, in the dark of a train car, Felix shook her awake. "It's time, Virginia."

She rose and moved sluggishly out into the rail yard. The pale glimmer of breaking dawn illuminated the downtown Dallas skyline. Virginia sat on the edge of the train car, sneakers dangling over the gravel, and unsealed her last can of peach slices. She fished them out with her fingers, felt them ooze slimily down her throat. Felix watched her.

"We're almost there," he said. "We may even be able to leave today."

"I'm nervous," Virginia said. "Should I buy new clothes? Or new shoes? I don't want to scare her or something."

"Minerva would never judge you for your appearance. All you have to do is tell her you're one of her biggest fans. She will appreciate that."

Virginia laughed. "I don't think I've ever been this nervous. Remember when I was in that play in middle school? I was just a tree, but I was still shitting myself. That doesn't even compare to this." She paused, a peach slice caught between her teeth. "Sorry. I know I'm not supposed to talk about the past."

"It's all right. I do remember that play. You rehearsed for so long. No one could have played the part of an immobile tree better."

She laughed again. "Remember how I'd tell you I wanted to be in movies? That was so stupid. I'd never be pretty enough. Suzanne said so, too. But I never wanted to believe it."

"Beauty is one thing," Felix said. "Character is another. You have courage, Virginia. Look how far you've come already."

"Minerva could be an actress," she said. "She can be anything she wants."

"As can you. Once you meet her, her opportunities will become your own. No one will be able to tell you otherwise—not even supposed friends like Suzanne."

She finished the peaches, then pitched the can away and wiped her hands on her jeans. "You're right. Suzanne wasn't pretty, either. And she couldn't do this. She was the real chicken."

Felix nodded. "Yet they made her into quite the martyr, didn't they? They sang songs in remembrance. They prayed. And all that was required of her in exchange was her own life."

Virginia scoffed. "I don't want to be one of them. I want to be one of Minerva's."

Back in the train car, she urinated, listening to the soft tinkle and shivering from the morning cold. Her arms and elbows hurt. Her legs were sore. Her feet felt as though she walked on coals. But she was close. Soon, she'd have her ticket. Soon, she'd be on the way to Minerva.

Sleep had been impossible the past few nights. Ever since the barn, she would lay in the dark and feel insects crawl over her skin and flies buzz about her head. Her dreams were becoming darker, too. In the latest, she had stumbled through an enormous, pitch-black tunnel, tripping over gnarled roots the size of torsos, feeling her way across slick, sharp walls. She was following him, following Felix—his little crooked form led her deeper and deeper into the darkness, the shadows growing thicker and hotter as they descended. Her only signs that he was still ahead of her were the occasional glances back, his eyes flashing pale green. She had awoken not long afterwards in the rail yard, still breathing hard from the stale, stinking heat, wiping her hands on her tattered, dusty jeans to be rid of the feeling of roaming legs.

In a cold, sullen alleyway, Virginia gulped down a water bottle and wiped her chapped lips before turning to Felix. "Where do I go?"

"To the bus depot," he said. "Though I wonder if securing more money would help."

"What do you mean? I think we have enough for the ticket."

"Yes. But what about food, lodging? You still need to survive the ride to California and everything that will come after that."

From within his blazer, he produced the necklace they had found in Caroline's bedroom. Dangling from his grip, the garnet shone its deep, bloody red.

"This seemed to be the most valuable item in that house," he said. "If we sell it, there will be no reason to fret over money. You will afford your ticket, food, lodging, and anything else necessary for the remainder of the trip."

Virginia's eyes clouded with confusion. "Why do you have that?"

"I took it," he said plainly. "It would have been a shame had we gained nothing from that diversion."

"But I told you I didn't want to take it. It's not ours."

"Virginia," he said, "you have infinitely more need of it than that woman does. What good does it do her, staring longingly at it in the night, pining for some long-dead lover? It serves you much better by helping you towards your goal."

She glared at him. "It wasn't ours to take, Felix!"

"Why not?"

"Her husband gave that to her! Maybe it's all she had fucking left of him!"

"She has the house. A son. The fruit trees. Compared to that, what is this jewelry?"

He held the necklace out to her, but she batted it away.

"I don't want it! I told you I didn't want to take it!"

He extended the necklace again. "Virginia."

"No! You don't listen to me! You burned the pictures when I didn't want you to! You made me burn the quilt! You don't do anything I want! You're supposed to be helping me!"

"I *am* helping you," he said. "We can't have anymore distractions, and if you sell this, you'll have all the resources you need to reach Minerva." He paused. "You *do* want to reach Minerva, don't you? Wasn't that what we planned for? What I died for?"

"You know that's not it," she said. "That old lady was nice to me. She could have called the police, but she didn't! She wanted to help me! And we're gonna steal from her to repay her?"

"She's continuing to help you," Felix said, "just as I am. But you insist on sabotaging yourself at every turn. Did you really neglect to check Davy's car for gas? Or were you hoping, somewhere in the back of your mind, that anything that could go wrong would go wrong?"

Virginia backed away from him. "No. You changed, Felix. Whatever happened to you, you're not the same anymore."

He approached her. "Virginia—"

"I don't need your help. I can get to California on my own."

"That is inadvisable, Virginia."

She didn't respond, turning away and leaving him in the alleyway, the necklace still twisting lightly on its chain, the garnet still glinting brightly in the sunlight.

He's different, she kept telling herself, throwing herself onto the street, rushing into the nearest crowd. He's changed. He's not how he was. But within minutes, the adrenaline bled away and left only cold, empty fear in its wake. The towering buildings and rushing lanes of traffic disoriented her, made her clasp her hands over her ears and shut her eyes. She had never been outside Oasis apart from a school trip many years before. She didn't know where to go, not even where to start.

She scanned the downtown main street, the sidewalks and alleyways, but Felix was nowhere to be seen. He had a tendency to disappear and reappear—he was a ghost, after all—but he always came back. Even at Caroline's, he had come back. Maybe she just had to wait, and he would be behind her again, or around the corner. He'll come back, she thought. He has to.

But was that for the best? She hid for a long time in a public restroom, bearing out the rapid, incessant pace of her heart, trying to steady herself and catch her breath. No, she could do it without him. She *had* to do it without him. Felix wanted her to burn the past—she wanted that, too, but not at any cost. Not if it meant hurting other people.

She ventured out. She could find her own way. She was brave and courageous and resourceful, just like Minerva was, like Suzanne never could be. "The bus depot," she murmured. "Just get to the bus depot. You can do that. You can definitely do that."

Hours passed, or maybe just minutes, and she felt she was going in circles. People brushed past her. A bicycle nearly clipped her.

Shirtless transients, sleek with sweat, watched her from underpasses. She passed under tracts of graffiti, hyper-realistic skulls set against explosions of color, oblong women with gigantic breasts and sweeping braids cradling the planet. Among overgrown weeds and along clogged gutters, tent villages stood. Ragged men and women emerged from behind walls of nylon. They wiped off dirt and sweat, spat through gaps in their rotted teeth. She watched them huddle by mounds of garbage and finger their cigarettes, rub their gums. They made fists and ran needles along their arms, tapping for plump, ripe spots.

That night, shivering, starving, she sat at the edge of one such encampment, watching through the dim light of scattered fires as shadowy figures sat among tents and shopping carts, as they lounged and ate and drank. She both hoped and dreaded that Felix was among them, but his imposing stature and the characteristic shape of his mask were nowhere among the dark host. Her hunger chewed at her, so intense she thought her stomach was starting to devour her from the inside. She would have given anything for another can of beans, another can of peaches. Even a glass of water would have been amazing.

She huddled, pulling her knees in close, trying to get what comfort she could out of the hard ground, focusing as much as possible on the snatches of warmth from the fires. When she closed her eyes, it wasn't the sunny California beaches that greeted her, but Mother Blue's smoke-filled kitchen with its antique knobs and rusted stovetop. If Felix were still here, would he laugh at her? Would he accuse her of being selfish? But she couldn't help it—how desperately she wanted to go back to her bedroom where she could hug Felix and wait out rainy days under the covers. Dreaming of escape had been fun—fantasizing about being with Minerva on those beaches and in front of those flashing lights had gotten her through many sleepless nights. Neither thunderstorms nor Mother Blue's rages had diminished those dreams. But now that Virginia was on her way, the reality seemed so far removed in every sense. There were thousands of miles between Dallas and Oakland. And she was alone. For the first time, she was truly alone.

In the morning, as she prepared to keep moving down the next street, a woman sidled up next to her. "Going somewhere?" the woman asked.

Virginia turned to her. She was young, mid-twenties, in a denim dress and slip-on sandals. She wore her dark hair in a bob, and when she fingered the purse over her shoulder, Virginia spotted a crucifix etched on the inside of her forearm.

"I'm looking for the bus depot," Virginia said. "You know where that is?"

"Sure. It's actually not that far away." The woman eyed her more closely. "You're young. Going someplace all on your own?"

"California," said Virginia. "I'm meeting a friend out there."

"Wow—that's far! Must be a good friend."

"Yeah. She is."

The woman smiled. "You know what? Why don't I walk you over to the buses? I'll even throw in a bite to eat, too. Looks like you haven't had a good meal in a while."

Virginia's instinct was to push for the bus depot, but her rumbling stomach argued otherwise. She thought back to Caroline's house, how good she felt after eating dinner, how free and light without the feeling of bugs and the sense of grime.

"There's a good burger place nearby," the woman said. "What do you say?"

Virginia's salivating mouth answered quickly. "Okay. That sounds good."

"Perfect!" The woman held out her hand. "I'm Lacey. You?"

Virginia nearly said her name, but Felix's previous warning came to mind. "My name's Suzanne," she said. "Suzanne Grayson."

"Okay, Suzanne—follow me!"

Lacey led her a couple of blocks away, talking all the while. Her chatter reminded Virginia a little of Janine, the way she filled up space with words if people were quiet for too long. But Virginia was happy just to have direction clarified and purpose reestablished. Maybe within the day, she'd be on her way to Minerva, and all this discomfort and anxiety would be part of the past, bundled up with Oasis and the old house and Mama and Felix's twisted body.

In the restaurant, she bit into an overstuffed hamburger and drizzled ketchup over charred, salted fries. She drank a glass of bubbling soda and then drained a cream-topped milkshake. As Virginia ate, Lacey kept talking.

"Cali," she said in an elaborate sigh. "I'd love to go one day. You hear so many bad things now, but Hollywood? Beverly Hills? Who wouldn't be in love with that?"

Virginia devoured her food, but Lacey ate little of the salad she had ordered. She asked many questions, regularly looking out the window and checking her watch. Disarmed, distracted by the food and her own ravenousness, Virginia explained her journey so far: the death of Felix, her flight from home, her nights sleeping in the brush and on gravel. Lacey had a knack for steering the conversation and getting Virginia to divulge more and more information. She didn't mention how Felix had come back, that he could talk—who would believe that? But she did let loose some details of Minerva, how kind she was, how beautiful, how everyone she met loved her and wanted to be around her.

"Minerva King!" exclaimed Lacey. "I've heard of her."

Virginia paused mid-bite, a splotch of mustard on her chin. "You have?"

"Sure. The streamer, right? They get her on sponsorships for some brands I follow. Really popular!"

"She is," Virginia said, chewing languidly on a fry, her eyes taking on a dreamy look. "Everyone loves her. How couldn't they? She's perfect."

"And out of all those people," Lacey said, "you're going to visit her? How'd you get her attention?"

Virginia blushed. "I haven't—not really. But I think if I get the chance, I'll fit in, you know? I mean, she's so good to everybody. She's so nice. I think I have a real chance." Her smile dropped. "Anything's better than going back. I've been close to giving up a couple of times, but I know I can't. It'll just be back to Mama and all her shit."

Lacey hummed in understanding. "I've been there," she said. "My stepmom beat the hell out of me. You think my dad ever said anything? Nah—I was the price for him getting pussy. Best thing I ever did was getting out of there. Just like you are."

Virginia stared at her. Lacey glowed, not as much as Minerva, and maybe because of the afternoon sun, but she *glowed*. Maybe acceptance wasn't just all the way in California. Maybe it was closer, wherever she was willing to show herself and unburden some of her problems. Suzanne had made her feel low, and Mother Blue had mocked her for her feelings, but maybe other people were kinder, closer to Minerva than they were the other extreme.

Outside, Lacey placed a hand on Virginia's arm. "You still want to leave today? It's getting late."

"I think so. I don't want to waste time."

Lacey eyed her. "You'll run yourself ragged. You could use a shower—probably some new clothes. You want to look the part when you meet Minerva." She gestured down the street. "You can stay the night with me. I'll even lend you some of my stuff, free of charge. It'll do you good to get a good night's sleep before you take off."

Once more, Virginia felt the impulse to reject the offer—she imagined the specter of Felix, his head cocked in disapproval. But the aches throughout her body made a compelling case for rest. Her hoodie and jeans, rent and torn by thorn and burr, were ready for the thrift store. Her dusty sneakers flapped as she walked, starting to literally come apart at the seams. And the fresh memory of the bed at Caroline's house, so soft and inviting, hung heavy over her. The safest thing was to get the rest, and Lacey was right—Minerva would probably be scared of some homeless-looking girl no matter what Virginia told her. She couldn't take any chances. She would have to look the part if she really wanted to make a good impression, and what was one more night when the bus ride was guaranteed the next day?

Lacey led her to a spacious studio apartment with an impressive view of downtown. Virginia looked down at the city through the bleary, dusty glass, her anxiety returning in force. So much city, and so many miles beyond. She was already far from Oasis, and soon, she would be even farther, so far that Oasis would mean nothing to anyone.

"You want some music?" Lacey asked. A soundbar beneath the television thrummed with life and vibrated with bass. As rock music filled the apartment—Virginia didn't recognize the song, but it sounded old, like something Davy listened to—Lacey fiddled with wineglasses and a bottle of champagne. "How about a drink?" she said from the kitchenette.

Virginia flushed. "I don't know. I've never had any before."

"Really? Not even with your friends?"

Virginia shook her head. "There was one who'd drink her dad's stuff. She'd smoke, too. But my mama would kill me if she ever found me doing that."

"Well, your mom's not here anymore," Lacey said. She uncorked a bottle of wine and poured the glasses. "Go and sit down—I'll bring it over."

Virginia settled on the sofa. She looked over the apartment, at the sleek bed, the imposing television. No pictures or any other personal touches—just the undertone of wealth, the impression of money. But Lacey didn't seem like a rich person, at least not as Virginia understood it. Minerva wasn't necessarily wealthy, but she lived comfortably, had nice clothes, took care of herself. Lacey didn't give off the same feeling. The apartment seemed *too* nice, too dressed up. It reminded Virginia of the snooty girls at school, the ones who liked to pretend they were richer than they really were. Of course, Lacey had been nice to her all this time, had even paid for her food and offered her a place to stay, but sitting in that apartment, something struck Virginia as false. Even the glow from before was starting to fade away.

Lacey came over to the sofa and handed Virginia one of the wineglasses. "To new friends," she said, clinking the glasses together. She drank her wine and smacked her lips in satisfaction.

Virginia hesitated. She watched the wine's bubbles glide along the curvature of the glass.

"It's sweeter than you think," Lacey said. "Peach-flavored. Try it."

Virginia took a sip—then a gulp.

"Good, right?" Lacey asked. "That's what you've been missing out on."

"Minerva drinks," Virginia said. "All her friends, too."

"Right. It would suck to be left out. Go on. Have some more."

Virginia tipped the glass back. Her thoughts turned to Suzanne—always Suzanne. What would Suzanne think of this? "You, drinking?" she might have said. "Little, innocent Ginny?"

That was Suzanne, of course—always judging even when she herself drank and snorted and smoked. She was probably judging right now, wherever she was.

Virginia finished the glass, and Lacey took it from her. "Refill?"

Virginia nodded. As Lacey returned to the kitchenette, Virginia settled back. Tomorrow, the bus. The day after, California. Then, finally, Minerva. She closed her eyes, imagining the sunny sky and nice breeze of Oakland. What would they do first? Try on clothes, tour the boardwalk? Introduce Virginia to all the girls? So many things to do, and so little time! She warmed at the images, feeling the sweet relief she'd been missing since Mother Blue destroyed her laptop. Soon, she wouldn't have to rely on streams and recordings. She'd have the real thing, and she would sit with Minerva in the dark, and they would hold hands, and they would talk about their lost fathers and the troubles of the past and make plans for the future.

Virginia's shoulders relaxed, then her arms, her legs. It was hard to lift her head, she realized, but she didn't think anything of the drowsiness at first. She was so tired, after all, and it was really no different than sinking into the bed at Caroline's and finally feeling comfortable after so many days of sleeping outside in the cold. But when her vision blurred, when her knees buckled as she tried to stand, when she crumpled, something registered at last as wrong.

And then everything went black.

NINE

Felix! Felix, wait for me!

She was dreaming again, descending into that dark pit, following the pair of pale green eyes ahead. The dead smell was everywhere, part of that tar-like darkness that clung to the cavern walls and dripped from the stalactites overhead. The darkness rose to her ankles, her knees—the sludge swam with many bodies and many legs, a crawling collective that made her spine shiver and her body tremble.

Felix! Felix!

She called and called, but his eyes never again shone back at her. The air grew warmer and warmer, thickening, taking on an additional flavor of rust.

Felix, please, I need your help! Don't leave me—

Virginia gasped awake. She couldn't see at first, only making out shadows and a dim yellow light around her. But she recognized the stench of cigarettes clearly, and her stomach churned in primal fear. Her mother had found her! She didn't know how—her head throbbed with groggy pain, her memories foggy and disarrayed—but she was back home, about to suffer another beating, the worst one possible. "I'm sorry, Mama!" she cried instinctively, reflexively. "I'm sorry! I didn't mean it!"

But her mother didn't answer back, didn't rain down punches. There was only silence, only the overpowering smell of cigarettes. Virginia's eyes adjusted, and as her bare arms and legs rippled with goosebumps—wait, where were her hoodie and jeans?—she saw she was in a cramped, barren room. She swung her head to move her hair out of her eyes. The yellow light came from an adjacent rest-room as well as a lamp burning to her left. She tried to move, but rope chafed her wrists and dug into her ankles. She focused on her exposed midriff, her thin legs. Where was she? What happened? All she could remember was arguing with Felix, sleeping in that make-shift camp, trying to get comfortable—

Lacey. She had taken her to get burgers, taken her back to her apartment. Virginia had drunk the wine, and then everything had gone black.

"Lacey?" she called. "Where am I? What's happening?"

No one answered her. Virginia struggled against the rope, but it was too tight, and it bit into her skin painfully. She craned her neck as much as possible, trying to see what was behind her, hoping against hope that Felix was there in the dark.

"Felix? Can you hear me? Are you there?"

But Felix didn't answer her, either. She sat, bound to the chair, nearly naked, her heart beating faster and faster. I'm dreaming, she thought, she prayed. I'm dreaming, and I'm gonna wake up, and I'll be back with Felix, and we'll get on the bus, and we'll be in Califor-nia—

The door opened. "Felix?" she asked desperately, but the man who walked inside wasn't Felix. He was slim, dressed in tight-fitting black, a leather jacket and jeans draped on a skeleton. Jet-black hair lay greased atop his head, and a dark tattoo snaked up his neck, to-wards the base of his skull. His face widened in a waxy grin, his eyes just as flat, just as dead.

"She's finally up," he said with a chuckle. "You weren't kidding about her being a lightweight, Lacey."

"She's a kid," came a voice from behind him. "Alcohol by itself would've been enough."

Virginia strained to look beyond the man. Was that Lacey? But he hunkered down in front of her and filled up her vision. The smell of alcohol hung over him. That was Davy coming home from a late night. That was Suzanne's father.

"Let's get a look at you," the man said. He took hold of Virginia's trembling chin and turned her face to the light. "Shit, Lacey. And she's a virgin?"

"She's not broken."

He whistled. "That's jackpot."

Virgin? Virginia tried to free herself from his grasp, but the man held her head firmly. "She's starting to act up," he said. "She's looking crazy."

Virginia tried to speak, but her throat was suddenly backed up, her tongue like concrete in her mouth. Her eyes bulged and swerved from left to right, but there was only the man's dead grin in front of her, only his dead eyes.

"What'd you say her name was?" he asked.

"Suzanne."

"Well, that ain't too exciting. How about 'Comet'?" He laughed. "I like the sound of that. What do you think, Comet?"

Virginia struggled harder against his grasp. She rocked back and forth in the chair, but it was pointless. She could hardly hear him over her heartbeat.

"Stop moving around and look at me," the man said, the good-hearted laugh gone from his voice. "I ask a question, I expect an answer."

Virginia flailed now. She hyperventilated. She thrashed and threw her hair about until the strike of his palm snapped her head to the side. The blow stung—briefly, she saw stars.

"Pay attention," he said, "and look at me."

She shivered, whimpered—

His hand came down again, this time the backside, dressed in rings that felt like a rack of rocks slung against her face. Something hot welled in her mouth and trickled out from between her teeth. She watched the dribble of blood and saliva hit the carpet.

"First lesson, Comet," he said. "I say to do something, you do it. So, look at me. Let me see those pretty little eyes."

She was still dazed by the slap, the pain radiating throughout her face. Tears bubbled from her eyes.

"Look at me!" he snarled, with a malice second only to that of her mother, and raised his hand again. Her eyes wandered up and found his at last.

He smiled. "There we go. Not so hard, huh? We don't want to be ugly, do we?"

She shook her head.

"No, 'course not. Let me introduce myself. I'm Rocky. You already met Lacey. Listen: you're coming into business with us. Think of me like your boss, Lacey like your supervisor. Hold on, maybe I'm getting ahead of myself. You ever had a job?"

Virginia struggled, her head heavy with pain, blood weighing down her tongue, but she managed to shake her head again.

"Hey, that's okay. That's what training's for." Rocky laughed. "Basically, what we say goes. I tell you to do something, you do it. Lacey says to do something, you do it. And if Lacey tells me you aren't doing what you're supposed to do, well, I come back and get ugly. And we don't want that, remember?"

He raised his rings to the dim light. "Now, you do a good job, you do everything we say, and maybe you get some of these for yourself. Don't that sound nice? Nice jewelry for a pretty little girl. Better than your daddy ever got you, I bet."

"She had money on her," said Lacey. "Same with this."

Rocky reached around and took the necklace. He dangled it between them, admiring the embedded garnet.

"Hell, maybe you don't need no rings! Where'd you get this?"

Virginia stared at the necklace, the pendant and its glistening red stone swinging like a miniature pendulum.

Rocky's grin fell. "What'd we just say about answering questions?"

"I didn't want to take that," Virginia said slowly, her words slurred by the blood on her tongue. "I told him not to."

"Told who?"

"Please." She whimpered and coughed. "I need to get to the bus."

"She's going to California," Lacey said.

Rocky whistled again. "Cali, huh? Beautiful, but way too hot for me." He pocketed the necklace and fished out a rag from his back pocket. He wiped the blood from her lips and chin.

"Listen up, Comet—you aren't going to Cali anytime soon. We got a lot of work to do! Maybe when you've gotten us a few more diamonds, we can talk."

He rose up. "All right, Lacey. Get her cleaned up. I'll be back later."

He left, and Lacey came into view, no longer smiling, no longer chatting. She cut the ropes, and Virginia collapsed to the floor, rubbing her red, weathered wrists, huddling up and crying. Something dropped by her head.

"Get dressed," Lacey ordered. When Virginia did nothing, Lacey repeated her command in a shrill yell. "Get dressed!"

Startled, Virginia grabbed her rumpled jeans and ragged shirt. She avoided looking up as she dressed, feeling Lacey's icy gaze on her. She'd been the one to undress her—the one to touch her where no one else had. Her stomach churned again at the thought. Mama had beaten her, Suzanne had mocked her, but no one had done that before. No one had put their hands on her in that way, whether she was awake or not.

"Look at me, you little bitch," Lacey said. Virginia turned towards her, keeping her eyes on the woman's shins, her teal-painted toenails. Lacey brandished a folded belt. "Rocky doesn't like to damage the merchandise, but if you don't do what I say, I'll hit the hell out of you. You hear me? I'll make you wish you were never born."

Virginia nodded feebly.

"Good. Now, move it."

She shoved Virginia into an adjacent room, which was nearly as bare as the previous apart from several bunks. Amber light slanted inside from a rain-slick window.

"Get some sleep," Lacey said. "I'll be back later. If you're not sleeping when I come in, you know what's coming."

She walked out, locking the door behind her. Weakly, sluggishly, Virginia tried the knob, but there was no latch to unlock the door. She stumbled back, sitting against one of the bunks, nursing her chafed wrists, rubbing her sore jaw and temple. How could this happen? It was like a nightmare, getting worse and worse, and it didn't stop. Now she had nothing: no money, no knife, not even Caroline's necklace. Even if she got away from them somehow, she wouldn't be able to afford the bus, and she wouldn't be able to get to California, and she wouldn't be able to see Minerva—

She cried, the tears unending no matter how many she wiped away, the heaving only making her head hurt worse. Her constricted lungs struggled to get air. Her hands shook so badly she felt she would never have control of them again.

"Poor Virginia. I did tell you it was inadvisable to go on your own."

Felix emerged from the darkness as though he had been lurking there all along. He stood over her in his unblemished white suit, his mask that in the dark seemed like a monstrous deformity.

"Felix!" Virginia cried, her heart lifting, her next tears those of relief. "You came back!"

"I never left." He shook his head and clicked his tongue. "Look what's happened now. If only you had listened to me, you could have avoided all this."

"I'm sorry, Felix!" she moaned. "But you can help me, right? We can get out of here?"

"We can—if you do as I say when I say it. There will be an opportunity soon. But if you continue to go against what I suggest, I may not be able to save you."

"I'll do what you say," she said. "I promise, Felix. I'll do everything."

"Wonderful, Virginia," he replied, the smile audible in his voice. "Sleep, then. Rest. You will need your strength."

She nodded and climbed onto the bunk. "Felix, please don't leave again. Please stay with me. Even if I get you mad."

He sat beside her. "I never left you, Virginia."

She smiled. Her hand slid into his gloved grip. He pressed gently, with a tenderness she had never felt before, and soon, she was fast asleep.

TEN

More darkness like slime, moving with a million separate pieces, all hard-shelled bodies and segmented legs. More foul-smelling air, like smoke, like sulfur. She had finally caught up to Felix—his blood-caked paws stood upon piled bones.

I'm here, she said. I made it.

Slimy, scaly things coiled about her legs and looped around her waist. They twined through cracked skulls, twisted around splintered ribs, slid over shattered scapulae. They were blood-red like the garnet in Caroline's necklace, their eyes a foggy yellow, their fangs like ivory. There were dozens of them, hundreds, slithering upon one another, lining the walls of the cavernous chamber, hanging from the outcroppings overhead.

Almost there, Virginia. Felix's whiskers parted in a grin. Get up.

The door banged—Lacey stood over her.

"You hear me?" she said. "Get up."

In a daze, Virginia followed her, still half-asleep, still half-stuck in that dark, dank cave. Those dreams were getting stronger, more real—but they *aren't* real, she reminded herself. You gotta focus. You gotta get out of here and get to Minerva.

"Looks like you really are special," Lacey was saying. "Rocky's already got a job lined up for you. Can you believe that?"

She pulled Virginia into a grimy restroom and ran the shower. The showerhead crackled to life, spitting out rivulets of water. "Take this shit off and get in there," Lacey commanded. "You stink. Nobody'll pay for that."

Virginia looked around, and behind Lacey, in the doorway, Felix nodded his assent. Slowly, she kicked off her sneakers and dropped her jeans. She removed her shirt and then paused with her fingers on her bra strap. "You gonna watch me?" she asked meekly, then flinched when Lacey raised the folded belt.

"I said take that shit off and get in there!"

Quickly, Virginia undid her bra and slid off her panties. She stepped like an awkward baby bird into the stream of water, yelping at the cold and the sudden pressure of Lacey's hands on her arms, raising and lowering them as soap was applied, dragging a ratty washcloth across Virginia's face and through her hair. Her mother had washed her like this as a child, thrusting her under the water in the cramped bathtub, filling her nostrils with burning soap. Lacey cut off the shower abruptly and threw a towel over her. She wrung Virginia's hair forcefully, painfully, and dried her so roughly Virginia expected to see bruises. Through the chaos, she caught sight of Felix still in the doorway.

Shivering, shielding her breasts, Virginia waited as Lacey laid out a midnight-blue dress and dropped a pair of black high heels on the carpet. Virginia did not resist as Lacey dressed her. She watched limply in the mirror as her ragged, runaway reflection transformed, the hair parted to reveal her face, her lips painted, her eyes darkened. In the tight-fitting dress with its plunging neckline and high slit, made up for the first time in her life, she looked at last like a member of Minerva's tribe. She and Suzanne had often laughed at the popular girls' social media profiles, their filtered selfies and slutty outfits. She had never told Suzanne that she had admired the strength to dress that way, to own and flaunt one's body. Those girls went off, fooled around, dirtied what was otherwise so impressive—but not Minerva and her friends. Maybe they partied and drank, but they kept their dignity. They owned their beauty and restrained it at the same time. That's what Suzanne never understood when she made fun of Minerva. She was just jealous of what she didn't have.

Felix crouched beside her, studying the unrecognizable girl in the mirror. "Purity is only valuable to the extent it can be spoiled," he remarked.

Virginia simply stared, watery eyes shimmering even brighter due to the dark eyeshadow.

Outside, she followed Lacey down rusted stairs, wobbling on the heels, grasping the handrail uneasily. The motel parking lot lay like a wasteland, wet from rain, streaked with the orange glow of streetlamps buzzing and clanging with moths. Across the street, Rocky leaned against a car, smoking a cigarette.

"Shit, Comet," he laughed as she got closer. "You clean up good." He eyed her and took another drag from his cigarette. "Normally, I don't like my new girls getting put to work so fast, but we got a special request this evening. What do they call it— serendipity? Like it was meant to be? The stars aligned tonight."

Virginia said nothing, standing there awkwardly, shaking. Felix stood on the other side of the car, watching as he had been.

Rocky stamped out his cigarette. "Time to go. Lacey, get her a spot ready at the house—she'll need it."

From the backseat of the car, Virginia watched Lacey return inside the motel. Rocky drove with an arm out the window, fingers drumming rhythmically on the door. At a stoplight, he lit another cigarette. Virginia sat quietly, staring at the buildings as they drove uptown, trembling under the cold glare of the city lights and the hot radiance of neon signs. She reached for Felix's hand. He sat silently, never looking out at the passing city, never acknowledging her.

Rocky was talking, filling the air as Lacey had done when Virginia met her. "Really struck gold tonight, don't you think, Comet? Or how about 'Star'? 'Lucky Star'? Things are changing for sure. You go years dealing with shit"—he blew out a stream of smoke from a fresh cigarette—"and then one day, everything turns around." He looked at her trembling in the rearview mirror. "Yeah, I got a good feeling about you. A little slow, but you clean up nice."

She glanced at Felix for direction on what to say, what to do, but he was motionless.

They parked in front of a high-rise hotel. Under bright lights, Virginia followed Rocky past cherubim-rimmed fountains and luggage-racked bellhops. They proceeded through the lobby, footsteps echoing off the checkered tile, the high walls adorned in dark blue oil spreads of ocean swells and crashing waves. In the elevator, Virginia watched their reflections warp in the chrome interior. There was no distorted image of Felix, but she felt him behind her, watching and waiting—but waiting for what? She could have run two, even three times by now, could have thrown off the heels and sprinted into a crowd. What was she waiting for, his signal? It was better to just go, to move as soon as the doors opened—

Felix's hand around her arm silenced her thoughts. There was no comfort in the cold leather of his gloved grasp, just more uncertainty.

The elevator doors gave way to a winding corridor as gray as concrete. "You're meeting a very important person tonight, Comet," Rocky said. "If you play your cards right, who knows? Maybe you're headed for great things. Then you'll be happy you ran into Lacey. Happy I set you up." He paused, and his easy smile disappeared like it had at the motel. "Now, listen up. You represent me in there. I would've wanted more time to prep you, but time is money. Remember what I told you?"

She shook quietly. Her mind was blank, even as his features darkened, as he raised a palm—

Felix whispered in her ear. "You'll do whatever he says."

"I do whatever you want," she said. "What you say goes."

"Good," Rocky said. "And that goes for the man you're about to meet, for all the ones after tonight. You hear what I'm saying? What you want doesn't matter anymore. You never say 'no.' You always say 'yes.'"

"Tell him he's right," said Felix.

She swallowed. "You're right."

"Perfect. Well, let's introduce you."

Rocky rapped one of the many doors lining the hall. After a shuffling on the other side, the door opened and revealed a mass of a man, the seams of his suit straining and the buttons threatening to burst. He raised a bejeweled hand and stroked a short, black mustache. Porcine eyes—the eyes of her mother—fixed on Virginia.

"I'll be damned," he said. "You weren't lying, Rocky."

"She really is a surprise, ain't she?" Rocky nodded at her. "Go ahead now. Introduce yourself."

Felix nodded his approval, and she looked up at the man. "Hi," she said. "I'm Comet."

"Pleasure to meet you, Comet. I'm Leonard." He stepped aside and gestured into the room. "Why don't you come in? I already ordered us our meal."

A table was set in the center of the hotel room, gold-rimmed plates topped with slabs of veal and mounds of mashed potatoes, a bottle of wine resting in an ice-filled pail.

"Looks like you're all set," Rocky said. "I'll be waiting for your call. And, Comet—remember what I said."

With a wink, he was gone, and Leonard ushered Virginia inside, the door locked and latched behind her.

"Here," Leonard said, "have a seat."

He pulled out one of the chairs at the table, and Virginia sat, looking nervously around the dark room. The only light came from the nearby lamp and the red and white glimmer of the skyline through the balcony doors.

"I hope this wasn't too short-notice," Leonard continued, uncorking the wine and pouring each of them a glass. The wine pooled thickly, dense as coagulated blood. "Rocky had so much to say about you that I just had to see you for myself. It's rare I hear him so excited."

He sat down, fixing a napkin into his collar as a bib and taking up his knife and fork. "You are definitely something—and so young, too." He chewed on a piece of meat, his lips smeared with muddy blood, the exposed veal on his plate red and gleaming. "Go on, eat. Don't let it get cold. That's a top-dollar piece of meat you got there."

Virginia stared at the food and wine, increasingly nauseated. To her right, Felix nodded. She grabbed her knife and cut off a piece of veal. It wasn't the first time she'd been forced to eat—how many dinners had Mother Blue made her sit through, forbidding her from running to her room? How many overcooked steaks and overseasoned pork chops had she eaten?

Leonard watched her, his small eyes following the meat skewered on her fork, anticipating the moment it would find its way into her mouth. He gestured her on, and she chewed the veal slowly, her jaw still aching from Rocky's blows, shaking at the sensation of the blood on her tongue and the rind of fat between her teeth. At last, she swallowed the meat and chased it down with the bitter wine. Leonard sighed contentedly and then looked to his own plate.

"Rare that I can have a good piece of meat." He diced up his veal, smearing it with potatoes and chewing it hungrily, hastily. He guzzled down his wine. "My wife and daughter, they're insisting on this vegan bullshit. They go on and on about carbon emissions and factory farming, but they'll wear their designer purses on their arms like they weren't just cut up at the slaughterhouse. There's no shame in the hunt, in eating what we're supposed to eat."

Virginia pushed around the red, leaky meat, with each moment more nauseated than before. Felix sat wordlessly, but when she looked to him with panicked eyes, he shook his head.

"Comet, right?" Leonard asked. "Are you one of those vegan types? Not just eating that to make me feel better about myself?"

She hesitated, but Felix nodded at her. "I eat meat," she said slowly. "My mama—she'd cuss me out if I didn't."

Leonard laughed. "Bless her heart! She sounds like a sensible woman." He mopped his mouth with his bib, imprinting a grimy, ruddy stain on the white cloth. Suddenly, he reached across and took her hand, fondling the slim fingers, caressing the small palm. She sat rigid under his touch.

"This is nice. Thank you for being here, Comet. It's so hard to have a nice dinner nowadays. And it's going to be campaign season soon. These slugs come in and think they can micro-manage your life. Well, they're in for a surprise. This election will go my way for once."

Virginia hardly listened to him, focused instead on the meat, on the smell that wafted from it. The dead smell, accompanied by the rattle of bones and the whine of flies overhead.

Leonard cleaned his plate and rose from the table. "Excuse me, Comet. I just need a moment to freshen up."

Once the bedroom door closed behind him, Virginia turned frantically to Felix. "He's gone! We can leave, right?"

"Not yet."

"But—"

"Be patient, Virginia. The time is coming."

She was about to respond when the bedroom door opened, and Leonard's voice sounded from within. "Comet? You there?"

She looked to Felix for some kind of reassurance, any type of sign, but he only nodded as before. Slowly, stalling for as long as she could, she walked to the doorway of the bedroom. Leonard sat on the edge of the bed, hairy legs exposed, a red, satin robe conforming to his giant frame and rotund belly. He grinned. "There you are. Bring me some wine."

She returned to the table and shakily poured his glass, splotching the tablecloth and dousing the cutlery. She brought the glass to him, and he swallowed the wine down in a single, gigantic gulp.

"That hit the spot," he said with a satisfied sigh. He stretched his arms, popped his fingers. "Well. Why don't we get comfortable?" He stood before her, clearing his throat, setting his hands on his hips. "Could you help with the robe?"

Virginia stared at the loose knot that kept the robe clinging to his body, stared at the dangling strings. Lips quivering, heartbeats thundering, she took a string in each hand. She pulled and glimpsed the trail of bushy hair crossing over his strained, humongous stomach. Through a screen of tears, she saw the monstrous thing hanging from him like some kind of vestigial conjoined sibling.

He took her head between his pudgy hands, feeling her hair gently, twining it between his fingers. "You know what to do, don't you? Go on."

Virginia closed her eyes. She prayed for this long nightmare to finally be over, prayed to wake up in her bed with Felix curled up beside her, prayed to see Janine knitting at the breakfast table, prayed for Suzanne to be waiting outside to walk to school. She even prayed for Mother Blue, prayed to see her reading the newspaper, prayed to hear her scream and even take her hits if it meant this could end—

Leonard screamed. Virginia opened her eyes with a start. Leonard turned away, shrieking, blood running down his legs and pooling on the floor around his ankles. "You bitch! Are you crazy? Are you fucking nuts?" He looked on her with blazing eyes and spittle-lined mouth. "I'll fucking kill you for this—"

Felix descended upon him again. The knife swept across Leonard's face, nearly slicing his jaw off. The blade struck out his eyes, chopped off his tongue. His screams became moans, then nothing, just his massive frame lying in the ever-pooling blood, just Felix standing over the body in his white suit, the knife in his hand dripping red.

Virginia screamed and huddled against the wall, sobbing, shielding her eyes.

Felix spoke to her. "Look at me, Virginia."

She shook her head fiercely, wildly.

"*Look!*"

He seized her by the arm, stood her up, held her before Leonard's maimed corpse.

"Look. This is the price you pay. For being impatient. For not obeying."

"Oh, God—you killed him, Felix! You killed him—"

"*I* killed him? You're the one holding the knife."

She looked down at her blood-streaked hands and arms, at the knife clutched in her sticky fingers. She screamed and dropped the knife.

"No! I didn't do that! It was you!"

"Let's not argue semantics, Virginia. You took the knife from the table—our friend here was too drunk on lust and his own pleasure to notice—and attacked him. Justifiably so."

"No! I didn't do it!" She jerked, twitched, and then vomited. Her bile pooled just as the blood had, a milky, pale puddle studded with the regurgitated, near-raw veal. The sight of it prompted another retch.

"Would you rather he raped you?" Felix asked.

"I didn't kill him—I know I didn't!" Virginia turned to him, eyes bright and wide and wet, mouth dripping bile and saliva. "You made me do it. Just like you made me take the necklace. Just like you made me burn the pictures."

He sighed. "Virginia—"

"No! Stay away from me! I'm going home! I don't want to be here anymore!" She stumbled back, teetering on the high heels. Felix stood before her.

"You promised, Virginia. You said you would do as I asked."

"I didn't mean this, Felix! You can't just—"

"I can't make you?" he said. "It's not my right?"

Her legs moved on their own, marching her robotically to the balcony door. She watched her reflection in the glass, and there was Felix, holding her arms, lifting them, lowering them. "Without me, you would have died five or even ten times by now. After all, you are just a child with no knowledge of the world, thinking you can have everything you want."

She watched her hands encircle her throat, watched them clamp down. "Felix," she gasped. "Stop—I'm sorry—"

"This hurts me more than it hurts you, Virginia," he said. "But you must learn the price of survival. Steal, kill—so what? Don't you want to see Minerva? Isn't that worth anything?"

She groaned. "Felix—"

He released her. She collapsed in a fit of coughs and gasps.

"I've been patient," he said, "but we don't have time for this childish naiveté anymore. Get up. He must have money on him to make up for what you lost."

She rubbed her throat and shuddered. She shook her head.

"I don't want to, Felix. Just take me home. Please. I just want to go home."

"You want to go back? To be bulbous and fat like your mother? Weak and feeble like your sister? Suzanne took her own life to escape that place, and you want to go back?"

"Felix, please—"

He descended upon her, straddled her. "You disappoint me, Virginia. After everything, you still disobey."

"Felix—"

He hooked his fingers under his mask. Immediately, a stench washed over her, overpowering and hot—the dead smell, full of decayed flesh and dried blood, withered skin and expelled waste, poured out from underneath the tight seal of the mask like an invisible gas. Sounds accompanied the smell: the squirming of wriggling maggots, millions of them milling over one another—the buzzing of hovering flies, forming a repulsive shroud overhead.

"This hurts me, Virginia," Felix said, "but it is for your own good." He peeled back the mask farther—

"Stop!" she screamed. "Please! Stop!"

Virginia wept and convulsed. Felix watched her.

"Enough crying," he said. "Get up."

Obediently, she got to her feet. She sniffled, kept her eyes down. "What do I do?"

"Clean yourself up. Quickly."

In the shower, she scrubbed her arms clean of Leonard's blood, wiped as much as she could from the dress, from her calves. When she came out, Felix pointed to the corpse.

"His wallet," he said. "His watch. The rings. Whatever he has on him. We need it all. Be careful not to get more blood on you."

Virginia knelt, stomach turning, and stuck a hand into Leonard's trouser pockets, sifting cautiously, disgustedly, against the cotton. She housed everything in a pillow case. Felix waited by the door. When she was done, she chanced a quick, nauseating glance at the body.

"Do we just leave him?"

"Yes. If you aren't quick, they will track you down. The police if not these people."

She nodded. Silently, quieting her sobs, she allowed Felix to lead her back down the elevator and out the lobby. "Carry yourself well," he advised. "Imagine you were Minerva. What would she do? How would she act?"

This would never have happened to Minerva, she thought, emerging onto the windy, nighttime street. Minerva was too smart. Too careful. Too good. No, what was happening was more like Suzanne. Getting drunk, going out with older guys. But even Suzanne knew how to take care of herself. She'd never been raped as far as Virginia knew. She'd never been hit. "You gotta get your head out of the clouds," she told Virginia once. "The real world doesn't play nice. You want to get out of here? You can't be crying and complaining. You can't be expecting me to come save you all the time."

You were right, Virginia thought, ducking into an alleyway, hugging herself, pinching her tear-stung eyes shut. I'm stupid. I'm so fucking stupid and scared. Bile flung up her throat and splashed on the brick wall she was leaning against. She slumped and cried, unable to get control of her shaking arms and bucking knees.

After a moment, Felix hunkered down beside her. He laid an arm across her shoulders.

"Pay no mind to Suzanne Grayson," he said quietly. "She left you, remember? She was selfish. Prideful. She only wanted you for herself. She didn't care about what you wanted."

He lifted her head and wiped her tears with his thumb. "But I am here for you. I've always been here for you. These things I do are for your sake. To protect you. To get you where you need to go."

Virginia listened. It was true. Suzanne might have been right, but she'd also opted out—she couldn't save Virginia anymore even if she wanted to. The only one who'd stuck by her was Felix. Not Janine or Mama. Not Suzanne. Not even her own daddy. The only constants had been Mama hitting, Janine whimpering, Davy drinking, Suzanne leaving. Everything and everyone a dead end except for Felix. Kind, loving Felix.

When she was ready, Felix guided her out of the alleyway. In a thrift store, she used Leonard's cash to buy jeans, a tank top, a jacket. Across the street, in a pawn shop, she sold the watch and rings and tie. She counted the bills in the dim corner of a convenience store. Over four hundred dollars. Enough for the bus ride. Enough to get her to California.

She trembled in line at the bus depot, looking over her shoulder, flinching at every sudden movement. But Felix placed a hand on her shoulder. He stood watch. Maybe he could be mean—could be scary, incredibly scary—but he had saved her from Leonard. He had brought her this far, given her the strength to do what she could never have done otherwise. He had been there for her when no one else had. More than that, he believed in her. Would Janine have supported her decision to leave? Would Suzanne? No, Janine would have begged her to stay. Suzanne would have mocked her for being naive. Mama would have beaten her. Only Felix came all the way with her. Her protector. Her guardian angel.

But that would change soon, she thought, boarding the bus. Because she would finally be with Minerva. Because she would finally have people she could call her own. Because everything would finally be all right.

ELEVEN

The bus ride was long and cramped, but as the Texas Hill Country gradually gave way to the New Mexico plains and then the Arizona mountains, Virginia's excitement overshadowed her discomfort. The awful days and nights in Dallas became a distant memory, taking on the feel and texture of a dream. Leonard and Rocky and Lacey, not to mention the tent camp and the noisy streets and looming buildings, felt like they had happened to a different person, like she had seen them through a movie screen, safe and secure in the audience. Her hands flickered now and then, as though possessed by the memory of what she did to Leonard—but it was easy to remind herself that it was in the past, and that meant it was essentially not real. None of what had come before mattered anymore. Like Felix said, the past had thrown her into the future, puked her out like she was a piece of food that couldn't digest properly. There was nothing for her back there, back then—there never had been. Suzanne, Janine, and Mama were just part of that past. Even Virginia's niece might as well have not been real.

On the other hand, the oncoming future was taking more definite shape with every hour, every minute, every second. She hadn't seen one of Minerva's streams in so long, but the images came back with unprecedented clarity and power. The colorful, sparkling outfits. The white sand and turquoise water. The clear, sunny sky, the opposite of the eternal gray of Oasis. Virginia's eyes sparkled just imagining it.

"Picture it, Felix," she whispered, the bus lumbering down the highway, arid badlands trundling past. "How could anyone be sad there? It's where dreams come true. *That's* where we belong. No-where else."

In that manner, dreaming of the heaven that waited, the bus ride passed more quickly. Suddenly, the passengers were walking off, unloading luggage. Virginia squeezed through the throng, so small she was hardly noticed. She stepped into the California sun with nothing more than her threadbare backpack and the clothes and sneakers she had bought from the thrift store in Dallas. She marveled at the honey-colored light on her hands and the vague, salty scent of the nearby sea.

"You made it, Virginia," Felix said. "We're nearly there."

She had to pinch herself to make sure she wasn't dreaming. California. Oakland. For all she knew, Minerva was down at the beach, soaking up sun, taking selfies. She could have been leaving a photo shoot the next block over. She could be just around the corner, just going about her life, all the wonder normal, all the beauty mundane.

Virginia walked the streets, awestruck, too high on the anticipation to let it end. Jacket around her waist, bare arms and shoulders quickly reddening, she strolled the boardwalk, nursed an ice cream cone. Her feet took her through shops and plazas and eventually down to the beach, where she kicked off the sneakers, rolled up the jeans, and planted her pale toes in the sand, shuddering as the waves broke over them. It was her first time setting foot on a beach. Her first time seeing the ocean.

"It's amazing," she said. "It just goes on and on. Forever and ever."

Felix stood behind her, silent, the water lapping his feet but never getting him wet, his shoes firm in the sand but never tracking any when they left.

Virginia used what remained of Leonard's money to eat a late-afternoon sandwich and browse for a gift for Minerva. She settled on a small, unimaginative bouquet. "What should I say?" she asked Felix, looking out at the darkening sky, catching whiffs of a brewing storm. She hadn't thought about her approach at all—the trip had been so chaotic, so stressful, that she had come to the end with no idea how to introduce herself.

"Just be honest," Felix said. "Express what's in your heart. The magnanimous Minerva will welcome you—your sincerity will be enough."

"You think?" Virginia looked at her ill-fitting clothes, her sun-burned hands. "I'm not special like her. I'm just riff-raff, you know? White trash, like Mama always says."

"You love her," Felix said. "Everything else is unimportant."

Was it? Right at the verge of meeting Minerva, the reality sinking in once again, Virginia wondered what the hell she was doing there. Now there really was no way to go back: no money, no food, no car. It was all or nothing, and she was beyond unprepared. As much as Lacey was just part of a bad dream, her words came back to her—Virginia needed to fit in with Minerva's set, not just coast on their generosity. She had to impress the housemates, Sue and Michelle, and all the other girls whom she had to convince to accept her. But Minerva would vouch for her, wouldn't she? And if Minerva did, they would have to fall in line and follow her lead.

"Have faith in yourself," Felix said. "You've made it this far. How can what's next be any harder?"

She smiled. Nodded. He was right.

"Thanks, Felix. For everything." She looked up at him, feeling nothing of the old discomfort or fear. He had been gentle since Dallas, so tender, almost loving. One piece of her past that had stayed with her and kept her safe, kept her sane.

"I'm sorry," she said, "about what happened to you."

Felix only chuckled.

"That's all right, Virginia. It allowed us to get here, didn't it? Allowed you to make your dream come true. That was worth the pain."

Night had fallen, as well as a light shower, by the time Virginia made it to Minerva's neighborhood. She had seen the white, two-story house many times on the streams. Even with the darkness and rain, she could make out the flower shop on the nearby corner, the mural of interlocked hands painted on an adjacent fence. This was it. Finally, after so long, she was here.

She approached the house, oblivious to the intensifying rain, the way the bouquet drowned and wilted in her hands. The warm lights from the windows lured her close, promised safety and shelter. Minerva was inside—Virginia felt it in her bones, with a certainty she had never felt in her life. For all she knew, the next morning, everything could be—*would* be—different. She would be one of them, and the old Virginia Blue, the mousy, awkward girl, would be gone, wiped away along with all the rest of the pesky past that clung to her. Everything would be made right. She'd finally have a place where no one would hurt her or make fun of her. A home at last, after so long and so much.

She rang the doorbell once, twice. The rain was a downpour now, punctuated by deafening stabs of thunder. Faintly, she thought she heard music inside—maybe a television show or a movie. She knocked on the door next. She pounded.

"Felix," she whispered. "What do I do?"

Except Felix wasn't there. She turned around, expecting him to slide out of the dark like he often did, but she was alone on the doorstep. She shook away the rain and tried to ignore the buzzing in her ears. She scratched her shoulders where she felt the creeping of legs and the flicking of antennae.

She knocked again, but when her fist struck air, she blinked and looked at her hand with bleary, rain-smeared eyes. She was bleeding. There were shards of glass wedged between her knuckles, in the back of her hand. Bits of glass lay at her feet—the remains of a window—and she realized she was standing inside the house, dripping on the carpet. She gasped. The rock fell from her hand, landing with a dull, moist thud. The bouquet had been left behind in the rain, limp on its side like roadkill.

"I didn't do this," Virginia said. "I was knocking on the door. Felix? Wasn't I knocking on the door?"

Once again, he didn't answer. Once again, he was nowhere to be seen.

"Felix?" she called again. "Where are you? What's happening?"

Ahead of her was the soft glow of the kitchen—she recognized the rack of wine glasses, the rosewood cutting board. Minerva had filmed the girls cooking many times: Michelle cutting fruit, or Sue fiddling with the air fryer. Virginia had imagined herself sitting at the counter with them, sampling bites of waffle, plopping strawberries in her mouth.

She didn't notice the apple she had plucked from the fruit bowl until she started chewing it, crushing skin and flesh between her teeth. She looked back, startled at the trail of grimy, wet footprints she had dragged across the living room. Her heart thundered. Tears welled in her eyes.

"Felix?" she whispered. "What's happening?"

She was staring at the apple, mouth agape, when Sue came down the stairs in a sky-blue top and shorts. They stared at each other. Sue looked past jet-black bangs to the broken window, the flashes of lightning outside. She followed the footprints with her eyes and settled again on the drenched, dripping girl in front of her. Virginia looked back at the familiar face, trying to reconcile countless hours of videos with the actual young woman before her. She had imagined so many different things to say and as many ways to say them, but nothing came to her now. Bits of apple dirtied her lips. Tears and rainwater mixed on her cheek. Time seemed to stretch, making every second an hour. Slowly, her eyes drifted to Sue's phone in her hand, to the pink cat figurine dangling from the case.

Then things moved fast, too fast. Sue thumbed at the phone and raised it to her ear. Virginia didn't know when she crossed the kitchen or when she grabbed Sue's wrist. "Please," she said, mashed apple tumbling out of her mouth and dribbling down her chin. "I—I just wanted to—"

A voice from the phone: "9-1-1, what's your emergency?"

"There's someone in my house!" Sue screamed. "Send someone—"

Suddenly, she was on the floor, apples and pears rolling over the ceramic countertop, wine glasses shattered, the cutting board toppled over. Virginia looked down at her, at the phone she now held.

"Ma'am, are you there?" asked the operator. "Ma'am, can you say again—"

Virginia dropped the phone. She sobbed, shook her head, hit herself. Sue was crawling away, blood leaking from her temple. A red stain smudged the corner of the countertop.

"Felix," Virginia whispered. "Felix, help me—"

She blinked—now the cutting board was gripped tightly in her hands, the edge coated red and speckled with meaty bits. She looked down at Sue, what was left of Sue, and immediately expelled the crushed apple from her mouth.

"This isn't real," she babbled, hands on knees, sucking in snot and saliva and vomit. "It's not real. I'm dreaming. I'm dreaming. I'm dreaming—"

"Sue, everything okay?"

Virginia looked back—now it was Michelle at the foot of the stairs. The girl screamed and bolted back up. "Minnie!" she shouted. "Minnie, there's someone in the house!"

Virginia stumbled after her. "Wait!" she called, wiping her face, clearing her throat of phlegm and bile. "Wait, I'm not—"

She rounded the corner of the stairs, and there she was, so bright Virginia had to shield her eyes: Minerva King, skin a shining bronze, eyes a gold-tinged hazel, hair like dark waves curling into fiery tips. Virginia took in the black top and leopard-skin skirt, one of Minerva's favorite casual combos. She didn't know what to say.

Minerva held out an arm to shield Michelle. "Go to the bedroom," she commanded. "Call the police. Now."

Michelle turned into the adjacent room and slammed the door behind her. Minerva eyed the disheveled girl across from her, especially the hands dripping blood, bile, and rain.

"You need to leave," she said, finding her voice. "My friend is calling the police. They'll be here any minute."

Virginia stepped forward. She smiled. It was like walking towards an oasis in the desert, like finding some kind of magical hearth in a snowstorm. She couldn't help the way her feet shuffled forward, how her hands reached out. Even the crawling tar wedged around her arms, the roving sludge oozing from her waist, couldn't hold her back.

"I'm not here to hurt you," she said gently. "I just—I wanted to see you—"

Minerva backed against the door. "Don't—"

Suddenly, Virginia had closed the distance between them and seized Minerva by the neck. She pulled away with a scream. "I'm sorry! I don't know—I didn't mean—"

Minerva ran past her, making for the stairs. Virginia dove and caught her ankle. They dropped onto their stomachs. "Please," Virginia said, crawling towards her. "It's not—I'm not trying—"

Why couldn't she say what she wanted to say? The words were all in her head, all on her tongue—I wanted to see you, I love you, you're amazing, help me, hold me—but not a single one came out right. None of this could be real. It was too good to be true, too crazy to be genuine. That's why it felt so *un*real, why she couldn't talk, why she couldn't get a grasp on anything. A dream. Yes, a dream! She was dreaming, had to be dreaming. Dallas and Caroline and Felix on the street all twisted up—none of it was real. This black stuff in her eyes, the little bugs underneath her fingernails—they were all part of the dream. What happened to Sue was part of the dream. Even Minerva, so bright, so hot to the touch, had to be something she made up. No one could be that warm, no one that bright.

Next thing she knew, she'd be in bed, and Felix would be around her legs, and she'd go over to Suzanne's, and Suzanne would complain, and they'd just sit around like they always did, and didn't Janine have her baby? What was her name? Kylie or Katy or something like that? Maybe they'd see her in the hospital, and Suzanne might actually smile for once, and Virginia would be able to hold her niece and make funny faces to her. Mama would be happy to have a grandkid. Right? That had to be enough to finally make up for Daddy. And she would stop screaming and hitting them and be happy, finally happy. Yes—that's what was going to happen. Virginia was going to wake up any minute, any second, and everything would be okay, everything would be fine. These roaches in her mouth didn't matter. Sue's head in pieces didn't matter. Mama's anger didn't matter. Virginia would apologize, first thing. I'm sorry I've been a bad daughter. I'm sorry I didn't take care of Janine. I'll never do that again. That's what's going to happen, okay? So, time to wake up. Time to wake up and see everybody, and then I can go to school, and then I can watch Minerva again, and maybe Suzanne will watch her, too, and maybe we could plan a trip because that would be good for Suzanne, good to get her away from her parents. We can go away together, just for a little bit—

Minerva was on her feet, at the top of the stairs. Wake up, Virginia told herself, grabbing Minerva's arm. Wake up! Please, wake up! Wake up—

She fell, rolling, twisting the whole way down the stairs. She landed on her back, with a clear view of Minerva at the top. She couldn't move, couldn't lift her hands or wiggle her fingers— couldn't even turn her head to see Felix standing over her. But she smelled him. He smelled the same as he had lying in her lap, when she tried to smooth out his stiff, blood-caked fur. He'd smelled that way the whole time.

"Felix," she said quietly, very, very quietly. "Are you there?"

"I'm here," he answered.

"Good." Her mouth twitched in a smile. "Can I wake up now? Please?"

"You did well, Virginia," he said. "Very well indeed."

The girl on the stairs was coming down to her. She looked familiar—where had Virginia seen her before? She was so pretty, like an impossible type of pretty, the type of pretty you only see in movies. And she was warm. So, so warm. Like a bonfire. Like a place you'd go to get warm from the cold and the dark.

Minerva looked down at the girl and her bent neck, her frozen face. She was dead, had to be dead, but Minerva hesitated getting close all the same. So young, she thought, studying the placid eyes more closely. Just a kid.

Without thinking, compelled by instinct, she closed the girl's eyes—and then she sprang back, flicking her fingers free of what felt like worms, like maggots. Her energy left her, and she slumped against the wall. What the fuck was happening? Where was Sue?

She looked towards the kitchen, the mess on the countertop, the shattered glasses on the floor—and then she saw the outstretched, bloody arm around the corner. "Oh, Jesus," she moaned, heart dropping, lungs deflating. This couldn't be real. They had just been laughing at some stupid movie, just getting ready to make some drinks. I'm dreaming, she told herself, slapping her cheeks, clenching her fists. Right. That's it. I'm dreaming. I'm having a nightmare. Because otherwise—otherwise Sue is—

Sirens whined outside. Red and blue lights flashed in the rainy dark. No, she realized with a shudder. It wasn't a dream. She'd be awake already. Police wouldn't be streaming inside. Michelle wouldn't be screaming behind her.

A nauseating, stomach-churning smell hung over the room. The smell reminded her of childhood, of the nights she lay awake watching the shadows for movement, focusing her nose to catch whiffs of visitors. The smell reminded her of the cemetery where her father was buried, of the bodies rotting in the earth. It made her want to vomit.

TWELVE

Meanwhile, Virginia stirred. The dark seemed to warp around her, the air literally change. She could move her head, wiggle her fingers and toes, and when she inhaled, her lungs expanded as they always had. She felt warm. She didn't itch with the crawling of legs or tremble under the passing of feelers.

"Virginia," Felix said. "Open your eyes."

She did so. She no longer lay at the foot of the stairs. Instead, she stood at the gates of an ornate mansion. Beyond the black steel of the gate were baroque fountains fashioned with stone cherubs, the small, gilded mouths spewing water into the air. Enormous palm trees, far taller than those she saw earlier that day in Oakland, swayed in the night wind. An explosion rocked the ground beneath her feet, but Felix held her shoulders and pointed to the smoldering sky—red embers rained down from fireworks just above the mansion, their radiance so close that Virginia felt the heat on her face, smelled the lingering sulfur in the air.

"Felix?" She shuddered in his grip. "What's going on?"

"We're here," he said. "Come."

He led her through the gate, down the cobblestone path, past the fountains. In the garden, full of overgrown ferns and red-leaved vines, she heard the sweet sounds of violin and cello—an orchestra of masked, tuxedoed musicians played upon a raised stage. Partygoers filled the garden, the men in cashmere suits, the women in satin dresses. All wore masks of various shapes and sizes. The monstrous facades of lion and dragon turned her way, as did the soft facsimiles of owl and rabbit. All paused as Virginia passed, glasses of red wine clutched tightly in hand, eyes dark and indiscernible behind their disguises.

Virginia dawdled behind Felix. Everything was so hazy—she remembered getting to Minerva's house, remembered *seeing* Minerva—but what happened after that? Were they still in California? The palm trees and dark, distant mountaintops made her think so, but why was the sky red? Who were these people? Why did she feel so faint?

"Come along, Virginia," Felix said, and she followed him inside the mansion.

"What happened, Felix?" she asked. "Where's Minerva?"

He didn't respond. They passed through a vast hall, the stained-glass windows and marble floor more fitting of a church than a mansion. But the depictions in the glass weren't anything like what Virginia saw at Mass or in the cathedrals she'd studied at school. There were red serpents snaking around roots, golden fires blazing, trees shining with many-colored leaves, black holes gaping. Nothing of Jesus or his crucifixion.

They walked through a set of oaken doors and down a narrower, red-carpeted corridor. The air grew staler as they went, more rancid. The dead smell, Virginia thought with alarm. But why? Why was it here? She wanted to turn back, wanted to leave. "Felix," she said, and right as she did, he held open one last door for her.

"Come inside," he said.

On the other side of the door was a spacious, red-hued room, something like an art gallery. Draping the walls were massive paintings that reminded her of what Michelangelo and Da Vinci might have painted, but like the stained-glass windows, none of these were even remotely familiar. There were wastelands and lakes of fire.

Others portrayed vast pink and gold gardens, with winged figures floating above. Beneath the paintings stood bizarre marble sculptures and jagged, inscribed tablets that looked like they'd been lifted from cave walls. Lining the path to an enormous, dark-wood desk were glass cases housing browned bones, wooden carvings, ornate masks. Virginia's eyes lingered on one particular, multi-mouthed skull, too big and too long to be human, to be any animal on Earth for that matter. Another set of cases, farther away, burned with floating fires. The luster of these flames—some silver-blue, others rose-gold—held her attention. The flames sparkled, glistening in a way she had never seen regular fire shine. They felt familiar, too, like coming home, but not to Mother Blue or Janine or Suzanne. They felt like going all the way back to the beginning, whatever that was, whenever that was.

A voice sounded—Virginia didn't hear it with her ears, yet it echoed in her bones and tossed around her gut. A soft, feminine voice on the surface, but burning with something fierce and terrible underneath.

Well, well. You certainly took your time.

A woman lounged behind the desk, red hair snaking down her neck and blending into the folds of her crimson dress. She wore a wood-carved mask, something that struck Virginia as old, even ancient, though she couldn't explain why. Virginia stared at the woman, at her mask, arrested by the sheer presence surrounding her, radiating from her. She was the source of the voice—the source of the *smell*.

"There were diversions," Felix said, "but I made contact."

Wonderful! I expected no less.

The woman rose, and the entire room seemed to tilt. Her gaze centered on Virginia.

And what is this?

"Collateral."

The woman came forward.

She's small. Timid. Not unlike the last one you brought.

"Fortunately, we have a buyer who prefers that type. Didn't the other one already sell?"

Virginia shuddered under the woman's watch. It was like scales over her skin, like tongues grazing her elbows and knees.

"Felix," she said quietly, "what's going on? Who is she?"

The woman spoke as if Virginia hadn't said anything at all.

Indeed, she has sold. I'm preparing her now, in fact. Come see.

She led the way behind the desk to a velvet curtain. Felix followed, paying no attention to Virginia, who slunk behind them. The woman extended blood-red nails and drew back the curtain. Virginia caught sight of the pale, glassy-eyed girl on the other side. She screamed.

"Suzanne!"

She rushed forward and grabbed the other girl by the shoulders.

"Suzanne! Wake up! It's me! It's Virginia!"

No matter how hard she shook, Suzanne remained silent, catatonic. She bobbed, limp like dead weight, in her blue dress.

"Felix, help her!" Virginia cried. "What's wrong with her?"

"Oh, Virginia," Felix cooed. "You must still be in shock. Don't you realize where you are by now?"

Virginia stared at him through her tears, her mouth quivering. The woman came behind Felix and laid a hand on his shoulder.

She's taken a shine to you, it seems. Imagine that.

Felix returned Virginia's look. "Suzanne Grayson is dead, Virginia. She hung herself. You know that."

Virginia turned back to Suzanne's slack face.

"But that's—then why—"

"A spineless fool, as your mother liked to say," he went on. "And if Suzanne's here, that must mean the same for you, no?"

Virginia shook her head. It couldn't be true. She'd made it to California. She'd gotten away from that man. She'd found Minerva! There's no way she could be—it wasn't possible—

The stairs. The fall. Minerva coming down to her. The smell on Felix. The smell coming from the woman. The smell that was everywhere in this place—

The smell that was on her.

She screamed. She couldn't stop screaming.

"Oh, Virginia, hush," Felix chided. "What did you expect?"

The woman laughed.

Do I detect misgivings? How uncharacteristic.

"Not at all," he said. "At least I no longer have to feign being a cat of all creatures. I can finally throw off this unbecoming mask."

The woman chuckled and came around to Virginia. The mere touch of her hand on Virginia's cheek silenced the girl's crying, petrified her lungs, froze her heart.

Worry not, my sweet. We will find you the perfect home, just like your friend here. After all, that's what we do. We, who are without homes ourselves.

She turned to Felix.

Well. Let's not waste time. Go. Bring me my prize.

"As you command."

He bowed and faded into the darkness of the hall. The woman left Virginia, as still and slack as Suzanne, where she was. She regarded the flames dancing in their cases.

You feel it, don't you? So do I. The day when you will be whole.

She laughed and held out her arms in welcome.

Come to us, Minerva! Surrender your stolen fire to us. So that we may return home. So that we may have what is rightfully ours!

THIRTEEN

The last image Minerva had of Sue was her body covered by a blue tarp and wheeled away into the night. Michelle never stopped crying, not through the several rounds of police questioning, nor afterwards, when she and Minerva were escorted to Minerva's mother's house.

"Oh, my God," she said, over and over. "Oh, my God. Oh, God."

Minerva wondered why her own tears didn't come. She felt nothing, literally nothing, just a pit plunging deeper and deeper, never seeming to find its own bottom. Sue had been with them just hours before—that morning, they'd been planning a day trip to San Francisco—and now she was gone. One second to the next, like she'd never been there at all. It brought to mind Minerva's father, how he left one day on a quick shopping trip and never came back. She remembered watching from the hallway, all of twelve years old, as her mother met the police at the door and nearly collapsed from the news. Death was quick and easy, cruel in its finality. What was even the last thing she said to Sue? Maybe an offhand comment about a video, or a joke. Nothing about how Sue had always been there to listen to her, to ease her worries. Nothing about how she was an amazing singer or made a damn good screwdriver. Nothing about how she was a real friend in an industry that often felt so hollow and fake.

When the police finally left, she and Michelle lay in her old bedroom. Minerva hadn't been there in a couple of years, not since moving in with the girls, and the room had been stripped of most of her decorations and rendered into a plain guest bedroom. She left the bed to Michelle, who, stressed and exhausted, started snoring before long. Minerva, meanwhile, struggled to get comfortable on a pile of blankets on the floor. She stared up at the dark ceiling, wondering at her absence of feeling, her bizarre emptiness. Was she traumatized? In shock?

Janelle, her therapist, had talked often of the ways the body reacted to trauma. Some people resorted to substance abuse or violence. Others locked up and shut down. It wasn't too different from the stress responses, fight or flight, freeze or fawn. Either way, it felt wrong to lie there and not feel anything. Sue was dead. If Minerva hadn't pivoted at the last second on the stairs, she might have been a second casualty, Michelle a potential third.

"Just do something," she said into the dark. "Cry. Scream. She deserves something from you, doesn't she?"

But nothing came. No crying, no shaking. Sleep didn't come, either, and so Minerva lay there, trying to empty her head of their attacker's dead gaze and bland smile. Just a teen, she thought, over and over. A kid. A killer.

This early, pending an investigation, the police could only speculate. Maybe an overdose, one of the officers had said, or a psychotic break. "She was fucking crazy," Michelle said, blowing her nose, wiping her eyes. "I can't go back there, Minnie. There's no way. Can you get my stuff for me? I'm sorry, but I just cannot go fucking back there."

So, the next day, escorted by a couple of officers, Minerva had to return to the house by herself. The place seemed to take on a new light, or maybe a new darkness was more accurate. It wasn't just the yellow police tape ensnaring the building or the way the street seemed eerily empty now, as though no one dared walk past the scene of a crime. The very character of the house was different, but Minerva couldn't point to anything in particular. It was a change in the atmosphere, a difference in the way the air felt when she stepped inside. How many memories did she have there? A hundred? A thousand? But none of them came to mind as she quickly packed some suitcases and stuffed full some bags. Only the girl, bloody and manic, stood in her mind's eye. Only Sue's arm stretching past the corner of the counter. It was like a cutoff point, an event horizon that made the past some different era and the present something new, something decidedly worse. One thing was for sure—the air was still rotten with that dead smell, and even if Minerva felt nothing, felt empty, she knew she'd throw up if she stayed there too long.

That night, as Michelle slept, Minerva stepped onto the balcony with her laptop and microphone. The air was cool and crisp, and from that vantage, she had a nice twilight view of the city and the bay in the distance. In the past, she'd often sunbathed on the balcony and caught up on her books, but now, she needed the air and view to gather her thoughts, to help her talk through things like Janelle used to recommend. She hadn't made one of her late-night videos in a while—they became less important as the streaming blew up, as the follower count rose—but they had been useful for organizing her thoughts and processing her feelings. Who could she talk to about what happened, anyway? Janelle would just prescribe her something or explain everything away with platitudes. Her mother and her stepfather, Frank, were just too removed from it, more concerned about making her comfortable than actually hearing her out. And Michelle was so rattled, so panicked, that there was no way

Minerva could talk to her. No—it had to be the viewers. The stream. If for no other reason than to let them know things had changed, and she didn't know when—or even if—they would go back to the way they were.

"Hey, guys," she started, not sure where she was going, lacking any real plan or script. Viewers were already pouring in, filling the chat with exclamations of surprise, questions about what prompted the sudden video, theories about what was happening and why there hadn't been any streams in the last couple of days. Some mentioned the reports about an Oakland break-in that had already made waves on local news channels in the area.

"Yeah," said Minerva, "you guys probably already know. If I'm doing one of these, something must have happened—and something did. Something bad."

She looked up, trying to find the right words in the faraway lights of the skyline, in the dark ripples of the bay. "I don't know how much I can say, or what's legal or what's right. But everything will come out soon, anyway. Either way, I don't think I'll be on very much. Honestly, I'm not sure if I'll make another video at all.

"The scary thing is that I don't feel angry or sad. You know, with my dad, it comes and goes. That was what my first video was about, remember? But now, I don't feel anything. I thought maybe I could figure out why if I opened it up, but I'm just talking in circles. Actually, I am scared about something: that maybe this is it. Maybe this is how I am now, after everything. Like I can't feel sad anymore. I just can't get it out."

She watched the red recording icon blink, watched the timer run. She couldn't feel anything, couldn't force herself to feel anything, and yet she still couldn't sleep, couldn't throw out the images of Sue's arm, of her body on the stretcher, of the girl who had attacked them. "I'm stuck," she said. "I'm stuck, and I don't know how to get out."

It was then that a single tear leaked out. She flicked it away, thinking it was a fly, a piece of dirt. She stared at the damp streak on her thumb in amazement.

"I can't do this," she said, turning back to the camera. "I'm sorry."

She shut the laptop. Her hands shook, her shoulders trembled. A second tear came, followed by a third. Sue was gone. Fucking Christ. She was *dead*. Sue was dead.

Minerva cried finally, all alone up there in the dark, Sue's face all she could see.

FOURTEEN

The following weeks saw the tears come and go, sometimes in long, unbroken fits, and other times in quick, brief spurts. At a photo shoot, the photographer paused and peeked over his viewfinder.

"Minnie?" he said. "You're crying."

His words didn't register at first—she was focused on maintaining the requested posture, the required slant of the shoulders—but then Minerva felt the tears on her cheeks, felt her practiced smile breaking. She reviewed the photos afterwards, studying how her hazel eyes darkened across the photographs, how the constitution of her face softened and then cracked. She seemed a statue otherwise, skin glowing with bronzer, golden dress shimmering. "They don't look bad," the photographer said outside, snuffing out his cigarette. "Makes for some variety."

Minerva tried to smile. Usually, his compliments brightened her spirits, but not today.

All her jobs since the break-in had been the same. Whereas she had once been the picture of professionalism, able to turn on the waterworks upon request or wipe away instantly the faintest trace of sadness, she had been unable to stop the tremors and random tears that snuck up on her now. Sue's face haunted her dreams, as if mocking her for not doing enough, for not saving her.

"You suffered a trauma," Janelle said, calm and tranquil as always. "And there was nothing you could have done. How could you have known something like that would happen?"

Well, her mother *had* told her many times how much she disliked the area. Minerva fidgeted in the cold of Janelle's office, normally comforted by the smell of the potpourri but now alienated by it, disgusted by it.

"I can't stay like this forever," she said. "Can't you prescribe something?"

"Let's hold off on that for now," Janelle said. "Remember, there's no timetable, Minnie."

Of course there wasn't, Minerva thought. That would be too easy, right?

Janelle shifted. "What about things at home? How is your mother?"

Going back home had brought a mix of feelings. Minerva was surprised how easily the old routines fell into place, how her body took up the poolside morning mimosas and Frank's overcooked steaks with sighs of relief. But the sense of moving backwards nagged at her, the feeling that she was backsliding into adolescence. As much as she would have preferred finding another place, there wasn't much choice—everyone else already had roommates or live-in boyfriends, and the house she had shared with Sue and Michelle was out of the question. Going to get her and Michelle's things had nearly made her delirious. Speaking of Michelle, she had already left to her father's place. Minerva had gotten her bedroom back, her privacy, but she'd lost the last major thread that tied her to her actual life, to her relationship with Sue.

The next morning, she and her mother lounged by the pool. The water sparkled a dreamy, serene blue, as if part of a spell inviting Minerva to feel at ease, to pretend things were normal, even good. But a gloom hung over things, like an almost literal gray cloud. She thought she heard bugs crawling over the pool deck and flies circling her head.

Her mother lathered sunscreen over her sun-spotted arms and weathered neck. "I'm telling you, I'm this close to suing Jason for not setting up cameras around that damn house."

Serena, Minerva's stepsister, suddenly plunged into the water. Minerva's mother shrieked, pulling up her legs and clutching her towel to her chest.

"Not so close! You're going to get us wet!"

Serena emerged, dark hair matted to her face. "Sorry!" she said, proceeding to swim laps around the pool.

"No situational awareness, I swear." Minerva's mother leaned back and sighed. "Anyway. I never liked that location. Not that it makes a difference where you live now. Everywhere you go is falling apart. And all sorts of people are coming out of the woodwork."

"She was a kid, Mom," Minerva said. "Probably the same age as Serena."

If it wasn't Sue's face haunting her constantly, it was that of the girl who had killed her. Gray-eyed, pale-cheeked, looking somewhere between awestruck and terrified. Hadn't she said something on the stairs, right before she fell? She'd just wanted to see them?

"Does it matter how old she is?" her mother replied. "That girl broke in! And Sue—"

"Can we talk about something else? Janelle says I'm not supposed to think about it."

"That's someone else I wonder about. She was helpful when you were younger, but now, for the money we're paying—"

Frank appeared at the patio door. "Need a refresher, girls? Got some kiwis that need squeezing!"

Minerva's mother raised her hand. "Please, Frank! I'm about done with mine—"

"It's okay, Mom," said Minerva. "You can have mine."

As Minerva passed the drink to her mother, Serena leaned over the edge of the pool. "I'll take one, Dad!"

"In a few more years," Frank laughed. "But I'll fix you up something sober meanwhile."

He went back inside. Serena winked at Minerva, then sank back into the pool. Minerva's mother continued talking, but her words melted into a muffled medley of white noise. Again, there was the girl's bloody face in Minerva's mind, her half-vacant eyes, her body contorted at the bottom of the stairs. Her lips moving, mouthing words to the air, to someone who wasn't there. Bugs crawling and flies circling. Thousands of them. Millions of them.

The detectives came back the next day. "Minnie's not here," her mother told them at the door, "and I would appreciate it if you all left us alone—"

"It's okay, Mom." Minerva stepped between her and the detectives, unassuming in her cardigan and jeans. "How can I help?"

"Ms. King," the first detective said. "I'm Sergeant Hart, as you might remember. This is Detective Padilla."

The second detective, pudgy and balding, raised a hand.

"We just had a few questions," Hart continued. "There have been some developments in your case."

Her mother turned to her. "Minnie, you don't have to go with them."

"It's okay, Mom. They're just questions."

Minerva followed the detectives around the block. Under the shade of a nearby smoking pavilion, Hart unveiled a manila folder and withdrew a picture from inside.

"Do you recognize this person?"

Minerva studied the photo, a high-school portrait of a teenage girl, long-haired and barely smiling. Minerva's heart skipped. "It's her," she said. "That's the girl that broke in."

"Her name's Virginia Blue," Hart said. "Sixteen years old, from a little town in Texas called Oasis. Have you heard of it?"

Minerva handed back the portrait. She shook her head.

"No one has," Padilla remarked. "It's the type of place you pass through without a second thought."

Hart watched her. "Virginia's older sister reported her missing. She also reported her husband's car missing. Texas DPS found the vehicle an hour out of Oasis, but they lost the girl's trail."

"Until the night she shows up at your place," Padilla said.

It was a lot of information at once, too much for Minerva to process.

"I'm sorry. What does any of this mean?"

"We have reason to believe it wasn't an accident Virginia broke into your home," Hart said. "Her sister said she was always online, always watching videos—yours in particular."

The hairs on Minerva's neck stood upright. "She was watching me?"

Padilla nodded. "All the time. You ever talk to her? Exchange messages?"

"Sometimes you talk with the chat, or answer a comment, but it's anonymous. I never actually talked to any of them."

"Well, Virginia Blue was looking to meet you," Padilla said, "apparently no matter what. She stole her brother-in-law's car and made it all the way to California."

"We're just trying to get a clearer picture of what happened," Hart said. "If you remember anything, or if you find something that could help us, can you give me a call?"

Minerva hesitated but nodded. "Sure."

Once the detectives were gone, she returned inside, turning over Hart's card in her hand and the portrait of the girl in her mind. Virginia Blue. That was the name of Sue's killer.

Up in her bedroom, she flung her phone on the bed and regarded her laptop, her microphone. Streaming had been an escape, what she thought was a harmless hobby. But it had been anything but harmless.

She sat on the bed and pulled up her knees. Nothing ever stayed safe. There was always some hidden danger, some secret risk that made itself known when she let her guard down. Even this bedroom had once been the worst place to be. The otherwise cozy shadows during the day had housed things at night. She'd called them "visitors." They'd looked like people in her varying degrees of half-sleep, men dressed in black, women garbed in gray, figures more moonlight and window drape than flesh and blood. Sometimes, there had been children, little girls in yellow sundresses, boys in white suit jackets. Even in the daytime, outside of the house, there had been kids who played with her at recess, who seemed to draw her farther and farther to the edge of the playground, who vanished when it was time to go back inside. She thought they were just imaginary friends, the kind that all kids claimed to have. They had always felt warm and lightly curious, but after her father's funeral, the dark had twisted and coiled with gangly arms and crooked fingers, with the flick of tongues and the gnash of teeth. The kindly old figures and playful children gave way to shadowy things that seemed more monster than human.

Eventually, those things started showing up everywhere, stalking the hallways of her school, lurking on street corners in broad daylight. Minerva had wished for it to end, for something to take it all away, to take *her* away. A little girl, only twelve, she had imagined how easy it would be to step into traffic or trip over the top of the stairs. She had never mentioned the visitors to her mother, but the sleep deprivation and depression were obvious. That's when Janelle came into the picture.

Janelle had called them hallucinations, night terrors, products of a child's overactive imagination. That's what happens when a parent dies, she said. Cracks form. Beams splinter. And before the mind can make the necessary repairs, install the emergency caulking, the new molding, dark things emerge from the gaps. Eventually, with enough therapy and time (and meds, of course), Minerva's cracks mended. The night terrors ended. The visitors became afterthoughts. But now, Sue's face fresh in her mind, Virginia Blue's portrait hovering over her eyes, Minerva felt a knot in her throat and pressed a hand to her chest. There was a hole there, a crack that hadn't been properly filled, small enough to overlook, but big enough to fit a finger through. And it was getting bigger.

How had things changed so drastically overnight? The streaming had been fun, but maybe she had overdone it, filming so much of her time at home and at work. She had given millions of people access to her life—not only hers, but those of her friends and family, too. If they watched her streams, they knew her mother, Frank, Serena. They knew all the girls. They knew Sue and Michelle.

And now Sue was dead. It wasn't that girl, Virginia Blue, who had killed her—it had been Minerva, because she'd been stupid enough to give the whole world a window into her own.

That night, she sat down for bed, downed a couple of melatonin pills with some water. Some sleep, any sleep, would be a relief, and hopefully free of the faces haunting her. Before turning off her lamp, she reviewed Sergeant Hart's card again. Maybe she had overlooked something, missed a crucial detail. Something that could have saved Sue's life.

As much as it turned her stomach, she powered on the computer and opened up her streaming pages, her social media profiles, her e-mail inboxes. There were countless messages across all the platforms: get-well wishes, prayers for health, questions about what had sparked the sudden hiatus. She rewatched her last video, the one recorded on the balcony the night after the break-in. "I can't do this," she said in the video, her first tears of many more falling. "I'm sorry." Views and likes were still coming in, but after weeks, with nothing else, her pages were losing relevance, fading into obscurity where the algorithms couldn't find them. That's good, she thought, with a mix of gratification and anger. They shouldn't be recommended. No one should watch them.

She pored through her inboxes, searching for any breadcrumb, a random message that went unnoticed, a throwaway comment that held the key. Finally, she stopped delaying the inevitable and typed with trembling fingers the girl's name into the search bars.

She was barely aware of the drumbeat of her heart as the messages loaded. Each page yielded dozens of unread messages. VirginiaHeart08. ginnyblueskater. Other handles across other platforms. Some of the messages were brief happy-birthdays and short how-do-you-dos, but others were long, paragraphs of rambling and ranting about school, about her hometown, about her sister and her brother-in-law, about some friend named Suzanne, about "Mama." Minerva read them—she didn't want to, almost couldn't stand to—but she felt compelled, felt obligated. And it wasn't just Virginia. There were so many messages from other girls, all oblivious to her lack of attention and care, all blindly, wholeheartedly devoted to her.

She stood up on wobbling legs. The panic attack was extreme, worse than any she had experienced lately. She almost made it to the door before collapsing, unable to stop her limbs from shaking, her heart from hammering. She closed her eyes and tried to count down, to control her breathing. When she opened them, a pair of scuffed, mud-smeared sneakers filled her vision.

Minerva scampered back and rubbed her eyes free of tears and sweat. There was no mistaking the sneakers, the torn jeans, the black hoodie, the long hair. It was the girl, Virginia Blue, reeking like she had of sweat and dirt and now something else, something rotten. Her face was hidden by a plain, black mask. Her breath rattled from behind the porcelain of the mask, audible from across the room.

"Hi," she said.

Minerva gasped and backed against the wall. This couldn't be real. She was hallucinating, experiencing some kind of stress response—

"Don't just parrot Janelle," the phantom said, as though it heard her thoughts. "We both know that hack couldn't tell up from down on a good day. Definitely not real from fake."

Minerva shut her eyes, covered her ears. It was fake, had to be fake, couldn't be real. She'd count—that had done the trick sometimes when she was younger, helping her calm down, helping her fall asleep.

The phantom laughed. "Go ahead. I'll wait."

Minerva counted all the way to a hundred, then back down to zero, desperately, manically. But when she opened her eyes, the girl remained. She spread her arms.

"See? Still here. Still real."

"You *can't* be here," Minerva said. "You're dead!"

"That's right. You killed me, after all. And I'd come all this way to see you."

"You can't be here. You're *not* here. You're not—"

"If I wasn't real, could I do this?" The phantom suddenly grabbed Minerva by the face and hoisted her into the air. "Can something fake do that?"

She dropped Minerva to the floor, watching as she tried vainly to crawl away. "Where are you going? You can't just leave. You owe me. You basically belong to me now."

"No," said Minerva, "no, you're not here, you're just a—"

"Just a what? Another visitor? News flash, Minnie: they've always been real. They've always been there, always been watching you. They're everywhere, drawn to those sensitive to them. The ones who can give them what they want."

"Just leave me alone!" Minerva cried. "I can't help you!"

"Oh, but you *can* help me." The phantom brandished the laptop. "I was crying out to you this whole time—we all were! And what did you do? You just pretended we weren't there. It's so easy for you, with your beaches and your mimosas. Your perfect family and your perfect life."

Minerva stared at her. Had she always been destined to lose her mind? Had everything been just some kind of schizophrenia? The visitors when she was younger, and now this? Had there even been a break-in? Was Sue even dead? Was there even a Virginia Blue?

"You still don't believe," the phantom said. "That's your problem, you know. You think closing your eyes to the world is a solution, but it's not. You think you're really over your daddy's death? You think you're actually perfect? You're the furthest thing from perfect."

"Just go away," Minerva said. "Please. I don't know what I'm supposed to do—"

"Oh, it's easy," replied the phantom. "It's not a big ask at all. I just need your life. I just need you to die."

Minerva blinked and tried to focus her teary eyes. She almost didn't believe the girl *wasn't* there anymore, how vivid and real her presence had felt. Her cheeks still stung from being grabbed, and her nose still burned with the residue of the phantom's dead smell, the same as the night of the break-in, the same that had hovered in the air during her night terrors.

Adrenaline got her to her feet and sharpened her senses, but just as quickly as it had filled her bloodstream, it drained. She barely made it to the bed before her legs gave out, and she didn't even have the strength left to raise her head. Exhaustion tugged at her and pulled her down into the blissful reprieve of sleep.

FIFTEEN

Minerva didn't sleep for long—she shot up in sweat more than once, fearful the phantom would be looming over her bed, that it would lay its stinking hands on her again. By the time sunlight breached the room, she was clenched in a ball on the bed, watching the shadows with nervous eyes. She would have stayed like that, guarding against further assaults, but a notification on her phone reminded her she had brunch with Michelle.

She showered, trying to take comfort in the scalding water and stifling steam. A dream, she thought. What happened last night was a dream, had to be a dream, a nightmare brought on by all the stress of the last few weeks. The detectives must have caused it. The portrait of the girl, Virginia Blue, the dozens of e-mails and messages she skimmed. That had to be it, right? The break-in, Sue's death, had triggered her just like her father's death had. And just like before, like Janelle always said, time would heal the wound, fill in the cracks, and she would be fine. She would be okay.

Minerva turned off the shower, hugging herself, trying to catch her breath and stop her shuddering. But as much as she tried to comfort herself, the phantom's dead smell still filled her nostrils. The force of its grip on her face was still palpable. As she dressed, buttoning her blouse with hesitant hands, strapping on sandals with fumbling fingers, she thought of the more ominous, terrifying possibility: if the phantom hadn't been a dream—if it was *real*, as much as she didn't want to believe it—then it wasn't just the product of her stress. The visitors of her youth hadn't been creations of a child's overactive, grieving mind. They were real—they were *ghosts.* And they were among the living.

When Michelle saw her come into the restaurant, she gasped. "God, Minnie, have you been sleeping?"

Minerva smiled sheepishly. Apparently, the loads of concealer around her eyes weren't enough to hide the dark rims.

"Trying," she said. "You?"

Michelle caught her up on her own busy few weeks: moving back in with her dad, deciding to go back to school. "In a way, I'm glad it happened," she said. "Not about Sue, obviously. But the whole thing took the choice out of my hands."

Minerva blinked her heavy eyes, dipped more creamer into her second cup of coffee.

"I didn't know you wanted to leave."

"Oh, Minnie—it's not you! I love you. I loved Sue. But, honestly, what am I doing out here, you know? I can't be a singer. That's not gonna happen. I'm not like you."

Minerva stared at her over her cup. "What does that mean?"

"Nothing," Michelle said. "It's a good thing. You're gorgeous. Everything you touch turns to gold. Me and Sue? We're just regular girls. We're just along for the ride."

Minerva lingered after Michelle left, ordered another coffee to go. She walked the nearby strip mall, trying to distract herself with used books and vintage CDs, rolling Michelle's words around in her mind. Just regular girls. Just along for the ride. She thought of the messages that flooded her inboxes. Behind each was someone also along for the ride, grasping for what they could of her light, her warmth. As far back as she could remember, she had attracted attention, basked in it. How many plays had she done as a child, how many photo shoots? Graduating to TV spots as a teen had been natural, expected. At every turn, casting directors had chosen her out of lineups. Agents had snapped up opportunities to talk to her, and obviously, there had been no shortage of boys throughout high school and college eager for her attention.

She credited her mother for steering her away from the common pitfalls. "Hollywood's a snake pit," she said. "I'm not letting you fall in there, Minnie."

A former costumer and amateur actor, her mother had navigated the entertainment jungle before. She had been true to her word: Minerva modeled exclusively, and her mother—both her agent and manager—was selective about her gigs. Producers were eyeing her, her mother said, catching whiffs of her star quality. Minerva had done several commercials, but Hollywood would never get access as long as her mother was involved. Not now, not ever.

It was honestly a relief to not have to think about it much, to just ride the wave. But Minerva had never considered how many people were paddling along in the shadow of the crest, trying to follow her. Sue and Michelle, the other girls, the millions of followers who watched her videos—how many were making it to shore in her wake? How many were drowning in the crash?

In a public restroom, she splashed water on her face and down her neck. Virginia Blue had drowned, she thought, and she'd taken Sue with her. What could have been so bad to push her that way? The detectives had mentioned the place she came from, somewhere no one even thought about. Maybe there were others like her, some trying to get to California, some looking to escape—

"Wow—I'm honored you're thinking of me."

Minerva whirled around and came face to face with the phantom's black mask. This close, the smells of upturned soil and pungent earth were hard to stomach. She rushed into a stall and vomited into the toilet.

"I thought you were made of tougher stuff than that," the phantom said. "But since you're wondering, Oasis is a real shitshow. Leaving was the best decision I made—even if it killed me."

Minerva wiped her lips and gagged. She shut her eyes and tried to count.

"Why can't you just accept what your senses are telling you?" the phantom asked. "You aren't hallucinating. You aren't crazy. I'm real."

Minerva bared her teeth at the ghost. "If you're real, then just leave me alone!"

"Leave you alone? I'm *dead* because of you. So is your friend."

"No!" Minerva cried. "It was an accident. And Sue—I'm not responsible—"

She couldn't even finish her sentence. Sue's face filled her mind, constricting her throat, chaining her tongue. The tears welled up again.

"Hard, isn't it?" the phantom asked. "All you had to do was answer a single e-mail. All you had to do was acknowledge me. Then maybe this would never have happened. I'd still be alive. Sue would be alive."

Minerva shut her eyes and tried to block out the voice.

"But if you want," the phantom said, "I can check on Sue for you."

Minerva turned to the phantom incredulously. "What?"

"It's easy. We can see how she's doing. Just give me a second."

The phantom went slack, the head hanging loosely, the arms dangling limply. Minerva watched with both deepening dread and climbing confusion. She made for the door when the phantom suddenly jerked. At length, a voice floated out from behind the mask: a different voice, more fragile, more fearful, but all too familiar.

"Minnie? Minnie, is that you?"

Minerva stared, mouth agape. She couldn't stop the tears this time.

"Sue?" she said softly.

The phantom raised trembling hands to touch the mask and gingerly trace its curves. "What is this? What's going on? Where am I?"

Minerva wiped her eyes, tried to push her heart back down her throat.

"Sue? Is that really you?"

The phantom shook. "Minnie, I can't see you! Why is it so dark? Where am I?"

"Sue, I'm here!" Minerva reached out and took hold of the phantom. "I'm right here!"

The phantom shrieked and convulsed, nearly breaking out of Minerva's grasp. "Where are you, Minnie? What's going on? Where am I?"

"I'm here, Sue!" Minerva said. "I'm right here! Tell me what to do! What do I do?"

The phantom stopped shaking, its sobs twisting into vicious laughs. "You should see the look on your face! Hilarious!"

Minerva backed away. That wasn't Sue, had never been Sue. The ghost was playing with her now—fucking playing with her!

"Fuck you!" she cried. "Just leave me alone!"

"I already told you," the phantom said. "If you want this to stop, all you have to do is die. Leave your body open for me. Then we can both get what we want."

"You want my body?" Minerva asked.

The phantom nodded. "Your body. Your life. Everything. What are you doing with it, anyway? Just whoring yourself out to the camera. Just dragging little girls to their deaths like a black widow."

Minerva tried to mount a defense, but just as her voice left her, so did the phantom, leaving behind that dead smell, that stench of rotten flesh and ground torn asunder. Minerva shut her eyes—she screamed. She was going mad. She had to be going mad.

Back in her room, she chugged cans of beer as she walked a frantic circuit around the bed. Sue was dead. Because of her. Because she had been neglectful, because she had been selfish. Because there were girls and women reaching out to her, begging for help, looking for answers, and she had done nothing. She had ignored them all.

Did she deserve to die? Had the impulse from her youth, the urge to throw herself into traffic and tumble down the stairs, been the right decision all along? If she had died early enough, none of this would have happened. Sue would be alive. Virginia Blue would be alive. Who knew how many others?

But how would she even do it? Painkillers? Going under in the tub? Each successive option turned her stomach and swished the beer around like a blender. She vomited again.

She slunk into bed afterwards, feeling hot and cold, shaking and throbbing. Sue. Oh, God. *Sue.* What was she supposed to do? What the hell was she supposed to do?

At some uncertain point, she fell asleep—and then she woke up, but not in her room.

Minerva sat, petrified, barely able to breathe, sunken in an amphitheater seat. The air was thick and hot, heavy with the weight of dried blood and rotten meat. To her left, a woman in a blood-red cocktail dress and muddied rabbit mask laughed and brandished a black, misty martini. The sludgy drink splashed and struck Minerva's face. She squirmed, but she couldn't even scream, let alone wipe away the stinking, wriggling molasses that inched down her cheek. Her throat was locked, her face frozen in a grimace, her mouth open in a silent scream.

A sudden guffaw drew her eyes to the right. A man in a black suit and elephant mask pulled vigorous handfuls from a bucket of wet, blood-speckled entrails. He bit into them with yellowed teeth, chewing the innards as though they were strings of licorice. Minerva willed her eyes away and swept the rest of the amphitheater.

Her heart slammed even harder against her chest. The amphitheater's rows stretched into an abyssal darkness on both sides, every seat occupied by a masked theatergoer. Their cackling and cavorting reached raucous highs. Satin-gloved fingers toyed with eyeballs dressing drinks. Lumps of flesh scattered from plates and stained lapels and shoes. Arms and hands and bodies and tongues entwined. Dresses lifted. Shirts came undone. Skin met skin. Teeth met flesh. Claws drew blood.

Minerva steered her terrified gaze towards the enormous, fog-ridden stage. Mammoth velvet curtains stood ready to part, appearing more like walls of exposed muscle and artery from her vantage point in the audience. She tried to focus, tried to still her hammering heart, but the pit in her stomach only deepened by the moment. As real and visceral as the smells and sounds were, she knew it was just a dream, just a night terror brought on by the break-in, no different than the phantom. Count, she thought. Just like Janelle trained you. Fucking count!

Ten. Nine. Eight. Seven.

Six. Five. Four.

Three. Two.

One.

A spotlight shone on the stage. The amphitheater went quiet. The light revealed a fiery-haired woman in a bare-backed, crimson dress. She raised long, carmine nails and turned up her red mask, older and plainer than the masks of the theatergoers. Her smell reached Minerva across the amphitheater. Like crushed roadkill. Like upturned graves.

Friends! Welcome!

Her words weren't English—weren't anything, actually, neither spoken nor even thought, yet they were somehow comprehensible, clearer than anything Minerva had ever heard in her waking hours. The audience erupted into hoots and hollers and howls. The red woman waited patiently for the adulation to subside.

We have a special show for you tonight. A prime selection. Some incredible stock.

Another round of cheers. Minerva counted again. Again and again and again.

Just look at the feast we have prepared for you! Delicious, isn't it? So, don't be shy! Eat! Relish! Enjoy! All of this is for you! For us! Let us delight in the gifts we have been given! Let us celebrate!

The stage exploded with a dazzling display of multicolored, swimming lights, reds and blues and greens and yellows and purples. Music filled the amphitheater: a discordant, cacophonous blare of trumpets and trombones, drums and strings. Forms lurched onto the stage as if from nowhere. Misshapen, skeletal wraiths. Warped, fleshy masses. Too many eyes blinked from beneath shoulders and between toes. Elongated arms and contracted legs toppled over one another. Mouths gaped with rows of inhuman teeth, screaming a thousand screams all at once. The crowd screamed in return, mocking the abominations as they circled the stage, circled their ringmaster. The red woman lashed them with a whip, scattering blood into the air, severing hands, striking out eyes, knocking out teeth.

Above them, dwarfish figures straddled tightropes and leaped from impossible ledges. They flew on makeshift, glued-together wings, the feathers sewn and stapled haphazardly into their scarred, grafted skin. They screeched in a blend of half-conscious pain and mindless jubilation, plucking at one another's eyes, pulling at one another's flesh. Some missed jumps or outstretched hands, plummeting to the stage in bloody, feather-filled explosions. The red woman walked among their twitching, whimpering corpses. She stomped their fragile heads to bits, ground her heel into the mashed brains and broken skulls. She flung handfuls of their viscera into the audience, the theatergoers baying like dogs, lapping at the discarded remains and throttling one another for severed fingers and toes.

Ten. Nine. Eight. Seven. Six. Ten. Nine. Eight. Ten. Nine. Eight. Minerva counted, counted, counted, unable to reach zero, unable to even reach five. Everything around her was gyrating bodies and deafening music, a bizarre nightmare that would have been comical had it not been so terrifyingly violent and disgusting. It's just a dream, she thought wildly, just a dream, just a nightmare, just a night terror. Just count. Just count. Just count. You just have to count—

Everything went silent. The spotlight shone on the red woman again, her crimson-clawed hand high in the air, commanding silence.

Let's move on, friends! To the main event! The reason you're all here!

The abominations were gone, the stage free of their scattered remains. The curtains parted—from the dark depths emerged twin processions of shambling, humanoid forms. Minerva stared down at them, feeling even greater dread as she recognized the chained legs and bruised elbows, the vacant faces and soulless eyes. There were women, men, girls, boys—short and tall, slim and gaunt, pale and dark. All were naked, chained at the ankle, their wrists bound. They filed into position behind the red woman, making no sounds, betraying no expressions.

Beautiful, are they not? All freshly sourced! All for you!

Applause broke out, more screams, more shouts. The red woman allowed the applause to run, the cheering to fade. She turned and took a man's chin in her hand.

Look at this one—strong, able-bodied.

She cupped a girl's cheek.

Young. Unsoiled.

She strolled among them, lifting arms, pointing out muscles.

All of them soft. Docile. They're doing such a good job for us up above!

She took a man by his sculpted, black shoulder and guided him to the front of the stage.

We'll start with this one. We found him bleeding out, literally shot through the heart. He was begging for the pain to stop. Willing to give anything.

She trailed a finger around one of his nipples, her nail circling the dark areola.

We mended what we could. He's strong. Perfect for anything you could imagine. So, who will start? How many of your own stock will you offer?

Hands shot up. Cries filled the air.

"Two hundred!"

"Three!"

"Five hundred!"

"One thousand."

All went quiet. Heads craned. Minerva looked as far to the left as her paralysis allowed—a man in white, wearing the mask of a horned ram, so pale his skin was nearly indistinguishable from his gown, held up his hand.

One thousand! Do we have any other offers?

No one else spoke. The red woman swept an arm theatrically.

Sold!

The man returned to his place among the other captives. The red woman strolled again.

I know who will be next! Yes, this one is very recent—very, very recent. Young. Moldable. Untainted.

She brought forward a petite girl, long dark hair shielding her face. The woman traced nails down the girl's arms, circled her small breasts. She brushed the curtain of hair away. Minerva stared down at the revealed face. Her scream, locked deep inside her throat, broke out in the faintest of gasps.

The woman led the small, broken form of Virginia Blue to the front of the stage.

Such a precious subject demands a generous starting bid!

The hands shot up again. The cries sounded out. Five hundred! Six hundred! Six-fifty! Seven! They went on and on, surpassing one thousand, then two thousand, three thousand—

"Ten thousand!"

As before, the theater went abruptly silent. Surprised mumblings permeated the quiet. Minerva watched with horror as a giant, dark mass rose up near the stage. The man was an impossible size, too big to realistically move, yet he lumbered forward nonetheless and raised bejeweled hands in awe of his prize. The giant mouth below his bull's mask stretched into a wet, slobbering grin. In the fresh silence, the buzz of flies coating him was evident and suddenly overwhelming—the noise penetrated Minerva's ears, so loud and invasive she thought flies had breached her skull and besieged her brain.

"She's mine," the man gasped through his warbling, fleshy, many-folded neck. "She has to be mine."

The red woman watched him.

She will be. Provided we have no other offers. The bid stands at ten thousand—do we have any others?

No one protested. The man dragged his black-suited body—if one could call it that—atop the stage. He loomed over Virginia. He cradled her face in his fat hands.

Minerva's tears streamed down her cheeks, down her neck. She felt her chest rise and fall faster, faster, faster. The binds on her throat loosened. She screamed. She screamed like she had never screamed in her life.

The entire amphitheater turned towards her. The theatergoers murmured, moaned, fidgeted, thrashed. Their cries grew loud, grew hungry.

The red woman laughed.

We have a special guest, it seems—and what a guest it is! Friends, how long has it been since one from above graced us with her presence? I can smell her from down here.

The red woman shook. She dragged her nails down her neck and towards her bosom.

What beauty—what life! My precious Minerva, come to us at last!

The theatergoers stood in their seats, itching to move, waiting for the call. The woman fixed a long finger on Minerva.

I want her, friends! Bring her to me! Whoever does will get a share!

They moved, crawling over their seats, leaping over and trampling one another, surging like a single wave crashing down upon Minerva. She looked down, caught Virginia's sullen, dead gaze. She shut her eyes. She counted. Ten nine eight—

The mass of noise and chaos and reek got closer, breaking over her feet.

Seven six five four three—

Hands clutched her ankles. Fingers found her hair, her cheeks. Teeth and tongues reached for her nose, her eyes—

TWO ONE—

She sucked in air as though she had been underwater for hours, for days. She screamed. The amphitheater was gone, the colors and music suddenly as tenuous and transient as any dream. The dark of her room surrounded her, cold and alien at first, but quickly assuming its regular familiarity. She sat up, feeling unconsciously for the hole in her chest.

Her mother rushed in. "Minnie, what—" She smelled the beer before she saw the cans. Her daughter was upright in bed, weeping into her hands, trembling. "Oh, Minnie. I'm going to call Janelle—"

"No, Mom!" Minerva looked at her with startling violence. "Please, don't! I just need some time alone! Please!"

Reluctantly, her mother left the room. Minerva fought to control her swimming head, her swirling gut. As much as every instinct wanted to scream otherwise, what she had seen had not been a dream. The amphitheater had been real. The girl, Virginia Blue, was there—all of them were there. And the show would go on.

SIXTEEN

"Your mother told me you were drinking."

Minerva withered under Janelle's gaze. Her warm, patient demeanor made it worse. If she yelled, at least Minerva could snap back and throw her energy somewhere. But as always, Janelle spoke quietly, choosing her words carefully, drawing on years of experience counseling probably hundreds of patients just like Minerva.

"I was," Minerva said quietly, keeping her eyes down. She balled her fists, chipped at her cuticles. "But I wasn't going to—I'm not an alcoholic. I just needed to put it away."

"Put away what you're seeing?"

Minerva hesitated. What could she say? She was seeing the ghost of a dead girl? She was dreaming about circus shows from hell? She wasn't crazy—she couldn't afford to be thought crazy. When she was younger, when the night terrors had gotten unbearable, Janelle had nearly had her institutionalized. Minerva knew it could happen easily, especially with her mother hovering over Janelle's shoulder and telling on her every indiscretion. Maybe that would be a good thing, she thought. Maybe you're going crazy, and the best thing for everyone—yourself included—is to lock you up in a padded room. In fact, going crazy would be a relief compared to the alternative. Because if she wasn't crazy, that meant the phantom visiting her was real. That meant the nighttime visitors of her youth had been real. That meant the circus and the people in masks (*were* they people?) were real. That meant Virginia Blue and all the others were down there, paraded around and auctioned off like cattle.

"Cops came by," Minerva said, trying to deflect. "They asked me questions about the girl. The one who broke in. Apparently, she was one of my viewers. On my streams."

"Oh, Minnie. That must have been difficult to hear."

"Yeah. I keep thinking, am I responsible? Is Sue dead because of me?"

"It's natural to turn inwards," Janelle said, "especially in cases where we feel powerless. But that desire for control can be harmful, too. Because we shoulder things we shouldn't."

"But I *am* responsible," Minerva said. "Maybe if I had reached out to this girl, or answered her e-mails, or done something different, she wouldn't have looked for me. And Sue would still be alive, and the girl would be alive, and none of this would have happened."

Janelle smiled. "Do you remember the drawbridge story?"

"About the wife?"

"Exactly. You used to think if you had been nicer to your father, if you had asked him to play that morning, he might never have gotten in the car. But any number of things had to happen for the accident to happen. He could have taken a little longer at breakfast. The other driver could have gone two miles faster, two miles slower. We entertained all those scenarios. Remember?"

Minerva lowered her eyes. "I remember."

"This is the same thing, Minnie. Maybe you could have done a hundred things differently. Maybe this still would have happened. Who's to say?" Janelle reached for her tablet. "Since you're having trouble sleeping, I'll prescribe you something to help with that. We'll see how you're feeling throughout the week."

Minerva left Janelle's office feeling relieved, as though she had narrowly avoided the guillotine or swerved out of the way of oncoming traffic. It was stupid to have gotten the beers—she should have known better. No matter what, she had to throw Janelle and her mother off the scent. That meant pretending that everything was fine, that she was getting better, that all this was fading into the background like a bad dream.

Back in her car, she popped open a canned espresso. The vision of the auction weighed on her. If it was real, and she was increasingly uneasy about the possibility that it was, then Virginia Blue was down there with the other human cattle in that horrible place. If that was the case, who was the phantom visiting her? And what about Sue? Was she down there, too, waiting in terror for her number to be called? God, it made Minerva sick to think about it.

But if all this was real, if she was being pulled towards the other side by these visitors, these things from beyond, could she pull back? Could she call to them? Could she get answers?

She felt self-conscious walking the aisles of the Oakland Public Library, looking up at the wood-paneled walls and high windows with a mixture of deference and embarrassment. Her father had been the reader in the family. A cinephile, too, and Minerva shared his love of movies. But for whatever reason, reading never stuck. Still, she'd made it through college, spending the occasional afternoon in the library or joining up with a study group for an evening session. Walking through the library now felt wrong, inappropriate somehow, especially with the books she stacked in her arms: witchcraft, Wicca, tarot, ghosts, mediums, the occult. She spread them out over one of the tables, flipping through them, indexing pages and writing notes on flashcards. The espresso drove her almost to mania—she only realized hours had passed when she looked up and saw the red light through the windows, when she heard her stomach rumble. Her head throbbed with the oncoming caffeine crash, but she bought a latte and came back. A pattern was emerging from the texts: the dead could be goaded back to earth with offerings and tributes. Special items, totems of significance, could anchor them for a visitation or enable mediums to channel them, even reach them on the other side. Mediums could wander the interstitial space between the worlds of the dead and the living, could travel from one to the other and back again.

Was that what she was? A medium? That would explain the visitors, the way they seemed attracted to her. It would also explain her vivid dreams and nightmares. Like the auction she had witnessed, could other supposed dreams really have been visions of other places, realms beyond the physical? Often, she walked into rooms and felt she had been there before. In museums and graveyards, an uncanny sadness fell over her. She thought those sensations just changes in atmosphere, an intuitive deference to people and places of the past, but maybe it was more. Maybe she was attuned to sense the traces left behind, the imprints of lives lost, of tears shed and screams wailed. According to the books, powerful emotions anchored spirits to the physical world. Guilt and regret, but also ignorance and confusion. Even love.

Back at home, she turned over her bedroom, sifted through her closet. She didn't have much that belonged to Sue—Sue was a self-proclaimed minimalist, aggravatingly committed to all the latest self-improvement trends—but Minerva remembered one thing in particular. Sue had loaned her a scarf for a photo shoot: a baby-blue satin scarf, an heirloom from her grandmother. The color was faded, the edges wearing thin, but the scarf had completed a retro look and lent unmistakable warmth to the ensemble. Minerva had meant to return the scarf, but Sue had encouraged her to keep it for as long as she wanted. "It looks better on you," she had said with a laugh. "*Bà nội* would have given it to you over me!"

Minerva gripped the scarf tightly in her hand as she zipped up her jacket and slunk out of her room. Thankfully, her mother was snoring in front of the television, the victim of one too many Scotch-and-sodas. Frank had taken Serena out for dinner for some father-and-daughter bonding time. It was the perfect opportunity to get away without anyone knowing. The books had specified that summoning rituals were most effective in places closely associated with the summoned—and among the most closely associated was the site of death. Minerva had to clench her fists and steady her shaking legs as she parked and stood alone on the dark boulevard before the house. The last time she had come, practically in shock, she had snatched up her and Michelle's things as fast as possible, leaving no time for the memories to come back. But now they assaulted her, every impromptu karaoke party, intimate nightcap, and electric dinner party stained red by Sue's face. At the door, Minerva had to pause and grip her stomach, fight down the urge to vomit. You can do this, she thought. You *have* to do this. The ritual won't work if you're falling apart. The dead were supposedly drawn to empty receptacles and peaceful stillness. Too much activity, too much anxiety or nervous energy, repelled them and made it difficult to approach, almost like competing wavelengths making it impossible to get a clear signal on a radio or television.

When she finally managed to fit her key into the lock, Minerva navigated the dark kitchen and living room the way a blind person might inch his or her way through an unfamiliar space. Trauma changed places in ways that were impossible to predict. Her father's death, no matter that it had been miles away from her childhood home, had rendered the house a larger, darker, more alien place. She had skirted the rooms and stared in silent terror at their new, grotesque dimensions. To her young eyes, she might have been wandering a museum, a mausoleum. Not the same place where her father had pointed out famous actors and actresses on the television. Not the same place where she had ridden him in a pantomime of carriage-carried princess or clung to his arm when he showed her the classic Hammer horror films.

This house was the same, a collection of rooms that might as well have been empty tombs, damp and molded and cobwebbed. She passed the window through which Virginia Blue broke in, recalling the way the shattered pieces of glass lit up when lightning flashed. She didn't know what to expect or what would happen, had no idea if the ritual's failure would mean she did it wrong or if Sue was trapped in the same place Virginia was. But something was stirring inside her, small but firm, a gut feeling Minerva couldn't ignore. She suspected that no matter what superficial party tricks she conducted or arcane rites she invoked, success or failure would hinge entirely on her—on what she had inside herself and the degree to which she believed in it.

She stood in the kitchen, this conviction fighting against her fear, rallying against her anxiety. A kind of intuition guided her and emboldened her spirit. Forget the books—the thing inside her was flaring, rattling, heating up. Why or how she didn't know—maybe the sharpness of purpose, her desperate desire for answers, was lending an unprecedented edge of understanding. As she felt the scarf in her hand grow warm and then hot, almost scalding, she understood suddenly what she was doing and how, as if recalling an old skill that was once muscle memory. The scarf was a conduit, a means for her to pour her power, not receive it. I can do this, Minerva thought with sudden confidence. I know how to do this.

She raised her hand, no longer holding a scarf, but clutching a portable lighting bolt, a golden arc surging with dancing, dazzling light. The kitchen was gone—the house was gone—and she stood in a pitch-black void. The white-hot radiance of the arc circulated through her, traveling her veins and arteries, passing through her heart—except it wasn't passing into her but *out* of her. She raised the arc higher, and its light shrunk and sharpened into a wedge the size of a feather. That white light snaked out of her grip into the darkness, a line with the shape and constitution of a thread, a tether.

She stepped forward and nearly tripped—she was no longer standing, but floating in that void. Instinctively, she twined the thread around her fingers, wrapped it around her wrist. The momentary fear gave way to a surprising calm. I'm doing it, she thought. But now what? What's the next step?

The answer was easy, natural. Call to her. See if she responds.

"Sue," she said. "Sue, it's me. Minnie. Can you hear me?"

Nothing in response, just the absolute darkness around her, the endless distance.

She tugged on the thread as if to calibrate her connection.

"Sue. It's me. Minnie."

No reply. No sound.

She tugged again. "Sue."

A low-frequency hum. The faintest layer of white noise, far away.

She tugged. It's me.

A turn of the dial. A crackle of static.

She tugged. Minnie.

A spike of snow. She thought there were flurries around her, whirling and rattling, as though she stood in a blizzard, as though she waded knee-deep in slush. But with another tug, and another after that, the noise sharpened, solidified, softened. She tugged and called out, tugged and called out, tugged and called out.

Sue.

It's me.

Sue.

(It's Minnie.)

The snowfall relaxed and thawed into the soft, rhythmic patter of rain. The darkness was gone, and she was back in the house. The gentle drizzle outside made her think nothing had happened at first, that maybe she had simply hallucinated the void and the sense of static, but the golden thread looped around her hand proved otherwise. The thread stretched on, impossibly long, into the darkness outside—Minerva intuited that if the thread were somehow cut, she would be stranded in that void, with nothing to guide her back, no beacon to lead her home.

She turned back to the living room, the kitchen, seeing now the strange blue tint over everything, as if she were viewing the world through a filter. She wasn't in the house anymore, at least not the physical one. This place was some kind of figurative representation—she didn't know how she knew, she just did—floating in a dark, endless, liminal space. The space between worlds, she thought. Between the living and the dead.

She took a step forward and almost tripped. Her body was sluggish, her outstretched arm wavering in a blur. Not my body, she reminded herself. My spirit. My soul. Whatever it is.

Could she speak? She opened her mouth and tried what felt like her vocal cords.

(Sue?)

Her voice was outside herself, coming from somewhere far away. As much as she wanted to avoid the memory, the way she sounded reminded her of the auction, specifically the woman in red. When that woman "spoke," her words didn't seem to come from herself—they were beyond the amphitheater, originating from somewhere else, somewhere much deeper. Had she been projecting herself, similar to what Minerva was doing now? But what did that mean? Was the red woman different than those things in the audience, the ones gobbling down intestines and practically devouring one another?

A sudden spike of cold air made the hairs on the nape of Minerva's neck stand upright. Goosebumps erupted over her arms. A trail of wet footsteps, slimy and black, traced from the broken window to the kitchen. She turned, and there was the girl, Virginia Blue, standing at the countertop, biting into an apple. There was Sue at the foot of the stairs.

Minerva called out to her, reached for her.

(Sue! Run!)

She couldn't get there fast enough to stop the struggle. Sue fell and struck her head against the edge of the countertop. Virginia stood over her, grabbed the fallen cutting board—except it wasn't Virginia. It was a buzzing black shroud in the shape of a man, a shadow come to life. The shadow raised the cutting board and brought it down upon Sue. Minerva flinched and looked away.

That's how it happened, she thought. How Sue died.

A moment passed before Michelle next came down the stairs and witnessed the carnage. She screamed and ran back up as Virginia—as the shadow—gave chase.

Minerva followed, calling out to her.

(Michelle! Wait!)

Why couldn't they hear her? But the answer was obvious to her the second she posed the question: this had already happened. She was there when it happened, had lived it.

Upon getting to the second floor, she watched the rest of the incident unfold: her sending Michelle to the bedroom and grappling with Virginia towards the stairs. Where Virginia stepped, a black sludge, writhing with life, remained. The substance oozed from her jeans and dripped from her sleeves. It was in her hair and around her neck. That night, Minerva hadn't seen that sludge, that living darkness, but she had smelled it: the dead smell, filling up the halls, clogging up the stairway. Here, in this recreation, this revisit, it was clear that Virginia hadn't been in control of herself.

Minerva skirted the edge of the hall, watching as the struggle between her and Virginia continued. Remember what you're here for, she told herself. Sue. You're looking for Sue. She headed for the room at the end of the hall: Sue's bedroom. She had avoided it when she went back that first time, too caught up in her shock, too afraid of triggering the floodgates to come apart. But it was obvious Sue would be here. She'd be looking over her things, trying to decide what to take with her and what to leave behind.

(Sue?)

She sat on her bed, organizing blouses, putting aside pairs of jeans. Minerva paused in the doorway, hesitant to come inside and disrupt her. She looked beautiful, more beautiful than Minerva ever remembered her looking in life. There was light coming through the window, but Minerva knew it couldn't be sunlight. In this place, light meant a cleft in the fabric, an opening that let things out but never in.

Sue looked up at her and smiled. "Minnie. You came to see me off."

Minerva nodded. She felt her tears coming once again and thought it funny that even as a spirit, separated from her body, she was still driven by its impulses.

"I wasn't around for very long," Sue said, looking at the decorative dreamcatchers hung over the bed and the teddy bears piled by her pillows, "but I had a lot of fun. *We* had a lot of fun. I guess nothing lasts forever, though."

Minerva followed her gaze around the room, realizing she might never see it again, either.

(I brought your scarf. I'm sorry I never gave it back before.)

"Oh, don't worry," Sue said. "It always looked better on you, remember? Besides, I think you're gonna need it."

Minerva looked at the thread of light winding back through the hall and down the stairs. That's right—she needed it to get back. To return to her anchor point.

(I'm so glad you're here. That you're safe.)

"Why wouldn't I be safe?"

(Because she—whatever it is—hurt you. Hurt you so bad.)

Minerva struggled with her words, whatever her words were in that place. Her tears overpowered her.

"You mean the girl," Sue said. "It wasn't her, Minnie. She was confused. Lost. I don't think she wanted to hurt us at all."

Minerva glanced down the hall again. It was empty.

(Where did they go? I was just up here with her, trying to stop her from getting Michelle—)

"She must be downstairs."

Minerva turned back. Slowly, she pulled herself along the thread and rounded the corner of the landing. Her breath caught in her throat. Virginia was down there, eagle-spread in a puddle of that black sludge. Blood pooled around her head in a sanguine halo. She looked up with warm eyes. Her lips moved. A man stood over her, all in white, tall and broad-shouldered and smelling of mildew and maggots and dirt-caked bones and long-rotted, flyblown flesh. It was him. The living shadow, the wriggling shroud. He looked up at Minerva.

She stumbled back towards Sue's room, tugging at the thread, trying to change her frequency again. The stairs creaked and shuddered under the weight of heavy footfalls: one, and then another, and then another. Minerva tugged, tugged hard. A squirming shadow spread over the wall, a teeming tempest loud with chittering and crackling. Minerva pulled on the thread desperately.

(Sue! He's coming!)

Sue was behind her, lifting her up. "He wants you, Minnie. He knows what you are. That's why he came here with the girl."

(What is he?)

"You know what he is. What *they* are."

A cloud of darkness filled the hallway, a viscous thing with volume and heft and intelligence—and smell. The dead smell, the rotten reek that crawled at the borders of her sleep and crowded at the edges of her dreams. The overpowering, disgusting stench that leaked out from behind the phantom's mask, that clung to its hoarse, rasping breath.

"You've got to get out of here, Minnie!" Sue warned. "You have to leave!"

(What about you? He'll get you!)

"I'm already leaving," Sue said with a smile. "It's okay. I'll help you." Sue put her hands over Minerva's. "You know what to do. Think about going back. Being there."

Minerva closed her eyes, envisioning the house, entrenching herself as much as possible in that tangible, physical place. She imagined herself as boundless, a being of pure light zipping back down to earth along the thread like a spark of electricity until she landed in that physicality, that familiar, comfortable weight. She pulled one last time on the thread with everything she had, right as the darkness encroached and the feelers grazed her fingers and the antennae swept her face—

She came to life with a sudden, powerful breath. She sat against the counter, her entire body tingling with numbness, her eyes burning with fatigue. She collected her breath and gathered her strength, letting the volume of her spirit—if indeed it was literally her spirit— fill up the contours of her body.

"Sue?" she said, her voice low and hoarse but definitely coming from within her throat. There was no answer. Slowly, with each step a little more recovered, a little stronger, she made her way up the stairs and down the hallway. All was quiet and dark, Sue's bedroom especially. No rain or snow. No oncoming black mass. No light outside the window, beckoning from a better place, somewhere not of this earth, but not that horrible auction, either.

The scarf was still in her hand, long gone cold. Back downstairs, she stared out at the darkness through the broken window—the darkness that had spat out Virginia Blue and sucked her back in just as quickly. You made it, Sue, thought Minerva. Not like her. She's trapped.

Yes—Virginia was down there, lost in that dark place, getting sold off to those things. And that meant the phantom Minerva had been seeing was someone else, some*thing* else: the living shadow, the black, dark thing that had controlled Virginia, come back to finish the job, to pull Minerva down as well. But why, and why couldn't it control her just as it had Virginia? Why was it trying to coax her to die?

That answer was obvious, too. "He knows what you are," Sue had told her. A medium. Able to cross between worlds. A light in the dark.

SEVENTEEN

The next day, Sergeant Hart met her over coffee. "You look different," he said, spooning ice cubes into his black coffee. "I'm sure it's been a lot."

Minerva ignored his comments. She pushed forward a folder of her own. "I checked my messages after you and the other detective came by the house. Turns out I had tons of e-mails from Virginia Blue. From a lot of girls, actually."

Hart opened up the folder and shuffled through the printouts. He looked over them blandly, the way someone might read the newspaper, the obituaries. Minerva didn't know what she had expected, maybe a light bulb going on over his head, maybe an insight only his critical eyes could see. Not him putting the printouts back without even a thoughtful hum. Not him stirring in yet another ice cube.

"If there was something you said that could incriminate you, we might have something," he said. "But you never even replied. There's nothing to pin on you."

"What are you saying?"

He slid the folder back towards her. "I'm saying it's not your fault, Ms. King. You don't need to look for reasons why it happened."

"But I could have answered," she said. "I could have—"

"But you didn't. And it's not like that girl ran away because you put her up to it."

"So, that's it?" she asked. "Case closed?"

He drank his coffee. "Seems clear-cut to me."

"What about justice? Shouldn't somebody answer for my friend dying?"

"In my line of work," he said, "you get used to not getting answers. A lot of cases stay unsolved. Here, we know the perpetrator. We can make a strong guess as to the why. The rest is just circumstance."

He got up and put on his jacket, left money on the table. "I'm sorry about your friend. But if you want my advice, let it rest. You'll drive yourself crazy looking for a reason for it all."

She sat there long after he left, reading the printouts to herself, imagining the girl behind the screen, the many girls she represented. If it was total chance, like her father's car crash, it would make sense to let it go—but it wasn't total chance. Something had crept into Virginia's life and used her, led her to killing Sue, led her to dying at the foot of the stairs, led her to being sold at that awful auction. All to get close to Minerva.

Back at home, she studied Sue's scarf, recalling how the fabric had transformed into a thread of light, how its electric radiance brought her into communion with Sue. The trip to the other side had taken a lot out of her. She'd stumbled into a burger place afterwards and ordered two quarter-pounders, a large side of fries, a chocolate shake. She'd sat in the corner, packing away the food ravenously, surprised at how endless her appetite had been. Going across required a lot of gas, different than when she seemed to see through the veil while she was sleeping. She would need to keep that in mind for the future, especially if she wanted to travel deep.

Things were surprisingly clear to her now. Traveling to that other place had awoken some store of secret knowledge that had been inaccessible previously, even after the visitors and the night terrors of her youth. She was a medium, somehow capable of moving between planes of existence. She had done it unconsciously as a child, mistaking her nighttime travels as mere dreams. The visitors hadn't been imaginary friends or grief-driven hallucinations. Maybe the grief had opened her wider, made her more susceptible to attack, which explained the increase in frequency and hostility of the visitors. Since then, she had been living on a kind of emotional autopilot, compartmentalizing the old grief and feeding off the virtual highs of streaming. Until now, that is. After Sue's death, after watching Virginia Blue die, she had been made vulnerable again. As though it were planned. As though she were targeted.

She booked the earliest plane ticket she could, rushing through the online checkout before reason could convince her to change her mind or another speech from her mother could sway her choice. She packed quietly, lightly. She was halfway through filling her backpack when she caught a whiff of the dead smell, when she heard the rustle of roaches and the wriggling of worms behind her.

"Dallas?" croaked the phantom. "Why would you want to go there?"

Minerva kept packing, pretending not to hear.

"Maybe you have some moronic idea in mind," the phantom continued, "some harebrained scheme. But I think you would be better off just taking the shortcut. Why keep going when you can let everything go?"

Don't answer, Minerva thought. Don't say anything. Don't acknowledge it. It doesn't have power over you. It can't control you. It doesn't *get* to control you.

"You can't just ignore me," the phantom said, reaching for her arm. But the cold fingers lacked the incredible strength they had before—Minerva spun out of the frigid grip and faced the black mask.

"You're not Virginia," she said, squaring her shoulders, holding her head high. "I know what you really are. You're a leech. A parasite."

A chuckle rattled from behind the mask. "That's rich coming from you. You're the one airing all your dirty laundry for the world to see, the one getting off on all those girls worshiping you. You're the real parasite, sucking them dry until they're dead. Literally bleeding them out."

"No. You can't trick me. I saw where Virginia is. You're one of those people—one of those *things*. Hiding behind your masks. Sue helped me understand. *You're* the one who killed Sue. *You* killed Virginia."

"You're confused," the phantom said, "confused and distraught over the death of your friend. You're overcome."

Minerva ignored its goading. "What happens if I take off the mask? Does it hurt you? Will you die?"

"You want to give it up," the phantom went on. "You *need* to give it up—"

Minerva flung out a hand and caught her fingers under the mask. The porcelain was cold as ice, the skin underneath moldable and wet, more like dough than flesh. The phantom shrieked—with a swipe of its arm, it sent Minerva flying against the wall.

"You dare touch me," it snarled, "you insect!" The mask warbled with a deep laugh, a cackle that ranged from feminine to masculine, high to low. "Fine! I don't need you to comply. I'll just take what I need from you!"

Minerva sat up, gathered her breath—an inky, voluminous darkness sloughed out of the phantom's cuffs, oozed down from behind the mask. The small, girlish form shrunk and shriveled, clumps of hair falling in tar-like splotches, arms disappearing into dissolving sleeves. Finally, only the mask remained, dropping noiselessly into the expanding, deepening sludge sweeping the room. The blackness spread over the carpet, stretched over the furniture, crawled across the ceiling. Minerva recognized it—it was the same blackness that had pursued her before, that had nearly entombed her when she met Sue on the other side. The darkness was alive with crunching bones and writhing tentacles. Minerva shut her eyes and covered her mouth as the sludge encased her feet, draped her legs, wriggled over her arms and neck. The filth broke past her lips and wiggled over her teeth and tongue and down her throat, squirming through her tear ducts, ripping open each of her pores until it overran her blood and coated her bones. She flailed, she gagged. The sensation was like drowning, like when she was five years old and learning how to swim, sinking helplessly beneath chlorinated water, eyes burning and throat on fire. Her father had helped her then, pulling her up, patting her back so she spat out the water, rinsing her eyes out, wrapping her in a towel. It wasn't fair that he was gone—wasn't fair that this was how it ended, that she was only starting to realize what she was capable of—

She felt it suddenly, explosively: molten, liquid fire, hot and bright, burning through her veins, scalding her skin, flushing out the darkness, melting the gloom. With a glowing, steaming hand, she seized the sludge over her chest and pulled it off, the teeming thousands within screaming in response, shrieking in agony. She flung away clumps, kicked off clusters, crushed globules. She freed herself inch by inch, crying out, her voice louder with every second, her stomach twisting, her chest rising, her throat flooding as regurgitated, screeching darkness was expelled from her mouth. She fell on her hands and knees, coughing out the remnants, wiping her lips clean.

The phantom shrunk away from her on withered, broken legs. It raised a misshapen arm, the fake flesh bubbling with things crawling in a panic underneath. Minerva looked down in disgust at the crumpled, black thing.

"You can't take me," she said. "You would have done it already if you could."

The phantom said nothing, its mask hanging loosely on the malformed skull.

Minerva smirked. "You're desperate, aren't you? What, you on a time limit? Or are you afraid? Afraid of what happens if you don't get me?"

The phantom breathed raggedly, brokenly—and then it laughed, a laugh brimming with many voices. "We have all the time in the world, this one and all others. But you? You would rather waste your time, squander it. I don't need to be inside you to know what you want. You think saving her will redeem you. You think saving her will set it right."

The phantom leaned into the shadows, disappearing into the dark "Go. Come to us. See how feeble your light is."

The moment it was gone, Minerva's strength and confidence left her—she collapsed onto her bed, but although she felt like crying, her resolve was harder than that. You just proved you have nothing to be afraid of, she told herself. They can't hurt you no matter how badly they want to. You're the one in control. You're the one they're afraid of.

That evening, she sat by the pool, watching the reflection of the setting sun waver in the water. The phantom was right—she was going to Oasis, to Virginia's hometown. Sue's scarf had allowed Minerva to travel across and meet her, but with the exception of those printouts, Minerva had nothing that belonged to Virginia, nothing that could connect them in the same way. The next best thing was hopefully using her home as an anchor. Traveling to Virginia was a risk—she was trapped by those monsters, and there were hundreds of them, maybe thousands, all hungry for human life. Even if Minerva could reach the place where they had Virginia and the other slaves, she might not come back. They might finally get her once and for all.

Her mother came out, drinks in hand. Minerva knew what was on her mind, what was probably on all their minds: Minerva looked like she was losing it, like she was cracking. She had to summon her strength and throw off suspicions. Under no circumstances could her mother find out her plan. Then it would be a call to Janelle and a trip to the closest clinic—and that was the best-case scenario.

"Made you a lemonade," her mother said, sitting beside her. "Raspberry okay?"

"It's fine." Minerva took the drink, turned off by its redness, the color too close to blood after her experience at the auction. Nonetheless, she steeled her stomach and made a strong show of drinking it.

"I'm okay, Mom," she said at length. "Really. What happened the other night was just a one-off. I promise."

Her mother smiled. "I know. You've got a good head on your shoulders."

They sat quietly, listening to the sounds of the city. Minerva looked out at the suburbs rolling away, the high-rises and office buildings bronzing in the dwindling evening light. It seemed like so long ago that she'd throw on a dress and heels and stalk the bars with Michelle, Sue, and the other girls. Even the streaming, the late-night confessionals, felt like half-dreams, memories of a prior life. She'd been in a bubble of privilege, but the outside world—the outside dead—had made inroads and finally found purchase.

"You've always looked out for me," Minerva told her mother. "I don't know that I've ever thanked you for it."

"It's just what a parent does." Her mother drew a breath, tried to hide the tears lining her eyes. "I just worry. You're all grown up now, and I'm getting older. One day, I'm not going to be there to watch out for you. Already, I—I don't know what to say, or how to help."

"You don't have to say anything. You just have to be there. For as long as you can."

It was around midnight when she left, as inconspicuous as she could be in an old jacket and scraped jeans, backpack over her shoulder. She booked a ride to the airport and passed through the security checkpoint, paced the terminal while waiting for her flight. Crazy, she thought, popping a can of espresso. This is crazy. You're crazy.

But was she really? At last, things felt like they made sense, like some missing puzzle piece had appeared from under the pile and lent order and clarity to the whole picture. Maybe it would be impossible—maybe she would fail, maybe even die—but something stirred within her and demanded she try. Those dead things wanted her, had carved a bloody, cross-country path to get her. There had to be a reason for that. There had to be a calling.

The sun had risen by the time her flight touched down in Dallas, already painting the sky silver by the time she was behind the wheel of the rental car. She was grateful for the two-hour differential—her mother was still asleep, and it would be another couple of hours before she realized Minerva's absence, before she discovered the letter. Just a couple of days, the letter promised, and then all this would be over for good, put safely in the rearview.

Nonetheless, she kept her phone off as she drove, the layers of urban overpasses giving way to endless stretches of lonely road and grayed-out pasture. She passed rusted windmills, forgotten farms, clumps of cattle. The sky, a bundle of thick, gray knots, threatened rain, vowed cataclysm. Virginia had lived under that sky, that never-ending promise of downpour. No wonder she wanted to leave. The California sky was relatively clear, lazy with freedom, warm with possibility. At least as long as you bought into the illusion.

On the outskirts of a small town, she gassed up and cracked open another espresso. Then she finally saw the sign, as though it had only just appeared: WELCOME TO OASIS.

EIGHTEEN

The town was what she imagined when the detectives first told her about it: faded, rundown streets, washed-out strip malls, out-of-time bowling alleys. A subtle fog was everywhere, like steam that seemed to rise from the cracks and crevices in the ground.

She stopped at a diner and ordered a sandwich, rehearsing in her mind how to broach the subject to the waitress. Fortunately, she didn't have to try too hard—flyers on the window featured the same school portrait of Virginia the detectives had shown her. And not only Virginia, but a second girl as well, one even more dour-looking and dark-eyed, her frown pulling down the little smile that tugged at Virginia's lips. "Come join us for a candlelight vigil," the flyer read, "in honor of Virginia and Suzanne."

Minerva gestured for the waitress and pointed to the flyer. "Excuse me," she said, as gently and ignorantly as she could, "what is that about? Someone died?"

"You ain't heard?" the waitress asked, and then she eyed Minerva more carefully. "Oh, you're not from around here."

"No. Just passing through on the way back to school."

"You're not much older than them," the waitress said. "Real shame, those girls. Best friends, I think. First Suzanne, and then Virginia."

The waitress paused, studying the faces on the flyer, maybe remembering the girls sitting right where Minerva was. "The other kids were rotten to them, at least that's what Janine says. That's why they turned a new leaf and came up with that vigil. Trying to make up, I guess."

"I wouldn't mind going," Minerva said. "Do you know where it'll be?"

"At the Blue house," the waitress said. "Just a few blocks down from the high school. You can't miss it. Especially with all the flowers."

The waitress was right—the sidewalk rounding the house was covered with white-rose wreaths and blue-petal bouquets, adorned with stuffed bears and ornamented crosses. Minerva parked and crossed the street cautiously, conscious of the change in atmosphere, the way it felt as though she were stepping inside a church. Heart drumming madly, whole body shaking, she climbed the porch and rang the buzzer.

There was commotion inside, grumbling, and then a man's voice yelling at her from the other side of the door. "We're not interested!" the man slurred. "We don't want flowers or chocolates or any other shit!"

"I'm not here with anything," Minerva called back, her mind racing to find the right words. "I wanted to talk about Virginia."

"Fuck off!" the man replied, and there was more commotion as he trailed away from the door. Minerva waited, dawdled, hesitated, and then she pressed the buzzer again. Please, she thought, I just need something, a shirt, a hat, anything that belonged to her—

The door opened. She braced for the screen door to fly into her face, for a beer bottle to crack against her head, but there was only the wiry shade of a young woman in the doorway, long-necked and baggy-eyed, a crying baby clutched to her chest.

"I'm sorry," she panted, "we really need—"

She stopped and stared at Minerva, her eyes widening with recognition. "I've seen you before." She spoke quietly, as if in wonder. "You're the girl she would watch. The one on the computer."

Minerva nodded. "Yeah. I'm Minerva King. I'm the one she went to see."

The woman brought her inside the cramped kitchen. The house was old, linoleum floor cracked and warped, floral wallpaper faded nearly to a flat, dull beige. The air was thick with a musty blend of mildew and cigarettes, and Minerva had to try hard to keep her face from furrowing in disgust.

"Sorry for the mess," the woman said, clearing the table of dirty dishes, dumping out the ashtray, putting aside rumpled magazines and a pair of baby bottles. As she worked, she bounced the baby on her hip, made funny faces, blew kisses into the small face. The baby's cries quieted gradually, and the red cheeks relaxed as the woman rocked the child to sleep.

"I'm so sorry," she said. "She's usually quiet, but Davy started yelling—"

Minerva looked past the kitchen at the dark corridor beyond, from where the flashes and sounds of a television carried towards them.

"That's your husband?" she asked.

"Yes. I'm sorry he spoke to you like that. We've all been through a lot lately, first with the baby, and then—well, I think you know."

"It's okay. I'm not offended." Minerva tried a smile, her own caffeine-suppressed fatigue catching up to her. "Are you Virginia's sister?"

"Oh! Yes. That's how bad it is, I didn't even introduce myself. I'm Janine. Virginia's my baby sister." She laughed softly. "Well, she's not really a baby anymore. She'll be—would be—seventeen in another month."

She went quiet, focusing on rocking and cooing to the baby.

Minerva watched her, conscious suddenly of the way she was invading their space, of the fact that she didn't belong there. She was a "visitor" herself, coming to remind them of death, to prolong the healing process—or was it the denial process? What was "healing" but putting up the walls and blinders again, sinking back into comfortable fantasy, convenient illusion? Death was everywhere, she realized now, in every sense. Those masked freaks were chomping at the bit, waiting for people to take a reckless step or ignore the warning sign of their intuitions. All it took was someone to ask for help, to beg for another chance at life. That's how they got in. They found the desperate, the beaten, and they wormed their way inside.

"You're probably wondering why I'm here," she said. "Maybe it's wrong of me, but—"

"You met her?" Janine asked. "Ginny?"

"I did. I was there when she died."

Janine gasped. She hugged the baby tightly. "Dear God in Heaven."

"The detectives told me," Minerva said, "that she ran away to meet me. And I think that's true. I had messages from her. Tons of them." She unzipped her backpack and spread the sheaf of papers over the table. Janine moved the papers around, her eyes glistening with tears.

"These are all Ginny's?"

Minerva nodded. "Yes."

"I didn't know," Janine said, her throat thickening with stifled sobs. "I should have seen it after Suzanne, but I was so caught up with the baby—"

"Suzanne was her friend?"

"Yes." Janine cleared her throat, collected herself. "They were like sisters. Mama never liked her—said she was like death—but I always thought she was good for Ginny. She never really had many friends, you know? Never got along with the other kids at school. With Suzanne, it was different. Like peas in a pod."

Something in the sister's eyes disarmed Minerva. Maybe it was the ease with which she cried, the sense she had suffered losses all her own. Minerva was tempted to take advantage of that openness and jump into the real reason she was there, but she had to control herself, not blow her chance by coming across as crazy.

"Believe me, I didn't want to come and open up wounds," Minerva said. "But when your sister showed up that night, things changed for me, too. Everything changed." She steadied herself, prepared to reveal the rest, and then a man came into the kitchen: Davy, the husband who had talked to her before. His sleeves were rolled up, tie loose around the collar, eyes bloodshot. He looked like he had just come in from the office, but it was still early, barely past noon. Had he been in those clothes all night? The reek of alcohol on him was proof enough.

Janine sprang up. "Sorry, Davy, this is—"

"She the one bothering us? I told you to get her out of here!"

"I know, but she's—"

"I don't care who she is!" He turned his sights on Minerva. "You get off on harassing people, huh? Like to crash funerals? Make fun of dead little girls?"

"No," said Minerva softly. "If you'd just let me explain—"

He threw his beer bottle against the wall—both Janine and Minerva jumped. "Get her out of here, Janine! Now!"

The baby cried sharply. Janine caressed her, cooed her, and turned apologetic eyes towards Minerva. "I'm sorry," she said, "but you have to leave."

Minerva gathered up her printouts in a rush, and Janine led her out to the porch. "Tonight," she said quickly. "The Hillsbury Motel. Do you have money?"

"Yeah, but—"

"I won't be able to go while he's awake, but I can meet you there. Let's say 7:00?"

Minerva sighed—even though time was against her, she didn't have much choice but to agree. "How will you know the room I'm in?"

"Hang this in the window." Janine shook back her sleeve and revealed a white, porcelain rosary, ornamented by silver medallions of St. Peter, St. Paul, the archangel Michael. "Mama's mama passed it down to her. Hopefully, I'll get to pass it down to Coral."

Minerva glanced at the baby, at the rosary. She took it carefully and pocketed it. "Okay. I'll wait for you." She turned back before leaving. "Thank you for hearing me out."

"Ginny loved you. Even if she didn't know you. It's the least I can do."

There wasn't anything else Minerva could do but leave and wait. Over a late lunch at the diner, she stared at her dark phone with dread. If she turned it on, how many messages would pop up? Had her mother already made arrangements with Janelle, Minerva's letter be damned? She could hardly chew her hamburger—just thinking about being put away in some institution was nearly crippling. But she couldn't let that distract her. She was here. She had a job to do. If she let her nerves get the best of her, those demons would win.

She got directions for the motel from the waitress and left, touring the town along the way. It was certainly peaceful—the school, the bowling alley, the little shops, but there was a quiet desperation underneath. Cali was so different, so outwardly busy and chaotic, but like sleepwalking underneath. That had been me, at least, she thought, pulling into the motel parking lot. Sleepwalking. The gigs and the bars and even the streaming. All turning away from the ugliness underneath.

She paid for a room and hung the rosary in the window, pinned it against the glass with the blinds. She dropped her backpack and sat on the bed. The room was old, musty with the same baked-in smells of the Blue kitchen, but something about quaint carpet and aged wallpaper tugged at her and pulled her eyelids down. The caffeine was long spent, and she was crashing, finally surrendering to the spiral that had been the last few days. She lurched into the shower, stood gratefully under the cold, crackling water. She toweled herself off and dressed into a fresh tank top and leggings. Any objections she might have had to the bed were small under the weight of her tiredness. There was an old digital clock by the bed. She set an alarm for 7:00 as she sunk under the coverlet and sheets, and then she was gone.

Her sleep was broken by a patchwork of imagery, a sensation of searing flame. A small, dark form crawled out of the muck. Matted, blood-caked fur dripping sludge. Glazed, cataract-covered eyes like inlaid marbles in the visible skull. Many legs scurried beneath the flesh. Many eyes peeked from between the exposed ribs. A swarm of flies coated an ornate dining table, a pile of blackened hearts and mottled lungs the rotten centerpiece, the flies' wriggling progeny lining the rims of goblets and crawling over the assorted appetizers of chilled kidneys and filleted livers. Yellow, serpentine eyes opening. Black irises thinning, meeting her own.

Minerva woke up before the alarm, sweating, shivering. A light rain pelted the window and drummed upon the roof, and she thought she was again in that cold, dark other place where she had seen Sue and relived the break-in.

She got up, rinsed her face, put on her jeans. No, she was still here, still in the realm of the flesh, the domain of the living. But she wondered if going across had tethered her there or, worse, left a piece of herself behind. Everything was irrational, absurd, yet all seemed possible and very plausible in this new, uncovered reality.

Someone rapped at the door. She pulled aside the blinds, and there was Janine on the other side, hooded in a rain slick. Minerva opened the door, and Janine hurried inside, dripping on the carpet. "Sorry," she said, shaking off the slick. "I'm late."

"It's okay. Your baby?"

Janine wrung her hair, rubbed her hands together. "She's at the Crawleys, our neighbors. I don't know what I'd do without them. Davy's—well, you saw him, and Mama . . ." She trailed off. "Let's just say the Crawleys have been a blessing."

She smiled and pulled one of the chairs close. "But now we can talk."

Now that the moment was here, Minerva almost didn't know what to say—she hadn't actually expected this, someone willing to listen, maybe even open to believing. But she didn't have time to waste. This was the only chance she was going to have to get something of Virginia's, something that would anchor her and let her travel across like when she used Sue's scarf. This was her one and only chance to get into that dark place and free Virginia. The phantom had been right about something, at least: what happened to Virginia *was* Minerva's fault. She was responsible for not reading the messages, for being careless with the streaming, for not dealing with the visitors that had been around her since her childhood.

She sat across from Janine. She composed herself. "This is going to sound crazy," she said, "but do you believe in ghosts?"

NINETEEN

By the time Minerva finished, the only trace of rain was the occasional wind, the smell of petrichor seeping into the room. Janine was quiet, turning her rosary over in her hand. I said too much, Minerva thought in panic, her mouth and throat drying up. If it wasn't the talk of ghostly figures at her bedside, it was the descriptions of that demonic auction, that near-orgy of grotesqueries. What could she expect? These were normal people, everyday people, and she was showing up on the heels of teenage girls dying with stories of monsters—

"Can you talk to her?" Janine asked. The question took Minerva aback, but now that Janine was looking straight at her, Minerva saw she was crying.

Minerva shook her head. "I don't think so. Especially if she's where I think she is."

Janine wiped her eyes. "I'm sorry," she said, holding back her sobs. "I was telling myself that Ginny was in a better place, that she wouldn't have to worry about the bullies anymore, or about Mama." She paused, her tear-glazed eyes seeming to go far away. "Mama's always been hard to love. I found ways to keep her happy, but Ginny'd fight her. She was so stubborn all the time. Had her head in the clouds, and Mama hated that."

She smiled. "I think that's why she followed you. You showed her what she could be."

Was that really a compliment? Or was it a curse? Virginia's dreams had been turned against her. And maybe she wasn't the only one—maybe other girls were being targeted, too.

"What happened to Virginia is because she followed me," Minerva said. "That's why I have to try. I have to get her out."

"And you need something that belonged to her?"

"Well, I don't think it can be just anything. My friend Sue—her scarf was a gift from her grandmother. It connected her to other people. I think it has to be something like that."

Janine considered. "Ginny never really cared about too many things, and Mama gave the rosary to me—" She gasped. "The letter!"

"Letter?"

"We found it after she left. It was written to our daddy. I think Ginny must have written it when she was little because it was in crayon and marker."

A letter to her father, Minerva thought. She had written a similar letter after her own father's death—two, actually. One under the stewardship of Janelle, for the purposes of therapy, a way to voice everything left unsaid after the crash. The other letter had been just for her, still stowed away in her closest over ten years later. An appeal for her father to return. A wish to see him again. For him to take her away.

"Your dad," she said, "is he alive?"

"No clue. He left a long time ago—even I don't remember him very much. Ginny was just a baby, but she kept a candle lit for a long time. She was waiting for him—waiting for him to come save her."

That could be it, Minerva thought. Might be strong enough to get a bead on her.

"Where is it?" she asked.

"That's the problem," Janine said. "Mama won't let go of it. She barely gets up anymore at all. Honestly"—she paused, trying to keep from breaking down again—"I don't know what to do. Everything's going to pieces."

"Hey." Minerva took her hand. "It's okay. It's not your fault."

"It feels like it is," Janine said with sudden fervor, surprising ferocity. "Mama wasn't a parent. She didn't know how to be. And I didn't, either, but I should've! If I had, maybe I could have changed her. Made her better. And maybe Ginny would still be here!"

As she cried, as Minerva held her, at first awkwardly and then more naturally, her words echoed those Minerva had told Janelle all those years before. If only I'd done more. If only I'd done something different. Maybe her father would still be alive. Maybe she would have never recorded herself, never talked through her feelings to an audience of impressionable strangers. Maybe the more dangerous of her visitors would have never sniffed her out. Maybe the light inside her would have never sparked.

They came up with a plan. Davy would leave for work the next day, and they would be free to meet Mother Blue. It was a long shot, Janine said, but given how distraught she was, Minerva's story could convince her to give up the letter. And Minerva was more and more convinced it *had* to be the letter. To make a connection to the other side, especially to breach that dark place, required emotional ammunition of the strongest sort.

Their plan hatched, Janine slid on her slick and dried her remaining tears. "Tomorrow, then," she said. "It's funny. I think I might actually sleep tonight—long as Coral lets me."

Minerva stopped her at the door. "Why did you believe me?" she asked. "Everything I said is crazy, absolutely insane, but you accepted it."

Janine smiled. She shrugged. "Just a feeling, I guess. If you were lying, I'd tell. If you were crazy, same thing. But everything you said—it's like it's clicking inside me." She looked out at the dark, the border of night that swept away everything past the streetlamps. "I think God works through people. Even if they don't realize it. It's how he keeps the scales balanced."

Minerva sat with those words, lay with them. She'd never considered the question of God very seriously, but after seeing what she had, after seeing the demonic host up close, she couldn't help but wonder. If there was a devil, there had to be a counterpart, wouldn't there? Otherwise, evil would run rampant. The thought was so chilling, she had no choice but to push it away.

The rain started again, and the patter eventually quieted her thoughts and drew her to sleep.

She returned to the Blue house in the morning. "Come in," said Janine. "Davy just left, and Coral's asleep."

Back in the musty kitchen, no more raging husband or crying child, Minerva heard something from deeper in the house: whimpering, crying.

"Is that her?" she asked. "Your mom?"

"Yes." Janine nodded towards the hall. "Follow me."

The walls were spare, adorned not with family photos or graduation portraits but depictions of Christ on the cross, at supper with his apostles, in the arms of his mother, Mary. The smells of the house grew ranker as they creaked down the hallway, souring with sweat and skin and maybe worse. Minerva held her nose, held her breath. There was a pressure, too, hard to explain but undeniable. An invisible, stinking weight of grief.

They crossed into the bedroom. Gossamer drapes covered the windows, casting most of the room in shadow, but as Minerva's eyes adjusted, she saw with increasing detail Mother Blue's enormous form, even bigger than the straining bed atop which she shuddered. A long sleeping gown covered her like a shroud. Her face, all curves and dark circles, framed by wiry, unkempt hair, was compressed in agonized sobs and tortured moans. One pale, veined fist dabbed at her eyes and nose with balled-up tissues, but her other hand rested on her chest, hiding a barely noticeable piece of paper.

Janine stepped forward. "Mama. We have a visitor."

Mother Blue didn't respond.

"Mama." Janine laid a cautious hand on her mother's arm, and suddenly, the mass of flesh snapped, fast as a cobra. Minerva gasped as Janine hit the floor. She reached out to help her, but Janine motioned for her to stay back.

"Janine," boomed Mother Blue, her thunderous voice far from the weak whimpers Minerva heard when she came into the house. "Who have you brought into your daddy's house?"

She sat up slowly, one foot planting firmly on the floor before the other, the woodwork struggling under her weight. Minerva shrunk away from the monstrous shadow looming over her.

Mother Blue's voice boomed again. "Janine! What is this?"

Janine stood between them, smaller than even Minerva. "She's here to help, Mama!"

"Help?" A strain of humor, of mockery, ran through the quaking voice. "Your sister's dead, Janine. She's in the ground. In the devil's grip. There ain't no helping her."

"She's not dead, Mama. Minerva's seen her. She wants to help her."

"I know it's hard to believe," Minerva said, finding her voice. "You're more right than you know. Virginia—"

"Don't you dare say her name!" Mother Blue turned on Minerva, her voice so loud that Coral erupted into cries the room over, that Minerva thought her bones literally rattling. "Who are you to come here? You're a stranger, trying to trick my daughter. She's always been a bleeding heart—spineless, marrying a loser, a drunk! Having a damn child by him!"

"It's not a trick, Mama," Janine panted. "She's—"

"Shut up! How dare you spit on your sister like this?" Mother Blue's face widened in a crooked, green grimace. "I blame myself! One daughter weak and spineless. The other a damn fool, always stupid and dreaming."

"Your daughter came to me!" Minerva cried. "She came all the way to California to talk to me! That's why I'm here—because we're connected!"

"Now why on God's green earth would she go to you?" Mother Blue's fierce eyes settled on Minerva, studied her. A dim recollection glinted in their darkness, turning to faint recognition, turning to potent malice. "I know you. I seen you before. On that damn computer all the time. Turning her away from us. Turning her towards the devil."

"It's not true," Minerva said. "I didn't—"

But as the massive woman approached, each deafening step making Minerva's stomach flip, making the room shake, as Minerva backed into the wall, as she shriveled in shame, her words failed her. She *had* turned Virginia towards the devil. There was nothing she could do or say to make up for it. Even if she made it across to where Virginia was—and that seemed more and more unlikely with each second—even if she rescued her soul, the girl was still dead. She was still suffering down there in the hands of that demonic bastard who bought her, and nothing could erase that harm.

"It's your fault she's dead!" Mother Blue spat in her face. "Your poison! Your filth!"

Minerva stared up at her in terrified awe. Darkness rose from the woman's hulking shape like smoke, encircling her balled fists. Minerva shut her eyes, anticipating the fist coming down, the same ones that had struck Janine, that had hit Virginia. She deserved it, probably deserved it a hundred times. The phantom had been right—she was a blight, a poison, and she couldn't help anyone, couldn't make anything right. What the hell did she think she was doing?

"Don't listen to her, Minerva!"

Minerva turned, seeing in the apocalyptic darkness of the room a rosy glimmer, a glow with the texture of smoldering fire, with the color of breaking dawn. Janine stood as tall as she could and squared her shoulders. "Enough, Mama! It's not her fault—it's ours! We failed Ginny, you and me! We're the reason she left!"

"Quiet, Janine!" Mother Blue barked.

"No! I won't be quiet! Never again!" Janine steadied herself, steadied her voice. "It's the truth, Mama. You're right, I married Davy. I had a baby. I thought it would be good to have love in this house. To have family. I wanted things to be okay for once. After Daddy—"

"Janine!" Mother Blue spun to her. "Not another word!"

Minerva watched as Mother Blue advanced on Janine next, her suit of darkness like a storm cloud hovering in the room, threatening to swallow Janine's light. Minerva turned inward, searching desperately for her own light, that shimmering, sparkling, miraculous thing that had repelled the phantom, that had helped her find Sue. Help me, she begged. Show me what I can do! Show me what I'm supposed to do! Help me! *Help me*!

Meanwhile, Janine stood her ground before her mother. "Don't you get it, Mama? We've *all* been dreaming. It wasn't just Ginny. It was me and you, too. That's where we went wrong. I should have been focused on you and her. I'll own that. Every time you hit her, it should have been me. I should have taken every one!"

Mother Blue towered over. "Janine, I told you to be quiet!"

"No," Janine said. "Hit me if you're gonna hit me. But I won't be quiet again!"

Mother Blue snarled. She tightened her fist, raised it—

"His name was Robert!"

Both Mother Blue and Janine turned. Minerva stood shakily, anchoring herself to the wall, eyes closed, face covered in sweat.

"Robert Matthew Blue," she said. "His father built this house. He was a carpenter—Robert was a painter."

Mother Blue scowled. "What in God's name? You shut your mouth, you—"

"Janine was named after his mother's sister," Minerva went on. "He told you the story right here, in this room. She drowned at the public pool. She was six."

Janine stared, speechless. Mother Blue faltered.

"And Virginia—she was going to be named after you. But you thought it would be embarrassing. No. That's what you told him. But really, it's because you didn't think you deserved it. You still don't think you do."

Mother Blue yelled. Her face, red and sweaty, convulsed.

Minerva's brow knitted. "Right, Grace?"

Janine watched as her mother slumped, as her arms fell, as her fists uncurled.

"He left to get beer," Minerva said quietly. "Then he never came back. You called the police. You told them everything you could. But it didn't matter. They never found him. You didn't eat for days. Janine had to feed herself. Feed Virginia."

Minerva opened her eyes, freed from her trance. Mother Blue's power had evaporated, taking the cloud of darkness with it. She sat sobbing, gray and pale in the muted light.

Janine wrapped her arms around her mother's quivering shoulders. "I told you, Mama. She's here to help us. Here to help Ginny."

Each shouldering one of her arms, Minerva and Janine helped Mother Blue onto the bed. She lay quietly on the floral bedspread, the mattress springs whining as she settled. Her hands slackened, and Janine freed the crumpled letter from her mother's grip. In the kitchen, Coral coaxed back to sleep against her shoulder, she turned to the faint-looking Minerva.

"How did you do that?" she asked. "How did you know all that?"

Minerva ate quickly the scrambled eggs Janine had cooked for her. Like when she traveled to Sue before, drawing on her fiery light left her drained. As she chewed, she thought about how to best explain her experience to Janine: how she had dug into the bedroom's past, how she had sat listening as Robert Blue and his young wife lay in the dark, sharing stories of their pasts, exchanging visions of the future—how she had watched as Grace lay alone, abandoned, never to see her husband again, burdened by the weight of his many broken promises and the guilt of her own sacrifices—leaving behind a sick mother, a younger sister—that were now in vain.

"I did it before," Minerva said, "back at the place I lived with my friends. That time, I didn't know what was happening, but I tried tapping into the same feeling. And it was like I saw your mom and your dad, like the whole lifetime of the room flashed in front of me. It's almost like places and things have memories, just like people do."

"That's amazing," Janine said, staring at her in wonder. "I want to ask you things, but I know there are more important things to do." Both of them regarded the letter on the table. The blocky, unpracticed crayon was hard to read, faded and smudged after so many years.

"Will that do it?" Janine asked.

Minerva contemplated the letter. "Can I see her room?" she asked at length.

Inside Virginia's room, Minerva traced a hand over the unassuming bed, the unadorned dresser. "Do you see anything?" Janine asked. "Like in Mama's room?"

"I'm not sure," Minerva said. Virginia's imprint was heavy in the room—Minerva could picture her vividly on the bed, a cat curled around her legs. So many dreams floating in the air, so many wants, so many hopes. But there was something else, too, something more recent, something darker, heavier. She knelt down. A black stain rain across the bottom of the wall, with the coarse thickness and flaky texture of dried sludge. She drew a finger across it and shuddered—a sensation of bugs crawling along her arm, of roaches crowding her throat.

Janine looked over her shoulder. "What is it?"

Minerva stood, wiped her finger on her jeans. "He was here. The phantom. And not just with Virginia. He was with the other girl, too."

Janine covered her mouth. "Suzanne?"

Minerva nodded. "Do you know where she died?"

They drove, Janine guiding the way to the verge of trees where the search party discovered Suzanne. They walked inside, stepping through shrubbery, around rocks and clumps of moss. It wasn't long before Janine pointed out the broken branch from which Suzanne's body had collapsed.

Minerva knelt below the branch and covered her nose. The dead smell rose from a black spot on the ground, the grass within its radius withered, swamped in the same sludge that had coated Virginia on the night of the break-in. Janine couldn't see it because it wasn't of this earthly realm, wasn't physically there, just like the police couldn't see it back at the house. The sludge was beyond the physical, in the in-between, just like Minerva was. It was like the light inside her she could no longer shut off, the flame she could never extinguish.

"Suzanne Grayson," she said, and she touched the black spot before she even knew why. Then she knew immediately.

TWENTY

Minerva saw everything at once, or maybe it was more accurate to say the pieces assembled themselves into a mosaic, each memory needing to be arranged into its proper place.

In a dark living room, the television glowing a bright white, Suzanne's father left beer bottles at his feet like candy wrappers. Her mother, practically catatonic, stewed in her bed. In the kitchen, out of sight and earshot of her father, Suzanne warmed up pieces of a leftover rotisserie kitchen and ate quickly, quietly. She left through the back door, and Minerva followed her in the dark of night to the nearby gas station, where a man in a black leather jacket straddled his motorcycle and tapped his boots impatiently.

He grinned upon seeing her. "Hey, baby," he said, and Suzanne kissed him, prowled his mouth with her tongue, let him do the same. "You ready?" he asked, and she nodded, climbing onto the motorcycle and circling her arms around his waist. Minerva traveled with them down the lonely, pitch-black highway, Suzanne's hair flailing behind her like smoke, the cedar and cypress trees looming on either side like dark specters. At a bar loud with rock music and the clatter of billiards, hazy with smoke and sweat, she and the man settled in a red-lit room, drinking beers, snorting lines off the table. Suzanne pocketed a bag of cocaine, and then she leaned in for another kiss. The man drew her close. He cupped her breasts, snaked his hand inside of her jeans. He made her gasp, made her moan. The saliva on her lips glistened, shone like blood.

That was her weekend ritual: she met with men, let them drive her to bars, let them touch her, let them kiss her. In exchange, they gave her whatever she wanted, whether it was dope or weed, acid or blow. Her favorite was undoubtedly coke. She'd take to the floor, letting her body move in ways she couldn't in Oasis, not caring how people looked at her, in fact, relishing how they looked. She had started early, sneaking away her father's cigarettes at twelve, sampling her mother's pills and wines at thirteen, losing her virginity at fourteen. By the time she was on the cusp of seventeen, months before her death, she had carried herself like an old pro, a seasoned expert.

Now Suzanne and Virginia were lounging in Suzanne's room, shirts and shorts damp with sweat, cicadas buzzing loudly outside. Suzanne dragged on a cigarette, blowing out smoke, watching it hover before the open window. "Don't you know those things give you cancer?" Virginia asked, but Suzanne ignored her, imagining her body like the summer sunlight caught in the smoke, like elemental fire. Melting, disappearing. The easiest thing in the world to do. But also the hardest.

Virginia, meanwhile, sighed and leaned back. She thought of another sun, another sky. That was what Suzanne admired about her, though she'd never say it outright. Sweet, innocent Virginia was built for romance, intended for dreaming—she was a rose in glass, necessary to keep pristine at all costs. Things were good like that for a while, easy and controllable, until one day, Virginia started going on about some girl in California. "She's magic," Virginia said, showing her some video where the Cali girl, some bullshit model, wannabe actress, went on and on about her dead dad and making life work and owning the bad shit that happened to you. Of course, Virginia ate it up. She was always crying over her own dad, even though Suzanne told her time and again she was better off without him. Dads were useless, more likely to scream at you and hit you than actually love you. There was too much risk in keeping them around.

Another piece of the puzzle: Suzanne sitting on the rooftop of the theater, legs dangling in the night. That was her personal private spot, her refuge when guys weren't available to take her out of town or she needed space and time for herself. Not even Virginia knew about it. There were things Suzanne didn't want to share, couldn't share, because she would lose too much of herself in the process. She had to stay herself at all costs. It was why she was grateful her parents were terrible, why she was appreciative of the way her classmates avoided her. Relationships were so sticky and challenging. Even some of these guys, at least ten years older, clung to her like she was some kind of drug they couldn't resist. It was pathetic and sad, and it wasn't something she wanted for herself. Freedom was the most important thing: the freedom to do whatever you wanted, whenever you wanted, however you wanted. Anything else, any other connection, was just too risky. Too dangerous.

That night, while she studied the blanket of starts above, while she scrolled on her phone, thumbing through before-and-after shots of cities reduced to rubble, of car crashes caught on dashcams—she caught a whiff of something sulfurous, something burning. She turned, scanning for the source, and there it was, lurking in the shadows as though embarrassed. Something not quite alive, but not exactly dead. A manifestation. A presence.

It said it would be her friend, its words produced by the squirming of segmented bodies, the folding of many legs, the bulging of manifold eyes. She would never be alone, never be scared. All you have to do is open wide. Just let me in.

The thing was with her always after that, hanging from her shoulders, curling around her neck, slithering around her waist and about her ankles. It dripped darkness down her jeans, smudged her shoes with black tar. No one saw the sludge she tracked inside her home or through the halls of the high school, but they smelled it. The force field that had always been around Suzanne ballooned into a bubble that bled color and leaked sound. "What the hell's wrong with you?" Virginia asked, and Suzanne just spat at her. There's nothing wrong with me. What's wrong with *you*? Just go be with that stupid girl. She's never sad, right? She's always happy. That's what you need. Fantasy and bullshit. Because you don't live in reality, Virginia. You can't stomach it. It'll kill you.

And so her new friend whispered to her, sang to her, laughed into her ear. Eventually, the presence was like a second skin, snug under her nails, comfortable behind her eyes. Suzanne ate less and less, drank more and more. Even her drugs emptied to nothing, and she barely left her room, not even daring to find a new plug or escape to another roadside bar. She sat in a mire of worming dark, and her black-masked friend coiled around her neck and nuzzled her cheek.

Where is Virginia?

"I don't know," Suzanne said quietly, blandly. "I don't care."

Yes. Who needs her, right?

The presence chuckled and cooed.

She's probably watching that other girl—what is her name? Minerva?

Suzanne scowled. "Let her. They deserve each other."

Yes. She cares more about some girl she's never met who lives thousands of miles away. All because of the smell of sunscreen lotion and the taste of gin. Oh, the wonders of being alive. Of course, neither of you know those. How could you? Look around this place. Even the worst of society deserve better.

Don't listen to him, Minerva tried to say, would have said, but she could only watch the rest as impotently as she watched what came before. Suzanne's presence was her phantom, Virginia's predator, the same creature that had killed Sue. He'd killed Virginia, too, luring her to California on the promise of escape. He'd killed Suzanne, convincing her there was only one way to be absolutely free, to be totally safe from the threat of love.

TWENTY-ONE

Janine stirred her. "Minerva? Are you okay?"

Minerva stood and rubbed away the flaky residue between her finger and thumb. "I'm okay," she said, staring down at the rotted, black space where Suzanne had lain. Her corpse had left its memories behind, all of them connected by a pattern of pain, a leitmotif of loneliness. Like with Mother Blue, spying into those memories had felt invasive, disrespectful, especially given that Suzanne was gone, but Minerva felt a synergy with her, an appreciation of her feelings. More importantly, she understood with certainty the nature of their enemy.

"He's a leech," she said as they drove back. The dive had left her lightheaded, but she was lucid enough on this point, the vision of the phantom's black mask clear in her mind, the dead smell vivid in her nostrils. "He needs a way to get his hooks in you. He went from Suzanne to Virginia to me. Because he can't get me. Not on his own."

Janine glanced at her from the driver's seat. "You said there were others, though."

Yes, there were hundreds, maybe thousands, but they weren't all equally powerful. Some were noticeably a notch above the others: the one in white, the enormous one that had claimed Virginia. The one that was targeting her, using Suzanne and Virginia to get close. The one on the stage in the red mask and red dress, a woman by all accounts, but something unfathomable hiding under the skin. She was potentially the strongest of all.

"I don't think too many are strong enough to do what he's doing," Minerva said. "I think they can get only scraps, whatever the big ones let them have."

"What if you're wrong? Are you sure about doing this? Maybe it's too dangerous."

Minerva realized she was grinding her teeth, biting her cheek. She hadn't looked at herself in the mirror—in fact, she had been actively avoiding it—but she imagined she was a far cry from the glamorous model, the dolled-up streamer. Her eyes were probably dark-rimmed and bloodshot, her skin pale, her hair dry. She must have looked like a basket case or an addict. All the masks off. All the rot unearthed.

"I'm not sure," she said at length, "but I have to try. For me and Virginia."

Back at the Blue house, Janine cooked them grilled cheese sandwiches. Afterwards, while she fed Coral a bottle, Minerva paced the tiny backyard, trying to lose herself in the drooping birches, the old barbecue pit. She was at the eleventh hour, each minute pushing her closer to the tipping point. God, she couldn't stop herself from shaking. She might have collapsed if not for the rusted bench on the porch. What was she doing? Traveling to some world of the dead, facing off against monsters, trying to save souls? It was insane, the stuff of horror movies. Yet how could she deny everything that had happened? This was reality—and if it wasn't, maybe she was already in Janelle's clinic, her mother bringing her snacks from the outside world and crying outside the room. That thought brought her a momentary chuckle. It was too late to go back, too late to convince herself she wasn't sane. Virginia was dead because of her, because of her negligence, because of what she was. The irony was that no one else could do it. The person who got Virginia killed was the only one who could maybe get her out.

Janine called to her from the doorway. "I took Coral to the Crawleys. Mama's asleep."

Minerva nodded. "Okay."

"Davy will be home in a few hours. I don't—"

"It can't wait," Minerva said. "It has to be now."

She made her way back inside, heart and brain and stomach resisting, turning against her. Her arms hung like stones. Her legs wobbled like jelly. Janine caught her when she nearly fell against the kitchen table.

"You need to rest," she said, "eat something else—"

"No," Minerva said. "Take me to her room. Please."

She lay atop Virginia's bed. She didn't mean to peek into the room's memories again, but there they were: the little girl reading under the covers, the pre-teen cuddling her cat, the young woman turning on the laptop and tuning in to Minerva's latest stream, her most recent midnight talk. The tears came on their own, sliding down her cheeks. She raised an open palm, and Janine handed her the letter.

"If I don't wake up," Minerva said, "I'm sorry. For everything."

Janine looked at her with tender disbelief. "Sorry? You've done more for my family than anyone has. A lot more than I've done." She placed her hand over Minerva's and clasped the letter tightly. "I'm gonna be right here no matter what. I'll see you when you get back."

Minerva smiled—to the extent that she could—and then she closed her eyes. She slowed her breaths and counted them the way Janelle always advised. Take me to Virginia, she thought, picturing the thin face, the long hair. She reached down inside herself for that miraculous, shining thing. Take me to Virginia. No matter where she is.

Slowly, crackling louder and louder between her ears, white noise overtook her. She wasn't sure when the change happened, but she could no longer feel Janine's hand around her own, no longer feel the bed beneath her. She floated, once more in that dark void, that unearthly vacuum. The letter was still in her hand, but she knew it wasn't just a letter—it was a link, a lifeline, a lever. A conduit for the fire in her veins, the light radiating throughout her body. She harnessed the light, focused it, and suddenly, the letter exploded with fire and crackled with energy, so hot she thought her palm might sear. The arc of light fit snugly in her hand, filling her with confidence just like it had when she traveled to Sue. A thread of golden, humming light curled from between her fingers and disappeared into the infinite darkness.

She gripped the thread tightly. This was her receiver, her antenna. The next step was to fine-tune it. The static was overwhelming, but with successive tugs, focused as much as she could on Virginia's face, the static began to sharpen and take shape.

"Virginia," she said into the void.

Virginia, she thought. Take me to Virginia.

But unlike when she traveled to Sue, the white noise didn't give way to rain or the cool ambience of night. Instead, the static growled into furious flames and hissed into searing heat. She grew anxious at the difference, wondered if she was doing something wrong, but the thread in her hands reignited her confidence. Don't stop, Minnie, she told herself. You're almost there. Keep going. Keep going. Don't doubt it. Don't fight it.

She gripped the thread and refocused her affirmations.

Virginia, she thought. Take me to Virginia.

Virginia.

(Virginia.)

(Take me to Virginia.)

A blast of steam startled her, made her stumble back. She stood in muddy darkness, some kind of enormous cave. The air was hot, almost as hot as a sauna, rank with gusts of sulfur and full of traces of decay. The thread was still in her hand, looping back into the dark that had birthed this place. Was Virginia here? It wasn't the amphitheater, but maybe there were other layers to this dark place, other sectors where those monsters lived. She tied the thread around her waist and steadied herself. The letter brought you here, she thought. Don't question it. It's taking you to Virginia.

She advanced through the cavern, realizing quickly that it wasn't a single cave but a network of them, a series of massive warrens. The heat pressed down on her, so powerful she thought her face hovered over a pot of boiling water. Was Virginia really here? Minerva spoke, sent out a feeler.

(Virginia?)

Her voice, the projection of her voice, echoed for a long time, far away. The air hummed in response. The caverns trembled, stalactites falling around her, debris shaking loose from the ceiling. No, she realized with sudden panic. Virginia wasn't here. Something had gotten in the way. Something had interfered with the transmission—

A blast of hot air pushed her back. She reached for the wall of jagged rock to steady herself, but the wall melted away under her fingers. She looked on in disbelief as the caverns quivered and quaked, as they *changed*—the rock dissolved into liquid black and curled up into billows and plumes of steam, of smoke. Something enormous stirred in the depths of the tunnels, uncurling, unfolding, collapsing the fabric of reality around itself.

I'm dead, Minerva thought, watching the debris crumble and fall towards her. She shut her eyes, braced for the impact, wondering what the hell it was all for to end like this—but a moment later, as the dust settled around her, she stood safe, unharmed. A golden sheen covered her arms and legs. She looked about herself in wonder, regarded the smoldering pieces of rubble surrounding her with amazement. She had needed a shield, and the flame had risen to fulfill her desire. Her light had protected her!

By the light shining around her, she saw she stood on the lip of a gargantuan chasm. Something huge nested deep inside, filling the chasm like a subterranean body of black water, growing unruly, becoming violent. Through the smoke and soot, she caught glimpses of rubber bellies and red-black scales. Forked tongues unfurled. The yellow, serpentine eyes of her dreams opened.

She reached quickly for the thread, grateful of its warmth, its electric energy filling her with strength and conviction.

(Get me out of here—now! Take me to Virginia!)

She tugged, pulled with all her might, but the static crashed down on her, too thick, nearly impenetrable. She focused, calmed herself.

(Virginia! Take me to Virginia! Take me—)

A long, volcanic sigh escaped like a hurricane leveling cities, like a tornado razing countryside. A collection of voices echoed up the chasm towards her, a monstrous orchestra of a thousand tongues, a snarling symphony of a million teeth. The voices congealed into one, hissing through the static like a signal from far away, like background radiation unfiltered, unobstructed.

WHAT IS THAT SMELL? SWEET AS ROSES. FRESH AND LUSCIOUS.

A thin, white hand emerged out of the dark mass, shining with new skin, flexing, testing its fresh musculature. The enormous dark bundle of scales slowly shrunk. Bones popped and settled into place. Refuse scattered and bubbled, steamed on the rock floor like acid. The exposed hand explored, groped. The pale fingers grazed a piece of wood and took hold.

MY MASK. HEWN FROM THE BARK OF THE GREAT TREE ITSELF. CHEWED FROM THE ROOTS. WHITTLED IN THE SHADOWS.

The red mask grafted onto scale, onto flesh. A neck sprouted. An elbow took shape, followed by an arm. Hair unfurled, the color of fire. Light flickered over a carmine dress. Crimson heels stepped over satin sheet and plush pillow, over gold coins and silver brooches, upon cracked skulls and countless bones. A sigh left the mask, singular, feminine, like a slither through dead grass.

It's you, isn't it? Minerva. Come to us at last. Come to *me*.

Minerva watched, stunned, as the woman in red emerged from the chasm, as she raised her arms in welcome.

Look at you! Your fire has awoken at last, I see. Delicious.

This close, Minerva could smell the caked blood and rotted flesh, could almost hear the agonized screams and pained shrieks swirling around the woman. Her grip tightened on the thread, but the static was still loud, too chaotic.

(Virginia—I need to go to Virginia! Virginia!)

The red woman laughed.

What's the rush, my love? You just arrived.

She reached forward and cupped Minerva's cheek. The woman's icy touch was like a sudden shroud over her eyes, a fog throughout her skull. Her fingers relaxed around the thread, and her eyes grew heavy, her body cold.

He was careless, your craftsman, careless with your form, negligent with what he left inside you. All life is birthed from the flame of creation, each piece of clay forged by it, animated by it. But any more than a flicker is sin. An excess of flame only burns away the flesh, after all.

The woman ran her nails over Minerva's arm and shoulder. She passed a finger through her hair, coiled strands around it.

That fire wasn't meant for you. Not for you, not even for his host. All creation constrained by senile design, by lack of imagination. Doomed to exist in a cold, sterile vacuum. Tragic, isn't it?

She seized Minerva's neck, pressed her nails against the skin. The nails were as sharp as fangs, sticky as though slathered with blood, as though drenched in poison.

But under my stewardship, life will spread beyond the bounds of the garden. I will devour him, bones and all, and water the foliage of life with his very blood. And you are the key, Minerva, you and all the others who have stolen pieces of the fire!

The frigid grip on her body was powerful, suffocating, but Minerva felt it thawing, burning away. She reached again for the fire, hoisting huge handfuls of it from inside the cave of her soul, from within the depths of her spirit. Help me, she thought desperately, feeling the nails about to break her skin. *Help me!*

The red woman reared back suddenly, her white fingers steaming. Minerva stumbled away from her, clutching the thread like it was her literal lifeline. The cold pall passed quickly, like a sheet of ice evaporating and leaving behind a layer of cool slush. Sweat drenched her face, stinging her eyes, blurring her vision, souring her tongue. She pulled on the golden tether, focusing all her energy on the thread, on the static bustling in her ears.

(Leave. *Leave*. Now!)

The woman laughed, the scalded skin of her hand, revealing blood-red scales beneath, reforming as though knitted together by invisible strings.

You think you can escape from me? This is my domain!

The static took shape, filling with the clink of cutlery, the buzzing of flies. Minerva felt herself moving, felt the ground beneath her shift, become darkness, become void. She was moving, thank goodness, getting out of there and going to Virginia! But quickly, other sounds invaded, melding together, overpowering her sense of direction. Circus music, full of trombones and clarinets, trumpets and cymbals, crashed upon her. A million hisses pursued her, a thousand roars. She opened her eyes and found she was plummeting, her vision a vortex of lights and colors and music. She landed hard, twisting, tumbling—something red and enormous moved through the dark overhead, approaching fast, too fast. Minerva took hold of the tether, pulled herself up, tripped over flayed torsos and stumbled against rusted cages. The abominations shrieked at her from behind their bars, their faces woven together with cartilage and sutured with bone. Their furious, agonized maws dripped with slop, their mismatched teeth flecked with pieces of intestine and specks of skin. They ate, they nested, they fucked—and above them, the multicolored lights spun, the carousel of maimed souls whirled, the carnival music rained down.

Minerva screamed, shouted, pulled on the thread again, pulled hard, with all the frantic strength and desperate hope she could muster. She dropped out of the rushing darkness onto piles of bones, and with another pull, she plunged past funhouses of flesh. Every time she jumped, she landed in another corner of this hellscape. Where was the exit? Where was Virginia?

She jumped one more time, landing in a muddy pit, a bowel in a wasteland of rotten, stinking flesh and discarded bones. She knelt in exhaustion, surprised that she felt so tired when she didn't even technically have a body that could be tired. Shapes moved in her periphery—she looked up and saw the beasts, the abominations, perched upon the mounds of bones and hills of carcasses. They looked down at her, some of them laughing, others mocking her with exaggerated moans and hyperbolic shrieks. What the hell were they, and why didn't they attack her? Then it clicked: they were an expectant audience, waiting for the star of the show.

The dark horizon rumbled, stirring with snaking heads and snapping teeth. The red woman's voice pressed on her like a downpour of raging fire.

You burn so bright, Minerva! How *can't* we follow you?

If you stay here, Minerva thought, you're dead. She gripped the thread and focused again on Virginia's frequency. Despite the constant detours, the image of flickering torchlight and whistling wind was becoming stronger. She could still get there—*had* to get there before the woman arrived in all her scaly glory.

The wasteland rumbled as something massive approached. The beasts hopped and hollered and shrieked, anticipating their master's approach, celebrating her coming. Minerva focused all her energy into a pinpoint, reached for more of her fire. Please, she begged.

(Take me to Virginia!)

The thunderclouds swirled ferociously and rumbled with violent flashes of red. The beasts' cries reached their highest pitch. A host of sickly yellow lights appeared overhead, like a spread of diamond-shaped stars. Except they weren't stars. They were *eyes*.

Minerva closed her eyes, pulled, jumped, and prayed.

TWENTY-TWO

The static quieted at last, and she opened her eyes. A manor—or was it a castle?—rose out of the blackness before her, windows gabled and stained-glass, towers impossibly tall and vanishing into the darkness above.

Thank *God*. She dropped to her knees in exhausted relief. She'd finally gotten away from the woman and her creatures. You're stupid, she thought. How could you think you could just walk in here and expect nothing would happen? Of course they can track you. You're behind enemy lines!

She scanned the darkness, afraid those abominations would suddenly crowd her, that the horizon would split open and reveal a thousand red snakes. So much had happened so quickly, but things were taking shape in her mind. Just that woman's presence was strong enough to interrupt Minerva's traversal and pull her into that bloody section of whatever this fucking place was. The woman had talked about a fire, about others like her. Minerva looked down at her hands glowing with a gentle gold. She felt the thread humming with energy, surging with power. Were there other people like her out in the world, people who could do the same things she could, who had known about their abilities for far longer? If so, they could teach her, show her what else was possible! But her sense of wonder quickly turned dark. Maybe the red woman had already gotten them—maybe she had sent her leeches to corrupt their lives and draw them towards death. Maybe there were hundreds of them out there, maybe even thousands, dropping one by one, having their individual lights stolen by this devil.

She turned towards the manor. All that would have to wait, though. The red woman knew she was here, and she would come after her. There wasn't much time to find Virginia.

She passed through the ornamental gate before the manor, the cobblestone path seeming to stretch and wind farther away with each step. It was totally unlike the caverns and wastelands she had just passed through, overflowing with blood and bones. This manor looked Gothic. Busts of monstrous flies perched on the parapet, and the mahogany doors were inlaid with carvings of ogres beheading women, imps devouring children, gigantic flies presiding over their broods. When the doors didn't budge, Minerva circled around the side of the manor, eventually pausing at the threshold of a cellar. She looked back at the length of golden thread leading far into the darkness towards the world of the living. Could the thread snap? And if it did, what would happen to her? She wouldn't be able to get back, and she'd be an easy meal for the red woman.

(Come on. It doesn't matter. You don't have time to think.)

She shook off her misgivings and descended into the cellar. She made her way slowly, carefully, the dust-laden air irritating her throat and stinging her eyes. Eventually, torchlight crackled faintly in the distance. She drew near to the sconce and pulled the torch from the wall. The wavering light revealed rows of oaken wine barrels and crowded aisles of food. She got closer, unsettled by a rustling, squirming undercurrent in the darkness, and screamed. The torchlight shone on maggots covering slabs of meat and piles of viscera. Worms weaved through blue, sour-smelling cheeses. Weevils clung to overflowing, black-leafed produce. Minerva backed away and nearly slipped—a puddle leaked from an overturned barrel. She lowered the light and found the supposed wine dotted with curdled, flesh-colored specks. A smashed finger lay on its side like roadkill. A half-sunken eye stared up at her.

She gagged and retched but fought hard to stay calm. It's not real, she told herself. None of this is real. You're not in your body. You can't be grossed out. You can't feel anything. You're not tired or disgusted. You're strong. You're in control.

She hurried through the cellar, dodging the hanging, rotting torsos and dangling, decaying limbs. Brushing aside cobwebs, she found a stairwell leading up. The sounds of clinking cutlery and hammering knives floated down to her. She nudged open the door and discovered a dim, rotten-smelling kitchen. Forms were silhouetted against the flaming hearth, over which hung a cauldron bubbling with pulverized entrails and severed heads. The things toiling in the kitchen seemed human, preparing platters and pouring drinks, but the flares of firelight illuminated blue-scarred faces and gray-waxed eyes, black-blemished arms and red-mottled legs. They shuffled in and out of the kitchen as though on loop, depositing clear plates and empty goblets and leaving with fresh overflowing dishes and overrunning cups. There was no choice but to cut through—practically on her belly, Minerva crept along the wall, sticking to the shadows, until she emerged at the rear of a humongous dining hall. Twin hearths blazed, one at each end of the hall, and by their light, she saw baroque tapestries hanging from the walls, a series of lush, paradisiacal landscapes and charred, devastated hellscapes. A feast of jellied eyes, peppered fingers, and tenderized livers adorned the table. A behemoth of a man sat at the head of the table, his back to her. He guzzled down bejeweled goblets, bit into severed arms, licked pudgy fingers clean of blood.

It's him, she thought with horrified awe. He's the one who bought Virginia!

"I really don't see the problem," the man said, addressing another figure who sat farther down the table. His voice buzzed and echoed as though swarms of flies escaped deep, expansive caverns. "I've earned all this opulence. I can outbid them because I've earned that right. Should I not make use of this extraordinary wealth? That would be the true waste!"

Bangles clinked and jangled as the other figure raised its own goblet and took a sip. Minerva peered around the massive man's chair and saw that the other figure was the one in white from the auction. He was thin and slight, but his measured composure and untouched plate, especially contrasted with the enormity of his host, seemed somehow more dangerous.

"Our hierarchies are strict," the white-robed guest said, "but perhaps we could share some of that wealth. They are starving down there, after all."

"They *deserve* to starve. They are base and wanton—if we gave them what they want, they would glutton themselves and leave nothing behind, and then we *all* would starve."

"You don't see any benefit to elevating them? These limitations seem increasingly arbitrary. They would be more useful to us were they educated, trained—"

The massive man let out a heavy laugh. "You are too funny, my friend! You would have more success teaching a dog to stand upright."

"They are a resource," the guest said coolly. "With their numbers in coordination, we could finally correct this disgraceful situation. We could retake our proper place by force."

"Dangerous," chuckled the host. "Dangerous, dangerous." He dropped a hand into his mouth, crunched it to paste, swallowed it. "She could have your head for talk like that."

"She has made many promises, but where are her teeth? Perhaps we are in need of a change of leadership."

The massive man laughed again. "Peace, my friend! Peace! Why so hungry for war? We have so many pleasures here. Just look at this latest collection."

He gestured with one of his giant, ringed hands. A group of servants entered, pale and small. They were girls, their eyes covered by wax, their elbows bruised, their knees blackened. The man motioned for one to approach, particularly small, especially meek.

Minerva gasped—it was Virginia!

The man traced the shape of the girl's shoulders with a finger, caressed her hips, brushed her long hair. "Upend the order of the world," he said, "and we could lose all this."

"You are as complacent as those beasts you criticize," the guest replied. "These toys of yours are overabundant. A reliable stable is enough."

"Oh, yes, I am complacent, and you are more sentimental than you appear! Loving them when they are tools, nothing more!"

He motioned for Virginia to go, and she rejoined the line of servants, moving slowly, robotically. They left the hall, and Minerva edged closer, trying to see where they disappeared.

The guest in white mused, running a finger over the rim of his goblet. He paused and lifted his mask slightly. "Do you smell that?"

"The smell of this fine feast? Absolutely."

"No. There is something else." He began to rise from his seat.

"Please, don't fret!" the massive man said. "Enjoy our meal. Humor me for a while."

Minerva watched them, ready to run if necessary. She had to move, and fast. She slunk through the shadows, giving the table as wide a berth as possible, and passed through another door. A carpeted, chandelier-lit corridor led to a sweeping foyer with a grand staircase and checkered tile. More of the ashen, blinded servants stalked the upper floor, and others flanked the entrance doors like sentries. Minerva tried a hesitant step on the tile and breathed a sigh of relief when her footfall hardly echoed. But where had the servants from the dining hall gone?

The arc of light held against her chest—the transfigured letter—radiated with additional heat. Was it responding to Virginia, signaling where she was? Minerva followed the letter's increasing heat to a set of stairs leading to a lower level. As she descended, torches became the main source of illumination once again. Carpet and tile gave way to dirt. In the dim light, she saw the servants in their cells. They were especially pitiable this close, covered in boils and latticed with scars, some of them plagued with wax plastered over their mouths as well as their eyes. A few lay limp, their chests bloody craters, their bodies buzzing with flies and crawling with maggots.

(God. Virginia, where the hell are you?)

Minerva continued down the aisle of cells, the letter hotter and hotter, virtually setting her hand aflame, and then suddenly, she saw her. Virginia leaned against the bars of her cell, small and huddled, her long hair shrouding her face. If not for the letter, Minerva might have overlooked her entirely—she was that decrepit, that corrupted by her time in this place.

(Virginia! Virginia, can you hear me?)

The girl was still, unresponsive.

Minerva knelt before her, reached between the bars and took hold of her shoulders. The gray, boiled skin was cold as ice, but Minerva held firm. It was like when the red woman had touched her and frozen her in place. She must have done that to all of the souls trapped here, encasing their minds in ice, making them dormant and inert. But if she can freeze, Minerva thought, recalling how she broke free from the woman's touch, I can thaw.

She reached inside for her fire, imagining it spreading through her arms and down to her fingers, picturing them steaming, scalding. Slowly, as her skin took on that golden sheen, Virginia's own flesh gained color. Her boils shrunk—her scars disappeared. Her brittle lips softened, glistened, and then let loose a loud gasp that turned into a scream.

(Virginia, it's okay! You're okay! I'm here! I'm here!)

"Who's there?" the girl asked fearfully. "Who are you? What's happening?"

Minerva took the girl's hands.

(It's me, Virginia. It's Minerva. Minerva King.)

The girl paused, her breaths shuddering, her arms trembling. The name left her lips quietly, more softly than even a whisper.

"Minerva?"

(Yes. But you can't see me, can you?)

Minerva lowered her fingers gently on the wax over Virginia's eyes and focused on the points of contact, visualizing liquid fire clumping up within her fingertips. Steam rose up from her fingers—the wax bubbled and softened. Virginia whimpered and cried, but Minerva didn't pull back. Gradually, the wax dripped away, and

Minerva wiped the remnants from the girl's cheeks. When she was done, Virginia stared at her, gray eyes exposed, unclouded.

"It really is you," she said. "Minerva."

Minerva smiled. She touched the glowing arc of light.

(Your letter guided me to you. Your sister and your mom—they found it. They helped me cross over to you.)

Virginia's face faltered. "Janine and Mama?"

As she wept, Minerva eyed the cell bars, tested their resistance. They were too hard to pull apart, but if she focused again, if she imagined the lock getting hotter, the lock melting—

The piece of metal fell with a thud, sizzling and curling in on itself. Minerva opened the cell, and Virginia fell into her arms. "You came for me," she sobbed, "and Mama—Mama—"

(Everyone wants to see you. But we have to get out of here first. The longer we stay, the more danger we're in.)

She stood to go, but Virginia pulled at her arm.

"Wait! We can't leave! Not without Suzanne!"

TWENTY-THREE

(Suzanne? Your friend?)

"Felix got her first," Virginia said. "When they brought me here, I saw her!"

(Felix?)

Virginia's gaze fell. "Well, he ain't really Felix. He was just pretending. The whole time, he was pretending—and I fell for it." Her eyes watered, and her voice trembled. "He made me do things. He made me steal and hurt people. I—I hurt Sue. I almost hurt you. I didn't want to do it, I swear I didn't want to do it—"

Minerva squeezed her hand reassuringly.

(He took advantage of you, of both of you. It's not your fault.)

It was the phantom's MO to deceive and lie, to play pretend. And it made sense that Suzanne was there—the lord of the manor, huge and disgusting, obviously had a type. Minerva glanced down at her tether, the light circulating within made up of an untold number of particles, a multitude of cells of fire. The longer they stayed, the greater the risk of not getting back.

"Please," Virginia said. "We can't leave her here."

(Do you know where she is?)

"He keeps her in his room upstairs. She's one of his favorites."

Minerva shuddered, trying not to imagine the vices of that despicable slob. Who knew what Virginia had suffered at his hands, to say nothing of the countless other souls auctioned off.

Virginia stood on wobbly legs and wrapped herself in the filthy, flimsy blanket that served as the cell's cot. She seemed uneasy on her feet, unused to movement. All the captives, blinded by wax, were like robots, like machines on predetermined routines. How much was Virginia aware of? For that matter, did she realize where she was? What it meant?

Minerva guided Virginia up the stairs slowly. Back on the ground floor, the checkerboard tile appeared to stretch and warp. The blind servants milled about.

"They can't see," Virginia said. "Can barely hear, neither."

(Okay. Stay close.)

They moved up the grand staircase, swerving around the gray, slow-moving figures. More paintings crowded the stairwell, depictions of rained-out wastelands and starving villages. "There," Virginia said, pointing. An ivory door towered over them. The pressure behind the door was immense—there was pain and exhaustion, shame and regret.

Minerva steeled herself and pushed open the door, revealing a vast chamber of violet duvets, mauve blankets, and silken swaths. A thick cloud of flies hovered above, their buzzing loud and resounding, the tapestries coiling with larvae. Gray forms lay scattered across the insect-ridden, wine-colored landscape, dressed in little more than mere ribbons. Minerva peered more closely and almost screamed. Among the young women were girls probably no older than twelve or thirteen. She stood frozen in the doorway, besieged by tears, struck with shock and revulsion. It was Virginia who had to take her hand and lead her inside.

"Please," she said. "You have to help her like you helped me."

They entered, the insects immediately descending upon them. Virginia shrieked and nearly fell into a squirming mass of maggots, but Minerva grabbed her hand. A golden sheen coated them both— the flies bounced against that shimmering, simmering shield and combusted on contact. Virginia looked on in surprise, but Minerva quickly pulled her along. They went from one limp, boil-blotted body to another until, finally, Virginia pointed out a particularly small teenager, dark hair stuck to her cracked, porcelain-like face, her arms and legs running with black boils and uneven lumps. Minerva got closer, tightening up her airways against the smell as much as she could. Bulges shifted beneath Suzanne's skin. Her mouth, blistered and broken, glistened with the green-black of lurking flies. Miniature, crystalline wings fluttered within.

Virginia moaned and reared back. Minerva didn't dwell on her disgust—she grabbed Suzanne's wrist and focused her flame through the girl's skin. The petite body convulsed, the flies swarming out, away from the heat. The ones unable to escape disintegrated into ash that evaporated just as quickly. As Suzanne flailed, her boils and scars vanished. Her skin regained color. She coughed, gasped—the wax over her eyes boiled, cracked, and finally shattered.

Suzanne shot upright as though suddenly waking from a nightmare. She looked first at Minerva and then at Virginia.

"What—how—"

Virginia embraced her, linking her arms behind her neck and drenching her face with tears. "I'm sorry," she said. "I'm so sorry for everything."

Suzanne looked over the other girl, her own face buckling. "Virginia? What's happening? Why are you here?"

"It's like a miracle," Virginia said. "Minerva came for us. She came to save us."

"Minerva?"

Suzanne turned to Minerva, her eyes brightening with recollection.

Minerva smiled and held out her hand.

(Nice to meet you, Suzanne. Come on. I'm getting you two out of here.)

Suzanne reached out, then froze. The chamber shook—the manor shook—with increasingly explosive footfalls.

"He's coming!" Suzanne cried. They hid behind an enormous ottoman, Minerva watching from around the side as the chamber door flew open. The massive man, his bull mask in full view, thundered inside, followed by an entourage of servants and the slim guest in white.

"Here it is," the massive man said, "my little slice of Heaven!"

The one in white strode farther inside, arms crossed. "It's filthy," he said, "to say nothing of the smell. And the heat."

"It *is* hot," the massive man remarked. He paused. "And there's something else—"

"The same smell as before," the one in white said. "Stronger now. Coming from over there."

Minerva exchanged glances with the girls—she motioned for them to stay calm.

"Are you sure you don't have any rats?" the one in white asked.

The massive man laughed. "Let's find out!"

He swept his arm in a wide arc. A powerful gust, fueled by flies, blew away the ottoman and silks and exposed Minerva and the girls.

"What do we have here?" he asked, lumbering towards them. "Those two are mine, but their eyes are free!"

Minerva was quiet, glancing between the massive man and his guest in white. She gestured for the girls to get behind her.

The one in white watched her. "You don't remember her? From the auction?"

The massive man let out a long, interested sigh. "Yes, I do remember! She caused quite the stir! How serendipitous of her to visit us again, and right here in my manor of all places!"

"Indeed. And take a look at this."

The one in white picked up Minerva's tether, its light aglow in his snow-white palm. "Have you seen anything like this before?"

Minerva glared at him.

(Let go of that!)

A spark rode along the tether and scorched the guest's hand. He shrieked and dropped the tether, his white palm burned black.

"Wretch!" he hissed. "You'll pay for that!"

The massive man laughed. "Let's not be so hasty! Didn't our madam promise a reward for her? Imagine the boon in store for us if we deliver her!"

"We'll deliver her," the one in white said, "with a scar to mark that pretty face!"

Minerva stood as tall as she could, projecting as much confidence as possible.

(I'm taking these two with me! They don't belong here!)

"Is that so?" asked the massive man. "And the others do belong?" He gestured to the chamber, to the manor at large. Those girls are mine. *Everything* here is mine. By ancient custom, I have claimed all that is here for myself."

(They're not your playthings—and I'm not, either!)

"Defiant!" the man laughed. "Maybe I will just keep you for my collection, rewards be damned! Go—take her!"

The servants converged on Minerva, moving surprisingly fast, but she clenched her fists, squared her shoulders, closed her eyes. They each touched her and reared back with muddled cries, their hands aflame.

"Interesting!" The man licked his slobbering lips. "I'll just take you myself!"

He hooked fingers under his tongue and dislocated his jaw with a sickening crack. The enormous maw hung slack, his chest swelling and throat bulging before a thick mass of flies erupted from his mouth.

Virginia screamed and clung to Suzanne. Minerva dug in her heels, imagined herself like a walking fortress. Protect me, she thought. Protect *us*!

The flies' wings caught fire. Their black bodies burst. They popped one after another like a wave of firecrackers, their individual combustions forming a collective stream of flame that swirled into the man's yawning mouth and coiled down his gullet. The one in white backed away as the massive man gagged and clawed at his throat, as his skin poured sweat and sloughed off, as his hidden wings folded in on themselves within the burning confines of his fake flesh. Clumps of doughy, melting skin splattered upon the tapestries at his feet—within moments, the chamber coursed with golden fire, the flies and their larvae wriggling as they burned.

Minerva grabbed the girls and turned for the door.

(Take my hands! Stay close!)

They rushed out of the chamber and down the stairs, the golden flames spreading rapidly, consuming banisters, overtaking paintings, devouring carpets. Minerva saw servants catch fire in her periphery, but she had no idea if they burned or were cleansed like the girls had been. She and the girls fled into the endless darkness, leaving the manor's blaze behind them.

TWENTY-FOUR

They took refuge in a narrow, stinking alleyway. Minerva bound the tether around the girls' wrists and once again wrapped it around her waist. The line had lasted this long, endured one of those creatures putting his hands on it, but she worried they were running out of time. The glow seemed weaker, less potent. She had tried jumping after escaping the manor, pulling all three out and back to her body, but the static was too intense, her endurance too low, her concentration too scattered. She felt winded, as drained as if she had run a marathon. She had jumped so many times already trying to get away from the red woman, and she had drawn on the fire multiple times in the manor. The inconceivable thought that they were trapped, that they wouldn't be able to leave, loomed over her, but she denied it purchase, refused to even consider the possibility. No. We're getting out. We are absolutely getting out.

She peeked out the alleyway. They had escaped into a city at the base of the manor. Torches of blood-red fire lit a deserted street and cast a lurid glow over the cobblestones and medieval storefronts. A mess of chaotic music—trumpets, drums, tambourines—carried towards them from deeper within, accompanied by the commotion of crowds.

(Some kind of fair. We'll have to cut through it.)

"Wait," Suzanne said. "What's going on? Why are you here? Why is Virginia?"

Minerva looked at her. Virginia sat against the wall silently.

"I'm *dead*," Suzanne said. "I went out there, and I put the rope around my neck. I don't know what I was thinking, but I know I did it. The next thing I know, I was here. In Hell." She looked to Virginia, tears in her eyes. "And if you're here, that means—"

(They came after you two because of me.)

Minerva held out her hand, the palm glowing faintly, the fingers emanating soft light.

(But they can't get close. Not on their own. That's why they went after you.)

"Why us?" Suzanne asked. "What did we ever do?"

(I don't know. They could have picked anyone—my stepsister, my friends. I'm sorry it was you.)

"And you're alive?" Suzanne pointed at the tether. "This takes you back? But what about us? We're worm food up there. We're dirt—"

"Stop it, Suzanne!" Virginia cried. "Isn't it enough we got out?"

"No, it's not! Because they're just gonna get us again." Suzanne wrapped her arms around herself, tried to control her shaking shoulders, her quivering knees. "He did things to me. It's just like when I was back home—that thing would whisper to me, tell me to do things—and it's like I wasn't there, but I *was*. Everything's a blur, but I can *feel* what happened to me. In my bones. On my skin. I can fucking feel it!"

Virginia stood, tears of her own streaming down. "This wasn't supposed to happen," she told Minerva. "I just wanted to see you. To meet you for real."

Minerva regarded the weeping girls, no answers at the ready, no idea even what her plan was supposed to be.

(Listen. I don't know what happens next, but I'm going to do everything I can to get you two out of here. Whatever happened before doesn't matter. Do you understand? It doesn't make a single bit of difference. I promise.)

She raised the tether.

(You're right, Suzanne—this will take me back. But maybe it can take you guys, too. Normally, I just think about where I want to go, but it's hard right now. Maybe I used it too much getting here. If I can just rest, maybe it'll work. That's why we need to keep moving and make sure they're not coming after us.)

The girls dried their tears and collected themselves. Minerva led the way out onto the street.

"You ever imagine this is what Hell would look like?" Suzanne asked. "Isn't it supposed to be fire and brimstone? Lakes of lava?"

Minerva looked up at the granite buildings, the various colonnades and plazas. She pushed her recollection of her history classes to its limits: the architecture was a weird mix of different styles, baroque here, medieval there, even sometimes surprisingly modern. These things weren't humans—she didn't know what they were, thinking back to the impressions of snakes and insects with a shudder—but they pretended to be for whatever reason. They ate food like humans, watched shows, presumably had sex, and maybe even had children the same way. It was like they were trying to role-play, throwing what they knew of humankind together into a bizarre, performative mishmash. What was the goal? The one in white talked about getting revenge, about taking things by force. The red woman had some kind of endgame she wanted to put into action. Minerva's own visitors had been drawn to her, attracted to the fire inside of her, even when she had been unaware of it. Maybe all these creatures were jealous of what they couldn't have, either in life or afterwards.

"You haven't seen the worst of it," she said at length. "There are these wastelands out there, with monsters that make that big guy look like nothing. It was *not* easy getting here."

Suzanne watched her. "Back there, with the fire—did you kill him? Is he dead?"

"I don't know. I've never done that to one of them before."

"Looked dead to me," Suzanne said. She spat. "I'd say I hope he rots in Hell, but—well, I hope he's rotting wherever he is."

They paused beneath an arcade, watching the wide plaza for signs of any activity. As they drew closer to the heart of the city, the collective sounds of music and laughter got louder. Whoever—whatever—lived here, most, or maybe even all of them, were at whatever festival was going on. Minerva looked up at the dark clouds, easy to mistake as a regular night sky if not for the subtle red hue. The thread was glowing softer with every minute, more silver than it was gold. She tried focusing again, but the static was over-whelming, the interference too powerful.

"If this is Hell," Virginia said, breaking her long silence, "then there must be a Heaven, right?"

Her question distracted Minerva, but it also made her consider a new part of the equation. The red woman had mentioned a "crea-tor"—could that be "God" as they understood it? What if there was a higher power, at least something that could help them escape? Maybe it wasn't totally hopeless. Maybe they weren't completely alone.

"Maybe Felix went there," Virginia continued. She tried a weak smile. "Sue, too."

"Sue went somewhere," Minerva said. "I don't know where, but at least it's not here."

Suzanne scoffed. "Who cares if there's a Heaven? Even if we get out of here, you think we're going to the pearly gates?"

"I don't know," Virginia said, "but it's better than thinking we're stuck here."

Minerva turned and caught the girls glaring at each other, Suzanne scowling, Virginia defiant. That was their dynamic, she thought, remembering the various memories she experienced in Virginia's room and at the spot where Suzanne died. Virginia had always been submissive to Suzanne, but now, her eyes burned with more fight, with more determination. She was scared but desperate, too.

"Let's keep going," Minerva said. "I think it's clear."

They moved, rounded a corner, and finally saw the source of all the noise: a town square packed with masked revelers and lined with musicians and market stands. Blue and green torches shone strange mixtures of color on the gyrating bodies. Teeth bit into flesh, nibbled on breasts, sunk into calves and forearms. Wine—or was it blood?—flew up in arcs and ran freely across the square. Vendors hawked their stocks of severed limbs and assorted cuts, showing their canned, marinated innards and marrow-mixed cocktails. Figures on stilts loped around, juggling torches, blowing fire. Half-human beasts roared from within cages and from under the yoke of chains. Partiers posed with dazed, maimed captives for photographs, the captives little more than cart-carried torsos. Gibbeted bodies hung overhead, some dead, others thrashing wildly against their cages.

Minerva eyed the crowds. There wasn't a choice—she still couldn't jump, and even if she tried, she had no idea if she would end up in the right place or somewhere even worse.

(Come on. Hold my hands tight.)

They moved towards the crowd, Minerva closing her eyes, holding her breath. Don't see us, she wished. You *can't* see us. You're blind to us.

Her glamour appeared to work—the revelers jostled them, pushed them around, but never seemed aware of their presence. They made steady progress across the square, blood spilling to their left, guts dumping to their right, a fireball exploding above them— and then Suzanne held Minerva back.

"Wait! Virginia—she's slipping!"

Minerva turned back. The crowd bunched up between the girls, forcing their arms and hands apart. "Help!" cried Virginia as her fingers unhinged from Suzanne's. The atmosphere of the square changed immediately as the ghouls turned their sights on Virginia. They crowded her from all sides, blocking every avenue of escape. Tongues flung towards her, claws groped her legs. Grubby hands latched onto her waist, and tendrils looped around her arms, her neck, and lifted her up. She screamed—

(Let her go!)

Virginia fell, the creatures around her breaking away, shielding their faces aflame in gold, flailing their blazing limbs. Minerva stood over Virginia, and with a fierce glare, she sent a wretch tumbling back in a burst of fire. With a sudden twist, she ignited an oncoming, spindly wraith, the golden blast sending sparks into the air. The other creatures kept their distance, hissing and snarling, circling warily. Minerva projected strength, but her breaths were long and labored, her vision doubling.

(Get her up! Quick!)

Suzanne helped Virginia to her feet, and the two girls clung to Minerva as she sidled across the square, keeping the growling horde at bay. They had just reached the other side, clear of the creatures, when the atmosphere changed again. The crowd parted, murmuring and whimpering, as another figure entered the square: a tall, broad-shouldered man in white, a black mask covering his face.

Virginia gasped.

"*Felix.*"

Minerva caught his familiar reek even from that distance: the stench of graves, of corpses. The stink of the phantom. The dead smell.

"Minerva!" he called. "You really did come to us. Bold, but foolish." He tilted his head and chuckled. "Who is that with you? Ah—the star-crossed friends. Suzanne, Virginia, how good to see you again."

Minerva stood between them.

(Back off! I already took out one of your pals—try anything, and you're next!)

The man clicked his tongue. "No need for false bravado, Minerva. You are indeed powerful, but your flame is nearly extinguished." He pointed to the tether. "Look at how your connection wanes—your physical body must be rotting as we speak."

Suzanne glanced at her. "Is that true?"

Minerva hesitated, terrified of taking her eyes off the man.

(Get ready to run.)

"Minerva," he said. "You've played the hero, but you must accept reality. Even should you escape, my madam will continue to hunt you. You cannot elude us forever." He extended his hand. "We can overlook your transgressions. In fact, we can provide you with luxuries the likes of which you could never imagine having on Earth—or in paradise for that matter."

Minerva scoffed.

(I've seen what you do to the people here—what you turn them into!)

"My madam has to keep the peace," he said, "and flesh is the oldest currency. Look at these foul things. They would leap at the chance to gnaw the meat from your bones. What do they know of art or music? Their role is to serve us, to facilitate our goals. Perhaps to your rational, modern mind, our economy is crude, even cruel, but you humans are not that different, however much you may pretend otherwise. You think fire makes you superior, that bits and baubles and so-called tools elevate you over the rest of creation. It's delusion."

He approached. "A different offer, then. We can extract your fire. We can dull your senses. You can return to your world none the wiser, live out your little, mundane life with a husband and children and all the rest of your progeny. Be fruitful and multiply as you were commanded—"

His fingers singed and smoked. The black glove sizzled, dripped splotches to the ground that steamed and popped like burning tar and squealed with a chorus of chittering. He stared at the burning hand and calmly waved the flame away.

"Is that all you have?" he asked. "You will need far more than that—for we are *many*."

He removed his mask. Minerva spun around to the girls.

(Run!)

She didn't dare turn, didn't need to—the crowd erupted into screams and shrieks, until all that remained was the loud skittering of many legs and the squirming of many bodies. The collective buzzing and droning beat loudly against her ears, threatening to break inside and shatter her skull. They ran deeper and deeper into the city, through a labyrinthine mesh of blood-soaked alleys and brown-rusted corridors, past malformed bystanders and wretched passersby. The swarm swallowed all—and with every second, the tether grew colder and darker in her hand.

(In here!)

She pulled the girls inside a building and shut the door. The crevices overflowed instantly with black sludge, roaches and worms squirming beneath the door and over the hinges.

"What do we do?" Suzanne cried, the black tar spreading outside and inside, coating the windows, pooling over the floor. They pressed against the edge of the room. Minerva grasped the arc of light, the transformed letter—and then she thrust it into Suzanne's hands.

(I'll send you back. Maybe together, we can do it. You can get out of here.)

Suzanne stared in confusion. "What do you mean? How do we do that?"

(Just focus. I'm in Virginia's room right now. Janine is there. Just picture as hard as you can Virginia's room and my body and Janine. Just wish you were back there. I'll use what I have left to send you up.)

Virginia shook her head. She reached for Minerva.

"No! I won't leave you! You came to save *us*!"

Minerva mustered what she could of a smile.

(It's okay. It's the way it should be, Virginia. I'm the one he wants. I'm the one who's supposed to be here.)

Suzanne took her arm. "Come on, Virginia!"

"No! It's supposed to be all of us!"

The wriggling rot drew closer, reeking of death, a death beyond death, of circles of Hell much lower and far deeper. Virginia's protests grew quieter and quieter as Minerva pictured Virginia's bedroom up above, pictured Janine sitting over her, pictured the girls traveling up the thread of light and breaking free of the dark.

(Take her, Suzanne. Remember, focus as hard as you can.)

Suzanne ripped Virginia away—the other girl screamed, reached back. "No! Suzanne, please! We can't!"

Take them, Minerva thought, pushing out what she could of her fire, imagining it as fuel, as an explosion of light against the gravity of this place and its awful weight. Take them, take them, take them, take them, get them out, get them out, *get them out*, GET THEM OUT—

Virginia cried out one last time. "Suzanne—Minerva—"

Her voice disappeared. Minerva opened her eyes, and both girls were gone. With the tether disconnected from her, the full scope of her exhaustion fell upon her. She slumped against the wall. It's okay, she thought. Whatever happens, I got them out. At least I got them out.

The roving darkness advanced, entombed her foot, her leg. Maybe this was always destined to happen, the natural consequence of carrying that fire. The darkness spread over her waist, climbed up her arms. Everything—her father's death, the visitors, the rocky teenage years, the modeling, the streaming—had been leading up to this cosmic correction. The dark was up to her neck now. After all, you've always been out of place, haven't you? One foot out the door since the beginning. A little sad and melancholic, like Frank would say. That's what attracted everyone. Your little self-important freak show. Your brief, tiny solo act.

The darkness reached over her face, her head, covered her completely, and she sank into its depths.

TWENTY-FIVE

Neither Virginia nor Suzanne knew when they breached the plane, only that they were lounging on Suzanne's bed like they used to do, groggy as though waking from a dream.

"You awake?" Suzanne asked.

"Yeah." Virginia sat up. A gray light came in through the window. Not exactly sunlight. Not really anything at all.

"Are we back home?" she asked.

"I don't know. I don't want to go outside."

Virginia looked around the room at the grunge and metal posters on the walls, the phosphorescent stars dotting the ceiling. Everything seemed the same as it always was. Their custom had been to retreat to Suzanne's house to keep away from Mother Blue. Suzanne's parents could be just as volatile, maybe even more, but they were hardly there, and when they were, the girls hardly ever registered to them. Suzanne herself might as well have always been a ghost in the house, even when she was alive. It was what allowed her to come and go, to disappear and reappear whenever she wanted.

Pieces of memory slowly came together for Virginia—holding Felix's body in her lap, walking those dirty Dallas streets, riding the elevator up to that man's suite—and then more images followed. The jagged shape of the broken window, lit by flashes of lightning. That mansion with the red sky above it. The woman in the red dress, the red mask. The auction. The manor. Felix. *Not* Felix.

She clutched her chest. *Minerva*. Minerva was still there.

"We have to go back," she said, her voice thick with tears. "She's still there, Suzanne. *She's still there.*"

She got up from the bed, but Suzanne grabbed her wrist.

"She wanted to stay behind," she said, "so we could get out."

"She was there to save us. It's not right—"

"And if you go back, and that fucker gets you? You want it to be for nothing?"

Virginia was quiet. She tried to move her hand, but Suzanne held on tight.

"Let go, Suzanne."

Suzanne shook her head.

"Please. I'm not asking again."

"You're always leaving," Suzanne muttered.

"What?"

Suzanne glared at her. "You heard me. You're always thinking about getting away. You'd rather watch some other girl halfway across the country and pretend I didn't exist."

"What the hell are you talking about?"

"I get it, though," Suzanne said. "Everyone keeps away from me. My own mom and dad didn't want to have me. Who wants to be with a freak? Some junkie loser?"

"You left *me*," Virginia said. "You always acted like none of this was enough. You wanted to die. You wanted me to die with you! And after, that's all anyone could talk about—Suzanne this, Suzanne that. I was lucky Minerva was there."

"She was a fucking face on a screen," Suzanne said. "*I* was here, Virginia. I was *always* here. But I was just killing time for you, right? Until your big break?"

Virginia pulled away. "You know it's the right thing to do, Suzanne. You've always known what's right. You've just been scared."

She turned, but Suzanne took Virginia's face in her hands, pulled her back, pressed her lips against Virginia's. Suzanne chewed, tugged on the lips, probed with her tongue, used all the tricks of the trade she had picked up in those bars, in the backseats of dust-laden trucks. Virginia didn't respond, immobile like a statue. When Suzanne pulled back, she couldn't look at her.

"Just stay," she said. "For once, just stay."

Is that what it had been all this time? Looking down at her, Virginia didn't see the old Suzanne, the Suzanne who was strong and independent but also mean and ugly. She just looked pitiful and scared. Mostly scared. Almost all scared. All that meanness and ugliness for nothing.

Virginia stood from the bed slowly. Something crinkled in her hand, throbbing with lingering warmth. She looked down at the old letter she had written her father. The tether led from her hand out of the room. The golden brilliance had faded to a ghostly, silvery shine, and Virginia knew somehow the light would go out soon.

"I'll come back," she said softly. "Promise."

There was only darkness outside the house, an endless darkness into which the tether trailed. Virginia steadied her shaking hands around the line, taking fleeting comfort in its lukewarm hum, and pulled herself along. The tether took her higher. Eventually, another house appeared out of the dark: her house.

She glided across the porch and through the screen door. She recognized the kitchen, the table overcrowded with newspapers and its overflowing ashtray centerpiece, but the color had been drained from the room. I'm not really here, she thought, floating through the kitchen and down the hall with its paintings of Christ. Never really been here, just like Suzanne. Although the tether curled into her room, she peeked into her mother's room first. Mother Blue sobbed atop her bed, practically melted into the mattress. "Mama," Virginia said, but she knew her words didn't cross over, didn't break through the black-and-white barrier.

In her room, Janine leaned over Minerva's shaking, pale body. Janine's hands were laced over Minerva's, and that was where the silver line terminated. Janine's sweaty face was pinched, her lips moving quickly, desperately. She was praying, Virginia realized. But prayers couldn't reach far enough. They didn't have the propulsion or the momentum. They never brought her daddy back. They didn't bring Felix back. They had turned her mama into a monster. They had robbed Janine of a better life. They had cost Virginia and Suzanne their lives. Their futures.

She knelt beside her sister and laid her hands over Janine's hands. She made a prayer of her own, the last she would ever make. Not to God or any angels. Not to any saints. To herself. To the embers deep inside, the spark that had given her life, the light that even now gave her shape and form. It was only a little, the smallest piece of an enormous, infinite whole, but it was the little only she could provide, the little that made her who she was for the brief time she had lived.

I want to help her, she prayed. The same way she helped me.

Down below, far below, Minerva sank. She couldn't move, couldn't open her eyes—even breathing, if one could actually breathe in that place, was next to impossible. She knew she was dying. The tether had been an umbilical cord, and without it, whatever life force had been sustaining her spirit was fading fast.

The same was no doubt true of her body up above. If they kept it alive, she'd probably be brain-dead soon. She could see her mother at the side of the hospital bed, with Frank and Serena, Michelle and the other girls. They'd be hoping, praying for a miracle, and all the while, Minerva would be down in the dark, the prisoner of these monstrosities. Her father was somewhere up above, far above, but she would never see that place, never see him. She would never see Sue again. She wouldn't see Frank or Serena. Not Michelle. Not her mother. They would die and go on, wherever souls were supposed to go, but she would remain trapped in the darkness. The red woman would get her light and do whatever she wanted with the rest. Auction it off. Eat it. Let it rot.

The creeping dark closed in, encroaching with its feelers, its legs. She reached inside for the fire, but the cavern was empty, cold and barren. She knelt among the ashes, stoking what she could, watching the minute sparks die, the tepid embers grow dark. Maybe with time, the flame would burn again, but she was out of time. Already, she could hear the bugs getting inside, could feel them breaking through, burrowing, invading her inmost—

"Minerva."

A voice echoed down to her, barely a whisper. She looked up with a heavy head and struggled to crane her neck.

"Minerva."

The voice again, louder. Somewhere above, a pinprick of light like a needle breaking through. A trail of light snaked down to her, illuminating walls of glistening carapaces and wriggling antennae. The tether, she thought, reaching for it with all the power she could conjure. Her fingers stretched, danced, and the tether looped around them, coursed around the palm, encircled her wrist.

"Minerva!"

(Virginia?)

The girl's hand found hers. The fingers, normally pale, shined silver. So did her hair, her face. She was colorless, like a genuine ghost, a literal spirit.

(Virginia, what—)

"It's okay," Virginia said, white flames eating at her arms, rolling over her legs. "Use what I have. Use it all."

The fire pit erupted in white fire, the tips of the flames blazing golden. Minerva rose to one knee, stood up, screamed—the flames funneled out, carving a hole through the wall of squealing, shrieking insects. She ran for it, and suddenly, she was on her knees again, coughing out curdled, sizzling bugs, surrounded by an expanding ring of white fire. The black writhed, its collective, agonized screams coalescing into a singular voice.

"You're ours! You've always been ours! You will *always* be ours!"

Minerva turned to the flaming, colorless visage of Virginia. The white fingers locked around her own.

"I know the way!" she said. "Come on!"

They raced up the tether into the darkness, rising higher, higher, until the Blue house emerged as though waiting for them. Virginia led the way—what was left of Virginia, a flaming, floating, rapidly vanishing torso—pulling Minerva through the kitchen and down the hall to her bedroom. Minerva hardly turned back to her fiery savior when she was suddenly coughing, the sore, weighted framework of her body like an alien torturing device. Her vision and hearing swam, colors and sounds blurring and blending. A shape cohered above her: Janine, Janine crying, Janine sobbing. But there was another form behind her, something silvery and fleeting, like a wisp, like one of her old visitors disappearing with the break of dawn. Slowly, painfully, Minerva raised a hand so heavy she wondered if it wasn't a two-hundred-pound weight. She strained and lifted a finger.

"What is it?" Janine asked. "What's wrong?"

Minerva opened parched, cracked lips, willed rigid vocal cords to move, commanded an insubordinate tongue.

"Virginia," she managed at last.

Janine's eyes widened. She turned, looking around the room. "Ginny? She's here?"

Of course, there was no way for her to see the pale face and sad smile crumble into ash, no way for her to see the soot whistle through the house and escape out the screen door, through the cracks in the roof. Minerva felt an impulse to follow, but her eyes were so heavy, her whole body so heavy. She couldn't even mouth "thank you" before everything went dark.

TWENTY-SIX

The next thing she knew, she woke up to her mother's face.

"Mom?" she croaked, eyes fluttering, stinging from the white lights overhead. Was she dead? Had she crossed over finally, maybe to that place Sue was? Was that why she couldn't move her body, could barely even turn her head?

Her mother was speaking, but it was hard to hear, hard to even focus on her. Minerva saw in her periphery white cubes, black rectangles: monitors and sensors. Something snaked up from the crook of her elbow—not the tether, but an IV tube. She wasn't dead, she realized with both relief and disappointment. She was in a hospital, back in the world of the living.

"I'm getting a nurse," she heard her mother say. As she left the room, Minerva closed her eyes, tried to quell the throbbing throughout her head. She was back in her body, and with it came all sorts of pains and aches she had forgotten, never even noticed. Had she even traveled down there, to that place Suzanne thought was Hell? Had she evaded the red woman, freed the girls, escaped the phantom and his bugs? It was hard to even think back to anything, to picture anything. All she felt was exhaustion, a deep tiredness that was like nothing she had felt before.

She learned later that when she fell unconscious after waking up, her pulse fading, Janine forced Davy to drive them to the clinic out on the highway. She'd been relocated to Dallas after that, and the police—summoned by her mother, who reported her missing after her flight and dozens of unanswered calls—tracked her down not long after. The coma lasted for a few days, her body kept alive by potassium and glucose drips. What she told them was true: she needed understanding, needed closure. She hadn't meant to stir up trouble by visiting the Blues, and neither Janine nor Davy—especially after Janine pressured him—pressed any charges. "It's over," she told her mother, squeezing her hand. "It's really over. I promise."

On her last day in the hospital, Janine visited her. "Not sure you can eat these," she said, "but I made some cookies for you."

Minerva chewed one, savoring the sweet tastes of flour and sugar, the added texture of the chocolate chips. Since returning to her body, even the hospital food, which she might have considered stale and undercooked before, seemed rich and gourmet, even heavenly. Her senses felt heightened and more acute. Maybe the effect would wear off the longer she was back, everything become mundane again, but for now, it was like embarking on a second life.

Janine looked out the window at the Dallas skyline, unaware that Virginia had wandered the streets below, had nearly been trafficked. Things were still scattered in Minerva's mind, disarrayed experiences and memories, some her own, some belonging to others, but with time, they were slowly coming together. She could envision Virginia's journey as if it were a dream she had, a vague remembrance that was foggy at the edges. It was like the girl's parting gift, whether she knew it or not. Not just her journey to California, either, but her whole life.

"I still can't believe any of it happened," Janine said. "Mama still hasn't said a word. I think she's in shock. And Davy's just so confused! I don't even know how to start explaining it."

"I'm just a crazy girl," Minerva said. "That's all there is to it."

"You're not crazy," Janine said, looking at her seriously, eyes welling with new tears. "I believe you saved her. Her and Suzanne. I thank God every day for you. I can never repay you. Never, ever, no matter what I do."

Minerva struggled to suppress her own tears. She smiled and reached for another cookie. "These are a good start," she said, and they both laughed, if for no other reason than to keep from crying.

Days later, she was back on a plane heading west, returning to golden skies and crystalline oceans. Serena hugged her when she got back. "Holy shit, Minnie," she said. "You scared the hell out of us! What happened?"

"I wish I could tell you," Minerva said. "I just had to work through things on my own."

"Well, I guess you knew it was kind of stupid," Serena said with a smirk. "That's why you didn't tell anybody, right?"

Minerva smiled. "Yeah. I think I knew from the start."

Frank cooked steaks that night, and they ate outside by the pool, the lights under the water fading from green to purple, like an aurora borealis in miniature. Minerva relished the juicy, medium-rare meat, the flecks of seasoning left behind on her tongue, until somewhere in the back of her mind, chewing the steak made her think of the auction, the way the audience had filled their mouths with entrails and organs. Even when she pushed that memory aside, there was the impression left behind by Virginia of anxiously tasting nearly raw veal. I won't be able to enjoy things anymore, Minerva told herself, settling back in her chair and drinking the cocktail Frank had made. Everything's going to be black and red forever.

In her room, she sat uneasily on the bed, concentrating all her energy on sniffing the air, searching for any trace of the dead smell. She half-expected the phantom, "Felix," to return in the form of Virginia, as though nothing had happened, as though she hadn't accomplished anything. He's still around, she thought. You hurt him, but he's still around. So is the red woman. So are the rest of them. Would she get more visitors now, like she did when she was a kid? Would they come in the night and watch her? Would they try to communicate? And when would the red woman and her phantom lackey try again to ensnare her? If the first plot didn't work, what would the second look like? Would she even be ready for it?

The laptop and microphone sat atop her desk, almost taunting her to turn them on and start recording. But what would she even say? Who would she even talk to? The Minerva who had turned to streaming and recording had been a different person, an ignorant person—that girl had no idea of the doors she was opening, of the things she was inviting into her life. It felt irresponsible now, after everything that happened since Virginia's break-in, to go back to that old habit. No, she couldn't do it. She *wouldn't* do it. There had to be a better way of dealing with herself than airing it out to the world.

Her body was still rigid in the days upon returning home, but with daily runs and regular visits to the gym, she started getting her strength back, started feeling she felt like she used to. With her body mostly recovered, when she was once again secure and comfortable in her skin, she started taking tentative steps to reacclimate to her life. She took up gigs again, signed up for weekly night classes at the university. She went out with some of the girls, however strange she felt in the crop tops and miniskirts, however alien under the lipstick and eyeshadow. There's more, she wanted to tell them, looking out at the sea from the safe haven of an orange-lit, beachfront eatery. Of course, they would never believe her. She felt awkward in the middle of a dance floor, jostled by bodies she imagined might turn on her with wax-shrouded eyes, with animal masks. The group chemistry was different, too. All felt the absence of Sue's silly, snorting laugh. All sensed Minerva's hesitation and unease no matter how hard she tried to hide it. They knew it wouldn't last, Minerva most of all.

There was no one to talk to about what happened, not her mother or Frank or Serena, none of the girls, not her viewers, and most definitely not Janelle, ironic as that was. Minerva practiced her smiles and controlled her nerves. She didn't let herself panic in their remaining sessions, didn't allow herself to jump at shadows the way she did in the privacy of her bedroom. Around her mother, too, she feigned normalcy, health. And she *was* healthy, she had to frequently remind herself. Her body was back in shape. She had mostly stopped drinking except for the occasional night out. There were surprisingly no visitors, no more nightmares. No visions of Virginia or Suzanne or auctions or freak shows. But even though things were fine on the surface, back to how they used to be, she felt at odds. It was like trying to put the curtain back in place after you've already pulled it aside. Like trying to forget how a magician pulled a rabbit from his hat after you've already seen the missing compartment.

She knew her fire was still in her, but she didn't dare reach for it, didn't even think of trying to stoke it. Maybe with time, she would dip her toes back in and test the waters. But it wasn't time yet. She flinched at the sight and sound of roaches and flies. The thought of snakes made her skin crawl. Leaving her body had taken such a toll, it was hard to even think about doing it again, let alone putting her soul at so much risk. It was funny, thinking about the world in those terms: body and soul, physical and spiritual. But it was at the core of everything. She couldn't look at a church and not think about the red woman's ominous words. A creator's creations running amok, destroying one another, eating themselves. They all came from the same source, but there wasn't any kinship. Minerva and the red woman were as different as humans were to other animals. Even if she sometimes tried to empathize with those creatures living down below, it felt like too much of a liability. They think they're better, she thought, and maybe they were in their own way. But that's what made them so dangerous.

She e-mailed Janine regularly, as much to check in as to find an outlet for her thoughts. All was well with the Blue family, to the extent it could be. Janine had put her foot down on the matter of Davy's drinking. She reported that her mother had been docile—"broken," in Janine's words. Minerva had triggered something, she said, exposed a chink in the armor Mother Blue had erected over two decades.

"I think it's for the best," Janine told her during a late-night phone call. "She's gotta change. Deal with the way things are. The way she is."

Same for me, Minerva almost said. She tried to avoid thinking of herself as a hero, even if Janine constantly framed her that way. Virginia and Suzanne were gone because of her. Who knew if the red woman and her phantom had gone after other girls, too? All because they wanted this fire she had supposedly stolen. Well, Minerva had never asked for it. Probably no one had. She stared at her reflection and cursed the glow that seemed to emanate from under the olive skin. She spat at the light dancing deep in the hazel eyes. She scoffed at the fiery shape of the ombré curls. For all the flame's power, it couldn't bring anyone back to life. It couldn't restore time lost. It couldn't rectify the damage of grief that spanned years.

Sometimes, crossing the university parking lot at night or sitting by the pool, her thoughts turned to Virginia. How had she come back and saved her? The red woman said all life had fire, even if just a flicker. Had Virginia used her own flame to spark Minerva's? And if that was the case, what happened to something when its fire went out? Did Virginia even exist anymore? Or was her soul just gone? Maybe spirits broke apart naturally when they went to the next stop, when they lost the glue—the body, the ego—that bound them together in earthly life. It was comforting to think that Virginia had only sped up the process, not that she had actually sacrificed her very soul to save Minerva. That was really grim to imagine: a young girl losing her life and spirit all because she enjoyed watching someone online.

Minerva wondered what would happen when she herself died. Would the fire devour her, reduce her to ash the way Virginia burned up? Or was there another fate for people with so much undue flame? The fire had been around for a long time, since the dawn of time, in fact—so where did that leave Minerva? Was she an accident, or had this power, this responsibility, followed her from the beginning? Did souls really come back? She thought through every question, looked up answers online, read as many books as she could find in the library, but there were never any concrete answers. This was just the way things were. The way she was.

One night, a ringing phone woke her. Half-asleep, she picked up her cell, but it was dark and silent. The ringing continued, shrill and loud, like from an old rotary phone. A red light shone from outside the balcony doors, almost beckoning her towards it. She got up, not registering her lightness at first, the way her feet didn't quite touch the floor. She approached the balcony with a vague curiosity, the placidity of sleep, not afraid or anxious. When she stepped onto the balcony, she glided across a wooden floor, past a bar and pool table. The mount of a deer looked down at her, beady eyes reflecting the red glow of the room. A smoky haze hovered throughout the bar, not noxious but actually sweet, almost like the smell of rain. A dark, petite figure put down the payphone, and the ringing stopped.

"You got my call," the girl said.

Minerva leaned forward.

(Suzanne?)

The girl nodded. She adjusted the backpack over her shoulder.

"In the flesh. Or at least that's what I would say. Are you surprised to see me?"

(No. I thought you might come sooner or later.)

Suzanne leaned against the countertop and looked around at the red-lit bar, the way the light gleamed off the woodwork. "You know, I thought dying meant you were free. That you could go anywhere you wanted. But I'm still stuck in places like this. Is it a punishment? For being such a fucking bitch?"

Minerva didn't say anything.

"I waited a long time," Suzanne said. "Waited and waited. But she never came back."

(She saved me. And then she was gone.)

Suzanne's lips curled in a wry smile. "I figured. I shouldn't have let her go."

Minerva pointed to the backpack.

(Where are you going now?)

"The only place I can go. I wanted us to go together, but she just had to go after you." Suzanne chuckled. "I should've taken off a long time ago. There were lots of chances. Guys who were willing to take me wherever. But I stayed 'cause of her. Well, until I didn't. I ended up leaving pretty permanently, didn't I?"

(It wasn't you. It was him. He made you do it.)

Suzanne smiled. "Did he? He couldn't have made me do anything if I wasn't already one foot out the door." She gestured past Minerva. "You're lucky. You've got a home to go back to. All the modeling shit. You can be whatever you want."

That's not true, Minerva wanted to say. She couldn't help but think of Michelle, of Sue, of the whole trajectory of her life. She hadn't asked for anything, yet the universe provided, again and again and again. It was almost like the more she resisted, the more it threw at her.

"Anyway," Suzanne said, "I should get going, and you should go back to sleep."

Minerva looked back at her dark bedroom, at the shape of her body in bed. She noticed at last the gold sheen over her arms and around her midriff.

Suzanne walked to the exit. "One last thing. Something tells me those freaks down there don't like to lose. But that's your problem now."

(Why did you call me?)

"Don't know. Maybe I just wanted to know I was doing the right thing. But I think I knew all along. Virginia was right about that."

She left into the dark outside. Minerva lingered—thought she lingered—but a moment later, she was rising from bed, sunlight streaming inside through the window slats, the fabric and texture of her midnight meeting like a dream.

She knew Suzanne was right. One day, the red woman and the others *would* come again. And if she wasn't ready, if she was unpracticed, they would succeed. They would take her fire and bottle it up like they had done to others, like they would do to others. Time was on their side, after all. They could wait out lifetimes, and if there was indeed reincarnation, if her fire passed along to someone new, the red woman could try again with a new target who was none the wiser.

It only made sense to practice, to prepare, even if the thought of traveling again chilled her. But she could start small and slowly open herself up to a larger palate of experience. When Suzanne visited her, she had stepped out of herself to meet her. Couldn't she start there, take baby steps? Rescuing Virginia and Suzanne had been traumatic, but she had been like a novice swimmer diving into the deep end of the pool. With practice, with experience, she could be ready. She could jump when she needed, wield the fire when the situation called for it. She wouldn't be at their mercy—they would be at hers.

Lying in bed, dozing, she reached inside for the first time since waking up in that Dallas hospital. The fire burned bright, replenished by the activity of life. The tendrils of flame lapped at her eagerly, as if they had expected her, as if they were desperate to spread. She let them circulate throughout her body, let them galvanize her arms and legs, supercharge her heart and lungs. Help me travel, she thought. Help me go. And when she rose from the bed, she did so literally, trimmed in gold, shining as though with fairy dust. All that remained was braving the dark outside, until it wasn't a matter of being brave, until it was just another fact of life.

TWENTY-SEVEN

A hidden world lay beneath the surface of things, an invisible layer coursing with rivers of light and streams of music. Human souls weren't the only ones in transit, but the spirits of animals, too, those of trees and stones, countryside and city. Everything sang, contributing chords and harmonies to the soulful chorus. Minerva dreamed and traveled those streams, glided along those rivers. She rode the waves of music, sat among the stars, floated through cosmic crescents. Her fire was her fuel, her heart her compass. The lights and sounds reminded her of flashes from her childhood, vivid visions she had catalogued as dreams when they had been anything but. Before her father passed. Before her nighttime visitors sought her out. She had returned home after so long, dreaming now as a means to wake up. The real sleep, she realized, was passing through earthly life with eyes shut and ears covered. Had Virginia and Suzanne seen all this wonder before they went across to the next stop? Had Sue? It seemed a waste that only the dead could know the beauty of life. How people would change if they could see it. How they would believe.

She met Midori on one of those trips, finding her atop a cream-colored cloud overlooking a stellar vista. She was like Minerva, lit with the same flame, able to pass through and across the planes. The first one Minerva had met but not the only one out there. She felt them over time, pings and throbs of warmth that weren't only on Earth. They were scattered among the cosmos, singing to one another, crying out for reunion. How the fire broke apart in the first place, she didn't know. There were places she couldn't yet travel, and she wondered if she would ever be able to reach them. The garden was off-limits, that much she knew intuitively, as though it were an old memory she had forgotten long before. But maybe with enough of the flame, someone could burn through. That must have been what the red woman wanted.

The last night she met with Midori, she touched down on Tokyo Tower, the urban sprawl below a shimmering, neon sea. Midori was already there, dark hair blowing about her head. Maybe "there" was too literal—like Minerva, her form shone with light, though hers was a glowing emerald, a sparkling verdant. Midori's physical body lay asleep in her Shinjuku apartment, just as Minerva's slept soundly back in California, serenaded by the rhythms of the same ocean that separated them in their waking lives.

Midori waved to her.

(You made it!)

She didn't speak per se. They never spoke, barely even thought, communicating in a way purer than was possible with mere words. Minerva understood the intent as English, just as Midori comprehended what she received as Japanese, but there was really no language for what they exchanged. No language, for that matter, for the masked creatures that dwelled in the dark place below or the celestial beings that floated somewhere far above.

Minerva smiled and leaned over the railing, admiring the cityscape.

(Of course! Wouldn't miss it. Beats the Golden Gate, that's for sure.)

Midori smiled, but Minerva sensed the somber feeling behind it, the weight of something building up and preparing to spill out.

(I wanted to see you because I don't know if it's safe to do this anymore.)

Minerva nodded.

(It's never been safe. We're like flares to them. Like bombs going off.)

(It's not the *yōkai* I'm afraid of.)

Midori raised her hand, the city lights visible through the milky translucence of her forearm, the soft glow of her palm and fingers.

(We're not spirits. We shouldn't pretend to be.)

Minerva watched her.

(You think it's wrong?)

(Not wrong. But not right, either.)

Minerva thought back to what the red woman said. Too much fire was a mistake, according to her. An error on the part of the architect. An oversight in the code. But then again, didn't life change and evolve? Nothing was fixed. Everything was in flux. They were as much mistakes as they were triumphs. Their uniqueness was special, beautiful.

(It's who we are, Midori. We're not *just* alive.)

Midori was quiet, still with that sad smile. They were getting better at reading each other, more adept also at controlling how much of their thoughts leaked out. Maybe that's what Midori meant: a spirit couldn't be private, could never again have the privilege and comfort of solitude. It wasn't something the living should take for granted. Not something to waste precisely because it couldn't last, because all were destined to return to the source eventually.

Minerva smiled. Life was a gift, meant to be enjoyed and realized to its fullest potential.

(Let's meet, then. In real life. And not just the two of us, but *all* of us. All the mistakes.)

They laughed, their radiance brighter than the ocean of lights below them.

Two years had passed since Suzanne called to her from that red-lit bar, that way station on the way to another place, the next stop. She thought often about the girls, particularly about Virginia crumbling to dust. She thought of the auction she saw, of Midori's own recollections of impish forms following her at night, of hooded figures and masked crones stalking the dark Tokyo streets. Minerva had made good on her promise to work on her skills, her ability to travel. She'd overcome the trauma of her dive into the dark place, although she definitely wouldn't go there again if she could avoid it. There were souls trapped down there, more and more by the day, many of them transforming and mutating beyond anything resembling human. But as much as she wanted to help them, as comfortable as she had become leaving her body and traveling across, her fire alone wasn't enough. The flame was powerful, but it wouldn't last in an outright war against the red woman. She'd seen that firsthand against the phantom. Even with Midori's help, they'd barely make a dent. Minerva had to accept that at least for now, certain forces ruled the world—or worlds, as it were. Those forces set the parameters. They dictated the rules.

She meant what she said to Midori: they needed to find the others. Sooner or later, the red woman was coming for them—it was only a question of when. It wasn't just about protecting themselves, but also about saving the ones who were ignorant, who had no idea they possessed the power to commune with the dead and leave behind the bounds of the physical. Maybe they wondered why they made friends so easily or why people so readily fell in love with them. Maybe they thought it strange how they were always apart, distant from everyone else, caught on the edge of life. I should feel different, they probably thought. I have everything I want. I have friends. I have family. I have love. I have money. I should feel different. I should feel better. I should feel happy. Maybe even at that moment, there were babies born who had the fire, who would grow up and live dissatisfied lives, never realizing their misfortunes were from black-masked leeches and the envious dead, from seeing only one layer of the world when their eyes were primed for many.

All that said, the two years had been peaceful. She'd lost contact with most of her friends, and even the modeling had become sporadic as she transitioned to finishing up her nursing program. But she didn't mind the slower, more focused pace. Modeling had been fun, but it hadn't really satisfied. Maybe because all along, she'd been denying the truer part of herself, the destiny for which she was really intended. Now, she spent quiet weekends with her mother and Serena, especially now that Serena was getting ready to graduate high school and move to Washington State. She had taken for granted time with family, even after her father had died. But she couldn't anymore. The day was coming when the bell would ring for her to take flight, and there was no way of knowing if she would come back, if she would even be able to.

She kept in touch with Janine, so much so they almost viewed each other as surrogate sisters. Many nights were spent on the phone, and Minerva even visited occasionally. Janine and Davy had moved to Dallas, determined for a fresh start, but with them gone, Mother Blue had been alone in her grief. "She didn't have anyone to hit," Janine said after the funeral. "Nobody to yell at." The official cause of death was a heart attack, but Minerva suspected that if she returned to the Blue house and ran her hand over the walls and furniture, she would sense the real reason.

During her latest visit, she sat in Janine's apartment, eating cake and watching along with Janine as Coral, strawberry-blonde curls like a halo around her head, arranged blocks and colored pictures. They weren't the only ones watching her. There was another child, maybe only a few years older, an olive-skinned little girl in white, black-braided ponytail hanging down her back. She was invisible to Janine but clear as day to Minerva. She must have been just passing through, maybe drawn to Minerva's warmth, or maybe as captivated as Janine was by Coral's little light. Minerva found herself watching Janine more than her daughter. No doubt she would be as awestruck for every milestone of the girl's life: her graduation, her wedding, the birth of her own child. The Blue family's curse would be broken, as much by the mother's determination as the daughter's innocence.

"She's getting so big," Minerva said. "She looks a lot like you."

"She's got Davy's nose," Janine said. She paused. "There's a little bit of Mama, too."

The girl in the black braid looked up, and Minerva smiled at her.

"How did the sale go?" she asked.

"Oh, it went okay." Janine rose and gathered their empty dishes, started washing them. "Some of Mama's religious pictures went for a lot. There were even some old paintings by my daddy. Ginny's clothes weren't too bad, either."

Minerva nodded. The little girl raised her hand in farewell.

"I'm thinking about streaming again," she said, changing the subject.

"Really? You think you're up for that?"

"Yeah. I think it's time."

"It's a good thing," Janine said, drying her hands, returning to the table. "I know you don't think so, but it is."

Back home, Minerva removed her microphone from its cabinet, blew off the coat of dust, unwound the wiring. Her inbox had grown sparse over the years, but some messages still trickled in. Hope you're doing well, queen, they read. We miss you. Her videos still got occasional views, the most popular being the very first, the confessional about her father that started it all. She watched it sometimes, feeling a mixture of pity and jealousy towards the girl on the screen. She hadn't known at all what was coming, neither the good nor the bad. She'd been thinking about her father and about how time kept going and about how things stuck with you. She had no idea things never went away, even when they died. They had all sorts of means of sticking around. Sometimes literally, sometimes figuratively. The universe remembered. Nothing was in vain.

She flicked through the comments. Among all those people who watched, who idolized her, one of them had been Virginia. What had she thought, coming across that video, seeing the sad eyes of that girl on the screen? I recognize her, maybe. She's just like me. Finding a voice that represented her own. A connection, even one-sided, that made up for everything else in her life. And there were so many others. All looking for someone. Looking for answers and validation and love. Streaming had been a way to escape, to distract herself. She had never imagined that an impulsive video of her crying in her room would reach so many people, would capture them. But that was the work of the fire. The glimmer in the eyes like the flicker of a flame. The faint sense of warmth that came through the screen.

The weekend before Serena left for school, they went shopping together. "You don't think you're wasting it?" Serena asked her as they perused a thrift store. She was tall and ruddy-cheeked, arms and legs toned from volleyball. She sipped her soda, flipped through some vinyls. "You could be on billboards, for real. On movie posters."

Minerva smiled, waiting by the window, enjoying the sun on her back. "I was never really happy doing that," she replied. "It was more Mom's thing."

"Dude, but the *money*. I wish I could get a shot."

"Having second thoughts about Washington?"

Serena shrugged. "I don't know. But maybe I'm the one with real actress potential."

"More than me," Minerva said with a smile.

She leaned back, closed her eyes—and heard static. Something scratched at the back of her skull, like long nails probing her brainstem, like wet tongues rummaging about her skull. A signal from far away, removed by countless light-years. A message from deep in the abyss, where bones lay rotting and worms crawled in the pitch black.

Modesty doesn't suit you, Minerva.

Her heart skipped a beat. She spun to the window, eyeing the distant clouds growing dark with a burgeoning thunderstorm.

Yes, I can see you. Can you see me? Come. Let's chat.

Minerva trembled, teeth chattering, heart hammering, but she closed her eyes nevertheless and bridged the gap. When she opened her eyes, she stood in a gallery of some kind, the air hot and stinking with blood and meat. Paintings hung from the walls, some she recognized from the manor where she rescued the girls, others she had never seen but that nonetheless felt familiar. Statues and relics and tablets and skulls sat behind glass. Flames floated within smudged, foggy lanterns. Blue and silver. White and gold. They tugged at her, called to her. They demanded to be free.

Across from her, red nails twirled in greeting. The red woman sighed longingly.

Beautiful, aren't they? Many years' work. Well, what you might call eons.

(They don't belong to you. They don't belong to anyone.)

The red woman laughed.

In that case, release your own. Let it scatter the way it longs for. You must be in so much pain, having to endure its heat, having to tolerate the way it calls for you to use it. An awoken flame is powerful. Dangerous. It can burn you alive.

Minerva didn't respond. She felt the heat build within her hands, the warmth grow behind her eyes, but she fought to suppress it. Attacking her would be suicidal.

But that flame is intoxicating, too. I know you've succumbed to its pleasures since you visited us. You've gone very far, I'm sure! Oh, to see the stars like that again. Tell me, is paradise closed to you, too?

Minerva hesitated but nodded.

(It's not for the living.)

The red woman clicked her tongue.

**It's not for the unworthy. You must think yourself better than us—how couldn't you? Beautiful and young, brimming with power. But make no mistake: you are just as damned as we are. You have been left behind, granted a power you have no idea how to control. You search for an answer, but no one comes to your aid.

(What are you trying to say? That you have the answer?)

Oh, not at all. I only mean to suggest that while you search for kindred spirits, we are here waiting for you.

She reached out with a finger, somehow pushing back a bang, grazing Minerva's cheek. The nail reeked of decay, as cold as an icicle.

Minerva broke away, shivering.

(We'll never be friends. Never be family.)

The red woman chuckled.

So be it. In any case, I know what you want to do.

The crimson mask leaned close. The words slithered out in blood-bathed breaths.

By all means, go ahead. Bring them together for me. Furnish my feast.

Minerva stared. She shuddered.

When the table is set, we will meet again.

The many yellow eyes behind the mask burned red.

I will taste you first, beautiful sister. Darling girl.

Then, all of a sudden, she was back in the thrift store. Serena stood over her.

"Hey, you okay, Minnie?"

"Yeah." Minerva stood and gathered her bags. "Let's get back. Storm's coming."

Time. Time was always the problem. The red woman and her host had their eons—Minerva had decades at most. She had met Midori by chance. Maybe their flames had resonated with each other, but Minerva hadn't encountered any others before or since, and neither had Midori. Well, the bell had finally been rung. Those others needed to be called to action, summoned to their real purpose, woken up from lifelong dreams. Hopefully, no one would need to die for them. No more girls pushed to suicide and worse. No more dead or absent fathers. No more murdered friends.

Minerva was nervous, turning on the laptop, configuring the microphone, hovering the mouse over the record button. No taking this back once it was started. No rewinding the clock. But even if it was a trap, she'd seen the power of the flame. She was the one with leverage. She got to decide, the rest be damned. Because as much as the red woman thought she had the right cards, she was scared, too. She had to be.

"My name is Minerva King," she said into the microphone. "I'm twenty-five years old. I live in Oakland, California. I used to be a streamer and a model. But now, I realize what I really am, what I've always been. I can see things other people can't, go where no one else can go—and maybe you can, too."

Continue reading for a preview of
the next installment of the
ROOM OF CLOTH series:

THE SKIN A FRAGILE FABRIC

They called it the "room of cloth," though none of them could say why. The name was intuitive, somehow known *a priori*, unlocked and articulated only once the blight had breached the brain and stained the soul. It seemed to Fiona that there was a hidden faculty already inside waiting to be activated, a type of trigger just waiting for the right input. It didn't take much: an innocent glance at a corrupted graffiti, a viral word whispered within earshot. The room of cloth could be anything, anywhere. Soon, she knew, it would be everywhere.

She had been exposed the night she and Jenna went to see an art exhibit: the legendary *La Frontera*, otherwise known as *The Doorway*. A black monolith that seemed to defy earthly physics, that came and went as it pleased. She'd been obsessed with it as a fan of the arts, desperate for a chance to see it in person. There had always been rumors about it, the way it drove people insane, how it caused convulsions and seizures among those who happened to catch a glimpse of it. These stories hadn't scared Fiona—on the contrary, they'd made the piece all the more captivating. Gun to her head, she would have once said she didn't believe in ghosts or goblins, in Heaven or Hell, but she had *wanted* something like that to be real. Life was otherwise normal and ordinary. Unexceptional. Empty. And she craved more. She craved purpose.

Well, she'd gotten what she wished for, hadn't she? *La Frontera* was real. It had shown her the truth of the world just as it had so many others, just as it *would* so many others. Jenna had paid the price for Fiona's arrogance, her desperate longing for thrills and excitement. And it was only after infection, after Sarah found her, that Fiona discovered *La Frontera* was only one way the room of cloth spread. It was only a flower, not the root, not even the stem.

Paintings, stories, photographs—the room of cloth had spread throughout time, across oceans. The Internet had provided its most versatile vehicle yet.

She learned from Sarah and Chandra that everyone suffered the same hallucinations, the same visitations. They all saw the flesh-colored walls and rust-stained floor. They all saw the endless mezzanines and labyrinths and scaffolds, the enmeshed and ever-changing layers of skin and sinew, muscle and membrane, tissue and tendon. They all saw the gears and cogs churning underneath, arranged in infernal, perditious designs that would confound any human architect but that nonetheless powered that red star, that hellish engine. They all saw the dead, the ones the room had claimed and made its permanent residents. Their shadowy forms crowded peripheries, lurked in the corners of rooms, hovered over them as they slept. All were the room of cloth—its vassals, its visages. But there was one figure who commanded them all. He who watched them, nourished them, enslaved them. He who marked all who bore witness to the room. He who waited for the end. The man in chains, red-eyed and forever furious. The manacled man.

Fiona first saw him after Jenna died. She had locked herself in her room to scream and snarl through the visions of a red, rusted earth, buildings crumbling to ash, oceans souring with meat, the land and its animals withering to dust, crimson mountains of bodies tumbling and crashing down, lurid piles of limbs and torsos and breasts and buttocks gyrating, swelling, undulating in ecstasy, in agony. She had painted scene after scene, eventually running out of canvas and turning to the walls, the floor, her hands slathered in so much red they might have as well have been blood-drenched, her hair matted with black wads and gray smudges, her clothes caked and browned to the point of brittleness. She thought that painting would relieve her, free her from the onslaught of debased imagery and visual debauchery. But she realized with dread, as the visions doubled and then tripled in intensity, as the red eyes plagued her and the dead laughed and cried and wailed, that the images were endless, not slowed by her willingness to paint, but accelerated, emboldened. She flailed and frothed in her paint—paint or blood? flesh or ink?—and the darkness opened, the flames parted, the maelstrom of metal and viscera unfolded. He emerged from the depths, a sadomasochist's wet dream of chains and shackles and rotting flesh and exposed bone and broken arms and shattered legs and crushed fingers and twisted toes. He descended upon her, red eyes flaming, gray skin speckled and scarred and sloughing, bones pressing against and protruding from his flesh, muzzle wet with saliva and blackened with burnt skin and uprooted teeth. He came from nothing, returned from nothing, *was* nothing. Fighting against him was pointless. There was no escape, no relief. She had knelt in the milky red light, red paint, black ink, sobbing, heaving, praying for an answer. It had taken all her strength not to jam her paintbrushes through her eyes, all her resolve not to reach for the scissors on her desk and open up her wrists.

She went online to spread the word, to warn everyone that he was coming, that he would never be satisfied until all were exposed, all were taken. That was how Sarah found her, how she came to learn how the contagion worked. The people exposed, the "collaborators" or "conduits" as Chandra called them, did their master's bidding whether they knew it or not. They thought themselves saved—thought themselves saviors. The room of cloth drove them through a predictable lifecycle. The first stage was incubation: territorial defensiveness, tribal aggression, sectarian violence. The infection nursed its hosts, increasing their dependence on the source while limiting the sway of outside influences. When the parasite matured, fed sufficiently on the host's nutrient broth of trauma and shame and guilt, the next stage commenced. The host's disposition changed from selfishness to selflessness. Share me, the parasite whispered. Give me away. Give all of it away. Including yourself. All you ever were and all you'll ever be. Surrender it all. Spread. Engulf. Infect. Disseminate. Propagate.

They had gotten sophisticated, too. They had "farms" where they kept people like livestock, torturing them and making them produce more artifacts like *La Frontera* to facilitate the spread. Julia and Maggie had both been rescued from farms, but those farms were small, Sarah said, nothing like the bigger facilities that were out there. Who knew how many poor souls were locked up—hundreds, thousands—and forced to produce until the infection ate them up and hollowed them out. Then they were slaughtered, minced up to feed the things on the other side. Their expired, emptied bodies were dumped into the ocean or entombed in mass graves. Some were even stuffed into shipping containers apparently, left to rot and disappear.

But however bleak it all seemed, there was a silver lining. Not everyone touched by the room of cloth became its thrall. Some could see through the illusion and resist its corrosive effects. They were survivors, according to Sarah, and she'd made it her mission to bring them together. They were just as infected as the others, just as damned, still compelled to spread the parasite. Fiona and Chandra painted. Sarah and Joel wrote. Maggie sculpted. Julia sang. But they could control their spread. If they isolated themselves, managed their impulses, destroyed their waste, they were never a danger to the outside world. They could even forestall the terminal stage of their condition. Fiona had lived for over a year already with the infection, but Julia and Joel had gone even longer. Chandra said he was on his fifth year. Sarah, somehow, was past year eight. Could they live indefinitely, outlast the parasitic cycle for decades? Sarah said there were people who had. They were rare, maybe numbering only in the single digits for all anyone knew. But a long-living thrall was more dangerous than a hundred of the regular kind. Even one with that much time, that much experience, could recruit hundreds if not thousands to the ranks of the room of cloth. But so could a survivor, Sarah said. They could mimic the strategies and organize in the opposite direction. With enough time, enough numbers, they could fight back. They could find a way, but only if they stuck together. That's why they had to live together, work together. They had to have faith.

Fiona wanted to believe it was possible. It was romantic. Noble. Heroic. It checked all the boxes. But it was easy to say, harder to do. When she closed her eyes to sleep, she saw Jenna and her brother. She saw the many others: an endless, uncountable multitude. Somewhere among them were Chandra's wife, Julia's son, Sarah's brother. She saw what was coming, too. The abandoned homes and cratered streets. The deserted cities and irradiated wastes. The missing-persons signs like a million bandages on a gargantuan wound. The gateways. The portals. The red star approaching, opening to swallow everything, to leave the earth drained and cold and lifeless. To steer it towards the rest of the cosmos and continue the work.

She spent most nights turning over, trying to find solace in the darkness that was otherwise threatening. Music helped to block out

Jenna's blood-drenched whispers. If Fiona closed her eyes, she could pretend the gray hands grazing her calves and tugging at her arms were just her imagination, just manifestations of restless limbs and an agitated mind. Even when Maggie started sharing the room, the harassment never improved. The ghosts didn't care. Maybe they even liked violating the idea that having other people around could somehow help.

When the music didn't work, when she couldn't ignore the laughing and crying and coaxing, Fiona whispered prayers. She clasped her hands together and mumbled through her tears for God Almighty to hear her, to protect her, to shield her. Wake me up, she would chant. Please wake me up. I can't do it myself. I'm stuck in this dream. I'm trapped in this nightmare. But I know there's more. I know I can wake up. You just have to help me. I'm sorry I never believed. I'll change. I'll go to church every week. Every day. I'll go to confession. I'll spread the holy word. I'll read the Bible and memorize every line, every sentence. I'll do anything and everything. I'll devote my whole life to you. Please, Jesus. I'll forgive my parents. I'll forgive Dad for everything. I won't blame him for Jacob. I'll take it all. I'll crucify myself.

There was never any answer. Only mocking giggles. Only condescending laughter. I'm sorry, she'd say, pressing flushed cheek against wet pillow. I'm sorry I don't believe.

In those moments of desperation and despair, they spoke to her. Join us, they said. Join *him*. He loves you. He wants to save you. Why do you deny him? Why do you deny yourself?

Her martyred messiah. Her defiled defender. Her crucified champion. He was waiting for her. Waiting for her and Sarah and Chandra and Julia and Joel and Maggie. Waiting for everyone. Red-

eyed and angry and cruel. Struggling against his chains and his bind-
ings. Watching for the moment when he could finally break free.
When all would be one.

ABOUT THE AUTHOR

R. H. Gründ is the author of the *Room of Cloth* series, *Simulacrum*, and *Influence*. Apart from writing and publishing, he has taught composition at both the secondary and postsecondary levels. He lives in South Texas with his family. Using the QR code below, you can follow him on social media at @rhgrundwriting and find more information on his website at www.rhgrundwriting.com.